THE
SORCERER
WITHIN

WILL RICE

Copyright information

Book cover design by ebooklaunch.com

Editing services provided by Toby Selwyn

ISBN 9798524000828

Published by Will Rice

www.willriceauthor.com

For pp

I will divide my power into separate groups of effect and give power from one group only to each of my successors, to limit further the power of each sorcerer; I name these groups the Elements of Sorcery, and name each Element a colour.

Each Element provides the sorcerer with a type of control.
Yellow: Control of the mind
Red: Control of the sorcerer's body
Blue: Control of the natural world
Orange: Control of objects
Purple: Control of other people's bodies
Green: Control of the sorcerer's awareness of the natural world
Grey: Control of the sorcerer's self

Extract from *The Elements of Sorcery*, by Whitelock

PART ONE
RECRUITMENT

Two years before Kim's death

CHAPTER ONE

Arthan hoped this slack-mouthed boy wasn't the one. He couldn't bear the thought of spending his working hours with a cretin.

He drew on his cigar, watched the white honeycomb tip glow orange, then let the milky coils of smoke seep from his lips. The boy approached through the spinning fumes and dropped himself into the chair opposite Arthan's desk. Arthan said nothing. The smoke rose and the silence descended, each empty second meted out by the tick of the clock. The boy sat and stared, gawking at the room around him as though he had never been inside an office building before.

Arthan rested the cigar in its holder and half stood to shake the boy's hand, drawing in a breath to hide his stomach. The streaked mahogany surface of his desk was almost too vast to reach across, but that was the way he liked it. "My name is Arthan. I am the company director."

As he lowered himself back into his seat he let his stomach relax. For the millionth time he cursed the sour luck that had landed him with this podgy juvenile body for eternity. He could almost hear the boy's thoughts: *The company director? He looks the same age as me. Why is this chubby teenager wearing an expensive suit, smoking a cigar and claiming to run a company?* Arthan scowled.

The boy announced his own name and Arthan forgot it a second later. The boy's voice was as limp and clammy as his

5

handshake. Arthan scanned the application form, but it held nothing of interest. This was another dull-eyed laggard, another waste of time. There was only one more left, one more to find. Arthan knew it was now down to nothing more than luck, but all the same he felt an urge to act that made his neck itch. Every unsuccessful interview was an insufferable delay, every cretin a fresh annoyance. He had no choice. He had to be completely certain this simpleton wasn't the one, and so he pressed on with the banal routine. "How was your journey?"

"Fine, thanks. I live in Shepherd's Bush, so it was just the Central line then—"

"Good." Arthan was less than excited to hear an exhaustive account of the boy's train journey. He clamped his cigar between his teeth and pretended to examine the application form while he inspected the boy out of the corner of his eye, searching for some sign of intelligence and finding none. This one really was uninspiring; he wore the vacant gaze of the incurably dumb. Arthan wrinkled his nose. "This should be a short interview." The boy's attention swung back to him, like an animal catching the scent of food. "I am going to ask you some questions to see whether your skills align with our role profile. Provide as much detail as you can. Does that make sense" – Arthan glanced at the application form again – "Simon?"

"Yes."

At least he had answered that question correctly. It was beyond time to get to the point. Arthan asked the only question that mattered. "Tell me about your sorcery."

The boy's mouth flapped, making him look even more dull-witted. Arthan could hear his thoughts rattling around like stones in a tin can. "I'm sorry?"

"Describe your sorcery. Or show me, if you prefer. But please, nothing too dangerous." Arthan sucked warm, earthy smoke into his lungs, and then let it glide from his nostrils. "Remember, health and safety."

The boy's stupid gape confirmed what Arthan had already guessed. This was not the one.

"I'm sorry? Are you joking?" There was a sheen of sweat

now visible on the boy's forehead.

Arthan snorted. "Absolutely not." He set his cigar aside and glared across the desk. "Did you read the letter we sent you?"

"Yes. I—I thought that sorcery stuff was just marketing."

Not that again. Arthan had heard the same explanation from two other candidates that morning already. He frowned and tapped his pen on the desk. "Our letter was quite clear. It plainly stated, 'Applicants must be sorcerers. This is not a metaphor, a trick or a joke.'"

"I know, but I still thought that was, um, marketing."

"The letter also stated, 'For the avoidance of doubt, a sorcerer is someone with abilities that normal humans would consider supernatural. We are not referring to conjuring tricks.'"

Beads of sweat edged down the boy's temples. "I guess I thought it meant being a sorcerer at, like, time-planning, or communication, or business sense."

Arthan raised an eyebrow. "Yes? So are you a sorcerer with time-planning powers?"

"Um, no. But I'm very keen to learn."

Arthan laughed, then wished he hadn't. He hated the sound, a high-pitched titter that matched his body but not his mind. "You cannot learn sorcery. It must be in your blood."

The boy's eyes darted from side to side, as if looking for an escape route. "Can I give you some examples of when I have been part of an effective team?"

It was beyond time to move on. Arthan blinked, and felt his Control take hold of the boy's mind. He grasped the memories inside – the boy reading the letter from Arthan Associates, fidgeting on the train, squirming under Arthan's examination – and sucked the detail out of them, leaving a white fog of memory about an interview at a company whose name the boy couldn't remember. Arthan could do a neater job of removing the evidence, but he knew it wouldn't be necessary – humans refused to believe in sorcery even if they saw it with their own eyes. Keeping his talents a secret from the world was so easy it was disappointing.

The boy's eyes had taken on that glassy sheen, like the blank gaze of a doll. Arthan had once found it troubling to be faced with such a lifeless stare; whenever he took control of a human's mind they seemed to become a corpse. These days he found it a relief from the torture of mundane conversation. Lifeless dolls enjoyed silence as much as he did.

"The only thing we can be sure of in life is that we are never sure of anything," the boy said.

Arthan nodded. Despite the proof in those dead eyes, he found it reassuring to test whether he had full control of someone and hear the evidence from their mouth. "That is the first sensible thing you have said."

As he sent the boy traipsing out of the door, Arthan sank back into his chair with a sigh and reached for his cigar. He hated spending time with humans.

* * *

Three minutes later the next candidate was perched before Arthan's desk. Her skirt was too short for a business meeting, her make-up was too thick and her hair was too blond. Arthan imagined she would be attractive by modern standards.

"Thank you for coming in today. I hope you found our offices easily?"

"I came by taxi." She flicked a stray lock of hair over her shoulder. "Your assistant has taken details of my expenses. When can I expect to have them paid?"

What a distasteful creature. Arthan turned through the papers that Holly had left on his desk, took up a red pen and circled one section. This wasn't going to take long. "Before we get to that, I have noticed an irregularity on your application. Your date of birth. Is this correct?"

"Yes, that is correct."

Arthan gave her an icy smile. "We will only consider candidates who were born in the right year, as set out in the letter you received. Our researchers have clearly made an error – you should not have received an invitation to apply. You have wasted your time."

The girl raised her chin, her eyes bulging beneath caked black lashes. The stench of her perfume was evident even from behind Arthan's desk. "My father told me that it is illegal to only consider candidates born in a particular year. I could take you to court under the age-discrimination regulations."

How tiresome. Arthan blinked at her, and her eyes turned to glass.

* * *

The next candidate slunk into the room without a sound. If he hadn't been wearing a suit and tie Arthan could have mistaken him for a beggar: he was starved thin, his limbs hinged at angled joints. He had pale, milky skin and tufty, thick brown hair sticking out at erratic angles. When Arthan shook the boy's skeletal hand he felt the bones moving inside and noticed the muscles of the boy's face twitch and tighten.

"My name is Arthan."

"Gordon White."

The words were a throaty whisper, barely audible. Gordon folded himself into the chair opposite and bored his gaze into the floor, his thin chest rising and falling with laboured breaths. Arthan offered him a drink but he didn't respond. His knees had fallen together, his feet askew on the squares of grey carpet. Could he be the one? Surely someone like this, who seemed nearly terrified enough to faint, wouldn't apply for such an unusual job if he wasn't a suitable candidate.

"How was your journey?"

At first Gordon replied only by lifting his head. Arthan watched him gawk at the poster pinned to the noticeboard. It was one of the publicity posters Holly had printed last year. A soft-focus photo of a young businessman with a gleaming white smile was headed with the invitation to *Fulfil your potential – Unleash the power of your mind*. When Gordon spoke his gaze was once more glued to the carpet.

"Is this place real?"

Arthan felt the hairs rising on the back of his neck. This was it. He took a long pull on his cigar before setting it aside, examining Gordon's face again through the rising snakes of smoke. Was he imagining the likeness? Something in the angle of the chin, the shadow around the eyes?

"We are a business of sorcerers. We use our powers to offer services to the public, services that cannot be found elsewhere." *Not that the public appreciates our help*, Arthan added to himself. He drew paper towards him and readied his pen. "Tell me about your sorcery."

"I can move things."

An Orange Innate. He was the one. Arthan pushed the paper aside, leant forward and placed the pen on the desk near Gordon. "Show me."

Gordon recoiled from the pen as though it would bite him. His arm twitched, he clenched his jaw tight, and the veins bulged taut in his scrawny neck. For a moment Arthan thought that he was wrong, that this was just a strange and deluded boy and he hadn't found the last sorcerer.

Then the pen shook. And shook again. Then it tilted on one of its plastic edges to rest on its next side. Then it turned onto the next side. Then it began rolling along the desk towards Gordon. The pen reached the edge and carried on rolling, but did not fall. It rolled out into empty space and stopped, suspended in mid-air halfway between the edge of Arthan's desk and Gordon's white, rigid face.

Arthan walked around the desk, plucked the pen from where it hovered, subjected it to a brief look and placed it in his inside suit pocket. With conscious effort, he drew his lips into a broad smile. He hated smiling; it made him look young. At least he had something to smile about for once – he had found the last sorcerer. Belas would be furious. "Good news. We would like to offer you a position on our programme. You will receive an offer pack by post shortly. Speak to Holly about any necessary details."

Gordon looked Arthan in the eye for the first time. He stood on shaky legs. "I've never told anyone before."

"I expected as much, Gordon. Sorcerers are naturally secretive." Arthan finally let his smile drop, his jaw aching from the unfamiliar effort. "Do not worry, your secrets are safe here. You can look forward to a long and successful career at Arthan Associates."

Gordon's cheeks were glistening with tears. His arm was still twitching but all the tension had left him, like a puppet whose strings had been cut. His large, hungry eyes peered up at Arthan.

"Thank you," he whispered.

* * *

"Thank you for coming, but I am afraid all the positions have been filled."

The three candidates were lined up along the cream corridor wall on black steel-legged chairs. They gawped at him, perhaps wondering if he was another candidate. One of the three, a sweaty boy in a baggy suit, opened his mouth to speak, but Arthan cut him off with a blink and took hold of their minds with his power.

"Failing to plan is planning to fail," the sweaty boy said as his eyes turned to glass. He took to his feet without another word and sloped away down the corridor.

The girl in the next chair stood up, looking past Arthan with that same dead doll's stare. "In the midst of difficulty lies opportunity," she said, and followed the sweaty boy.

The other boy had not moved from his chair or said the words Arthan had sent into his head, and his eyes were still alive with interest. "Is this a test?" he asked.

A resilient one. Arthan closed his eyes and summoned power more deeply before trying again. "Well?"

The boy peered down the corridor where the boy and girl had disappeared, as if looking for help. "Um… it's difficult to find opportunities?"

Arthan frowned. Very odd.

The door to his left swung open. Arthan didn't need to look to know it was Holly. She never guarded her mind well enough; he could sense her approach.

"All written up now—Oh, sorry, I thought they'd all gone."

Holly glanced from the boy to Arthan, then looked at the floor. "Sorry."

She had her hair tied back today, as he'd asked her. He had been right – it made her seem older, and more professional. Her body looked almost as young as Arthan's, and while the gap between her appearance and her true age was nowhere near as extreme as it was for him, the principle was the same. He always wore a suit; it was always pressed, it was always clean, it was always appropriate attire for a man of business. She should dress according to her years of experience, not according to the age at which sorcery had preserved her body. Even with her ginger hair tidied away, her freckles and thin limbs made her look too girlish for clients to take her seriously. The dresses she wore didn't help. Arthan would have to persuade her to start wearing suits.

He brought his attention back to the matter at hand. "Gordon was our third."

Holly nodded. "Yes, of course."

"Belas has three." Arthan looked the boy up and down, searching for some clue to explain what had just happened.

"What's wrong?"

"And Olivia makes seven."

"Yes, I know." Holly put a hand on his arm. "Arthan, tell me what's going on."

Arthan held her eye for a moment, then removed her hand. It wasn't like her to speak to him in that way. When had she become so bold? "I cast a Control on this boy, and nothing happened."

The boy was watching them from his chair. "Excuse me, what is this about?"

"Persuasion?" Holly's brow wrinkled for a moment, then she shrugged. "It doesn't always work on humans with high Resistance."

"Perhaps. But my second casting was strong enough to overcome a sorcerer."

That caught her attention. She turned her wide eyes on the boy, who smiled, then reacquired a serious look when he caught

Arthan's eye. "You're sure you didn't miscast?"

Arthan snorted. He glared at the candidate again. Why was this human Resisting him? Why were his eyes not the lifeless marbles that Arthan had commanded them to be? No matter how hard he looked, the boy seemed normal. The way he sat suggested he would be tall when standing; he had broad shoulders, long arms. His black hair clearly had not seen a comb today; it tangled around his temples, framing a pale face with a sluggish expression and those wide brown eyes. Then, for an instant, something flashed across the boy's gaze that had nothing to do with Arthan's Control. It was something old, something different. A coldness that spoke of death.

"You could try more power."

"What?" Arthan was still looking at the boy, but his eyes were normal again.

"Some humans have exceptional Resistance." Holly gave the candidate a grin that was a little too friendly to be professional. Arthan would have to pick her up on that later. "Use all your power. No human could Resist your full power."

Arthan flexed his hands. "Let's see, shall we." He closed his eyes. He felt the familiar rush as his blood surged with streams of power yearning to be released, a hot fire in his throat. His skin prickled, his stomach coiled in anticipation, but he ignored the impulse to cast and summoned deeper. The streams became rivers, throbbing in his veins, heat rising in his ears. He focused, channelled and sharpened the power to a point, then thrust the full force of it into a Yellow Control. It was the same Control he had cast on the boy twice already, but this time the sorcery pealed from him like a crack of thunder, the release leaving him cold, his legs weak and his head thumping. He had to concentrate to keep his footing. When he opened his eyes he felt cool sweat running down his forehead.

The boy's eyes still weren't glassy; they were wide, confused and alive. The boy got to his feet. "I'm sorry, I think I'd better just go."

Holly watched him walk away with her mouth open.

"It would seem that at least one human can Resist my

power." If this boy really is a human.

But that was a question for another day. He considered for a moment. Human or sorcerer, the boy could prove useful. He called after him, "What is your name?"

The boy continued for a pace before turning. "Elliot."

Arthan recognised he might have given a less than welcoming impression to this boy, and so he would have to try to be charming. He tried to imagine how Belas would act, and approached Elliot with his hand extended, wearing the most genuine smile he could muster. "Elliot, I trust you will accept my apologies for behaving so strangely. I do believe we could find an extra space for you on our programme. Congratulations."

"Really?" A sudden grin broke across Elliot's face. "Thanks."

"You are welcome. You will receive an offer pack shortly. Holly will be in contact."

As they watched Elliot wander down the corridor and vanish around the corner, Arthan wondered if he had made a mistake. If Elliot was not a sorcerer but merely a human who was somehow resistant to sorcery, he might prove not only useless but also difficult to get rid of.

Holly was chewing her lip, a habit of hers. "Do you think he's one of the children?"

He took the folder from her and began leafing through the papers. "No. The other seven feel right." He paused, remembering the look he had seen in Elliot's eyes. "That one felt different."

"Who is he then?"

Arthan swept past her and pushed open the door leading back to his office. "I have no idea."

PART TWO
MURDER

The day of Kim's death

CHAPTER TWO

Arthan's office door swung open, interrupting him mid-sentence. He stared at the figure in the doorway, as did Elliot beside him. Holly stared back at them, her face blank.

He pushed his papers aside and went to her, his work forgotten at the sight of her hollow red eyes. The unguarded barrage of her emotions slammed into him, a sickening well that tore at his gut. When she buried her head in his shoulder he felt her fingernails dig into his side. Her skin was cold.

"What is it?" It was Elliot's voice, behind them.

Arthan held her tight and watched her dress flutter in time with her sobs. The state she was in had set his heart hammering, but the thought that she needed him, and that she had ignored Elliot, made him suddenly want to grin. While he waited for her to speak he sent subtle pulses of Yellow Control into her mind, knitting her frayed nerves, softening her raw thoughts.

"I knew something was going to happen – I felt it." Her voice was thick and sunken. "I felt it but I didn't know what… Sean called. He just got home." There was a wet sound as she gulped back tears.

"Tell me what happened," Arthan said. He kept his tone even; panic didn't help anyone. Elliot was beside them, his eyes wide.

"Kim." Holly choked on another sob. "It's Kim."

* * *

Kim's bedroom looked exactly as Arthan had imagined it

would: as tidy as her desk, as ordered as her filing. It was smart and practical. He lingered on the sight of the room's spotless and untouched corners, the pine units, the chunky woollen throws, the waxy green potted plant. But he couldn't avoid the inevitable. He dragged his gaze across the pastel wallpaper, over the white desk. A ring binder lying open, a pen beside it, and a chair lying on its side, stout pine legs splayed.

A blood-stained bed.

Her blood was darker than he had expected, a muddy brown, almost black. It was sprayed across the floor, across the thick white quilts, a cacophony of gore flung over the pristine brightness. At the side of the bed Kim slumped, unmoving, her clothes stained with thick black treacle. She didn't look like a real person but more like a shop mannequin. Her arms were bent backwards as though the shop assistant had forgotten to arrange her in a natural pose, and her head was missing. Her neck came to an abrupt end with a flat black stump, the head unscrewed to make it easier for shoppers to walk past the window and imagine Kim's blood-stained clothes on their own bodies.

The stench crawled inside Arthan's throat as he neared the corpse, but he made himself kneel next to her, inches from the twisted limbs. He looked at the space above her shoulders, unwilling to look down, although he could feel the glare of the grisly head from where it rested on the wooden floor. His stomach clenched and he closed his eyes against the nausea. He had to be strong. He had to be the man he was inside, not the boy everyone saw on the outside.

Behind him the door whispered open. He heard Holly's footsteps approach and felt her hand touch his shoulder. "Sean is talking now. But he wants some time alone."

Arthan nodded. Of all the sorcerers, this would be hardest for Sean: he and Kim had spent all of their young lives together; they were inseparable. Sean would have to keep hiding his sorcerer family from his foster parents, and would have to tell them his twin sister was dead.

"How do you feel?" Arthan asked, without turning from

the body.

"I don't know. I can't believe it."

"Believe it." Arthan stood. "There is a murderer out there, and not a human one."

"What do you mean?"

He surveyed the room again, trying to block out the smell and distance himself from the horror. "No human could have done this. The lock was opened without a key, but was not forced. Kim would have heard a human long before they entered the room; she would have restrained a human easily. There is little sign of a struggle – she was overpowered. It must have been a sorcerer."

"No, Arthan. It couldn't be. None of us would…" Holly's protests trickled away to be drowned beneath the pattering of rain on the window. Arthan had noticed a black sky following them from the office; she wasn't in control of her emotions.

"It was a sorcerer. I will conduct a full investigation." Arthan began turning the angles in his head, weighing the options for where to begin.

"I'll do it."

"What?"

He could hear the rain slowing. There was more colour in her blotchy cheeks now. She had pulled her hair back and only a few ginger strands escaped into her reddened eyes.

"I will lead the investigation."

"No, Holly. You are upset, you're not thinking." He touched her cheek. "You can't do this."

She bristled, and brushed his hand away. "I can. And I'll start by asking you a few questions, once I've spoken to the police."

He suddenly felt very conscious that her eye line was level with his. He pulled himself straighter, wishing he was just a little taller. He left the silence unbroken for a few seconds, expecting her to falter, but she didn't. He shook his head. "Forget the police. I've dealt with them already – they won't be involved. This is a crime among sorcerers; they wouldn't know what they were dealing with."

Holly opened her mouth, then just nodded. She looked a little shorter again already.

"You are right to question me," he said. "All of us are under suspicion."

She looked away, as if she could ignore the truth of his words. If she wanted this responsibility so much, she was welcome to it, but he doubted she would have the stomach for what it entailed.

"You should question us all. I will speak to Belas and he will cooperate."

"OK," she said to the floor.

He didn't let up. If she was going to do this, she had to confront it. "You must find the murderer, Holly, before anyone else is killed. You have eleven suspects."

Holly glanced at the closed door. "Eleven?"

"Yes. Sean is a suspect."

"But—" Holly lowered her eyes again. "Of course."

Arthan saw the moisture in the corners of her eyes, but he couldn't comfort her. "If you don't find the murderer you will be a suspect too."

The look that dawned on her face broke his resolve to be firm. He pulled her close, and she crumpled into his embrace. The head came into view over her shoulder, a pasty-white football of skin with matted clumps of stained blond hair. Kim's dead, glassy eyes stared straight through him. "Are you sure about this?"

"I will be."

A tear escaped Holly's eye onto her freckled cheek, and he kissed it away. "You should start by examining the body. Look for clues."

* * *

Rupert's hand shook as he reached for the telephone. The receiver was icy to his skin and the dialling tone cut a piercing note into his throbbing ears. The office walls bent in on him, a painful, glaring white. He put the receiver back down on the desk, removed his glasses and waited for the churning in his stomach to subside, swallowing to keep himself from vomiting.

Ian took his pause for indecision. "You have to tell them, Rupe."

"I know." Rupert heard his voice emerge as a croak. He wondered where Briggs had gone. He had vanished from the office floor after Arthan had called with the news, leaving Rupert and Ian alone. Naomi was apparently still at lunch, shovelling food down her throat somewhere. Rupert was glad Ian was the only one who had seen the sorcery take hold of him. He didn't like people seeing him like that.

Ian's broad face was pale, his eyes fixed, red and watery, but Rupert knew he must look worse himself. His shirt clung to him with sweat; his whole body burned. It had been bad this time.

He wished he could laugh the experience off. The lowest points in life were the most important times to laugh, but his stomach was too twisted and his vision too seared to leave any space in him for humour. He stared at the telephone to force it into focus. The nausea would pass soon, but he didn't have time to wait.

He swallowed again and dialled the number for Kim's flat. He half rose from his chair, but the room blurred with the ringing tone, swinging like a pendulum, and he fell back into his seat. The desks and chairs melted into a buzzing blur, Ian's figure stretched into a thin giant, like syrup pouring upwards. Ian would like this new look, Rupert thought; he wouldn't be teased about his weight any more.

"Hello?"

It was Holly. Her voice brought back the sharp, burning slicing, the trembling limbs, the scent of fresh blood, the fevered panting. How could anyone call these visions? Rupert had not just seen the future, he had heard the screams, and had suffered every moment as if the flesh torn by these nightmares was his own.

"Hello? Who is this?"

The room spun faster. "It's Rupert. I've just had a... vision." There was no response, but Rupert knew she was still there – he could hear her breathing. Familiar, shallow, desperate breathing. "Is Arthan there?"

"No. He's just left." He could barely hear her. Was she whispering or was the pressure in his ears making him deaf? "What did you see?"

"Tell her, Rupe," someone said.

His vision blurred beyond use, Rupert closed his eyes. "Is Sean there?" His own voice was a whisper too. Was he even speaking out loud?

"Yes."

He clenched his teeth to fight through the pounding in his skull. "I saw who killed Kim. It was Sean, and he's going to kill you next."

PART THREE
INDUCTION

Two years before Kim's death

CHAPTER THREE

"What's a sorcerer, El?"

Elliot froze, almost dropped the box he was carrying, managed to recover in time to catch it, and forced himself to keep breathing and keep walking. Surely he hadn't heard that right. "What?"

"What's a sorcerer?" Jay yelled again over his shoulder. They were strolling across the leaf-strewn lawn in front of Elliot's flat, the large cardboard box in his arms swaying back and forth above Jay's shaved head. He was nearly a foot shorter than Elliot, and slighter, which meant Elliot's view following him was mostly of the box and the large block letters outlined on its side, bobbing in and out of sight as they turned corners and sidestepped hanging branches. *TAKE CARE. THIS WAY UP. TAKE CARE.* Even from behind, Elliot felt like he could see Jay grinning. Jay was always grinning.

Elliot struggled along with his own box, which was digging a crease into his arms. He didn't know how to respond to Jay, so he focused on the glass-panelled doorway they were tramping towards. Once he reached the door he would think about how to deal with Jay's question. He certainly didn't want to say anything until they were inside. The tan-walled tower block was yawning with open windows, and he could imagine his curious neighbours sitting inside and listening. Each time the thick privet hedges rustled at his back he thought it was someone watching them. Finally they shouldered their way through the door and into the protection of his narrow hallway.

"Are you a sorcerer?"

Elliot still didn't answer. What should he say? He trailed Jay up the stairs and along the corridor while his head swarmed with questions. He had no idea how Jay had found out about sorcerers, or what would happen to Elliot if he let their existence be discovered by a human. He might lose his job and his chance to find out more about these people.

This thought was the one that made him sweat. His interest in the sorcerers had grown beyond a simple curiosity; he had become convinced that Arthan knew something about his real family. All the other new recruits at the company were abandoned at birth just like him, and they were all his own age. He could feel that there was a link, that he was connected to them. He had spent his whole life not knowing who he was, and now he was starting to feel a creeping familiarity, an echo of a feeling. The key to his identity was buried somewhere in that company, cloaked and twisted within the unnatural powers those people commanded.

They entered the poky room that would now be Jay's bedroom and crouched to release the boxes onto the carpet. Box by box, the muddy-white wallpaper was being hidden behind rising heaps of Jay's possessions. As if they were painting an identity onto a blank face, Elliot thought, picturing his own bare bedroom down the hall.

"Come on then, spit it out." Jay had settled in a leaning perch on an empty corner of a table, still waiting for an answer, but Elliot ignored him and headed for the door.

"We'd better get on." Elliot knew his tone was too terse, too abrupt, but he couldn't help it. He tried to think of a joke to distract Jay, but he could never think of jokes, and trying to force one didn't make it any easier.

By the time he reached the corridor, Jay's grinning face was at his shoulder. "Stop avoiding the question, El. Tell me about this sorcerer stuff. We're flatmates now – we have no secrets. If you didn't want me to find out, you shouldn't have left your papers lying around."

The letter. Elliot had left it on the coffee table in the lounge. He gave Jay what he hoped was an indifferent glance, and inwardly cursed his idiocy. He prayed that Jay hadn't read the whole letter. "It's nothing. Just a role-playing exercise from work, a team-building activity."

It was a plausible lie, but Elliot could see his friend hadn't swallowed it. Jay had that twinkle in his eye. Like most things in life, it looked like he was finding this funny.

"It doesn't look like a role-play."

Jay was right. It looked like what it was, a confidential letter offering Elliot a well-paid job at a company called Arthan Associates, on the condition that he had supernatural abilities. It was time to play the friendship card. Elliot paused by the door to the street outside. "Jay, I'm your best friend. Trust me, it's nothing. Please leave it alone."

The twinkle faded a little, and Jay patted Elliot on the shoulder. "Sure. No problem. Let's get on." With that he whistled past and set off towards the van.

Elliot let out a long breath and followed, trying to shrug out the tension worming into his shoulders. It seemed his secret was safe, so everything would be fine. After all, he couldn't hope for a better flatmate than Jay. They would do everything together, just like when they were at school. He knew there would be the occasional disagreement; there always was when you lived with someone for the first time. But he had been friends with Jay long enough that they would forgive each other for most things.

It was a shame he couldn't tell Jay about his job – he hated keeping secrets from him. But he had no choice. The confidentiality agreement was strict: no human should be told about sorcery without prior approval from Arthan. If Jay knew how much this job meant to Elliot, he would understand. Elliot had seen the tightening of Arthan's jaw every time one of the new recruits mentioned their foster parents. Arthan was the key to it all. There was some reason that he only recruited abandoned children. He must know something about who Elliot was. Could Elliot be one of them? A sorcerer? This job was his chance to find a place for himself in life, instead of drifting along on the tide as just one more piece of shapeless, faceless debris. A chance to finally exist.

* * *

"Beer?"

Elliot wiped the sweat from his forehead and nodded. He had been hoping for a break. His arms felt like jelly after carrying Jay's bed inside. It must have been made of lead.

Jay picked his way across his new room between the piles of boxes and headed for the kitchen. "What was your old flatmate like?" he called out to the flat in general.

Elliot followed, wiping his hands on his shirt. "He was an accountant."

"Sounds boring. Was he boring?" Jay passed Elliot a bottle of beer from the fridge. It was ice cold, the glass speckled with bubbles. Jay must have filled the fridge with beer the second he walked in the door.

"A bit." Elliot imagined that in Jay's eyes he must be boring himself. A thinker, a reader of books. Jay was a leader of groups, a teller of stories, a charmer of girls. Elliot was just a nobody on the sidelines listening to the stories. Despite Jay's crooked teeth, his shaved head, his height, he had that grin, and the grin always won people over. Elliot never felt he won anyone over, but had stopped being jealous years ago and accepted the obvious conclusion that they were two very different people. Maybe Jay would have preferred a best friend who was more similar to him, but he was stuck with Elliot. After a few years, best friends became as difficult to escape as family, and much more difficult to exchange than flatmates. Elliot smirked as he remembered something.

"What?"

"My old flatmate. He ironed his socks."

Jay sprayed his mouthful of beer. "Seriously?"

Elliot nodded. While Jay guffawed, he leant against the cupboard and sipped his beer, savouring the chill running down his dry throat. The tiny kitchen seemed a lot fuller with Jay in it, his vigorous conversation drowning out even the hum of the ancient boiler. His wiry body was always twitching with energy, like a bright-eyed terrier waiting for a ball to be thrown. He was one of those people who seemed to bring their personality with them wherever they went, while Elliot felt like a blanket that took the shape of whatever situation he was draped over.

Now, as usual, Jay was grinning. "I'd still like to know more about this sorcery."

"What?" Elliot started tidying the kitchen as his heart hammered. He'd hoped that Jay had forgotten about this.

Jay chuckled. "You seem to get very hard of hearing when I mention your job. El, stop putting things away – look at me." Elliot did, and was taken aback. An unfamiliar serious expression had descended on Jay's face. "Look, mate, as you said, we're best friends. You can tell me anything. You're hiding something from me, and that makes me worried. Are you caught up in something illegal?"

"Illegal? No, of course not."

"Then tell me."

How could he talk himself out of this? Jay had played the friendship card right back at him. Elliot needed a lie, a convincing lie, but he could think of nothing. "Please, let's forget it."

"Fine. I'll find out myself. I know where you work – I'll go and ask around."

There was no way out. Elliot swallowed. He suspected Jay was motivated by curiosity rather than his pretended concern, but Elliot no longer had any choice but to tell him. If Jay went to the office, Arthan would know their secret had been leaked and Elliot's career would be destroyed, along with any hope of finding out what Arthan knew about his birth parents.

"I can't tell you, Jay."

Jay grinned his wickedest grin. He must have guessed that Elliot had given in. "Surely you can. You told me when you wet yourself that time, when we were fourteen. If you can tell me that, you can tell me anything."

It was never the wrong time to tease, according to Jay. Elliot ran a hand through his untidy hair and sat on one of the battered wooden stools. "You can't tell anyone."

Jay's eyes lit up. He slapped his hands together and settled on a stool himself. "Great! So, what is a sorcerer?"

"Someone who uses sorcery."

Jay finished his beer and slung the empty bottle into the bin with a clatter. "So they actually believe they have superpowers?"

"Yes." *Because they do.* It was clear Jay didn't believe him. This was to Elliot's advantage: Jay was less likely to tell other people about sorcery if he thought it wasn't real. But all the same, Elliot felt a tension stirring in his stomach; surely he wouldn't be this dismissive if Jay had revealed a secret to him.

"And what do they believe they can do?"

Elliot sighed. He couldn't even think how to explain it. "Different things." He thought back to his first few days at work and tried to remember how he had felt then about the strange world he had discovered which now seemed so normal. How quickly the wondrous became routine.

"What a bunch of nutters."

Elliot shook his head. "They aren't nutters." He knew he should stop giving away details, but he found himself continuing. "They call the different types of sorcery Elements; each one is a colour. They all have a speciality, an Innate Element. One can change the weather, one can move things with his mind—"

"Change the weather?" Jay stared at him. "El, you really believe this."

There was no going back now; the truth came pouring out of Elliot's mouth. "I saw it, Jay. It's real." He had to look away from his friend's face; he could hear how stupid his own words sounded. It was like trying to explain electricity to someone from the past: he didn't know how it worked, he couldn't prove it worked, but he knew it did. He traced his finger in the condensation on his beer bottle as he continued in a low voice. "This guy, Briggs, he's a sorcerer who runs the other company, like a sister company. He asked the new joiners to show him their Innate Elements. None of them wanted to, but in the end this girl, Kim, she's the weather one, she went to the window and made it rain. She just stood there and it poured down. Then the sun come out, then it snowed, as easy as changing channels. You could see the weather was normal in the distance, but around the window she was controlling it. I don't know how, before you ask me."

"What about you then?" Jay tilted his head, smirking. "What can you do?"

Elliot shrugged. "Nothing. I don't think I'm one of them. But their sorcery doesn't work on me, so my boss thinks I'll be useful."

"Why doesn't it work on you?"

"I don't know."

Jay frowned. Elliot wondered if he was trying to think of the right question to expose sorcery as a sham. "How many of these sorcerers are there?"

"Thirteen. Seven of them are our age. Most of them work for one of the two companies, but not all." Elliot thought of something that would prove sorcery was real, and couldn't stop himself. "One of them is Olivia Gale."

"Olivia Gale?" Jay barked a laugh. "Well that would explain a lot."

Elliot spread his arms wide, amazed by Jay's scorn. "It does explain it! Have you never thought it's odd that an untrained young girl has broken world athletics records?"

Jay screwed up his face. "Everyone thinks she's odd. She's a freak. Or maybe a cheat. I bet she's not actually *untrained* for a start. Have you met her?"

"No, she doesn't mix with the other sorcerers."

Jay snorted. "That publicity company of hers has turned her into a brand. It doesn't mean she's a wizard."

"A sorcerer."

"Whatever." Jay leant back and took a swig of beer as though he had won the argument. "If the nutters pay you well, and you like working there, fair play to you."

Without warning, something burst alive in Elliot's head, like an invisible knife was slicing through his right eye. He jerked forward, his beer slipping from his hand, his muscles in spasm.

"Are you OK, mate?"

The attack on his body passed in a breath, and Elliot suddenly felt better. In fact he felt incredible. It was the same every time it happened, and it was happening more and more frequently. His eye still buzzed and stung, and there was a taste of burning in his throat, but he felt a sense of lightness as if his problems were trickling away down a drain somewhere out of sight. He felt his shoulders settle. "A migraine." He grinned, noticing the bottle in Jay's hand. "You have fast reflexes where beer is concerned."

Jay chuckled and passed Elliot's beer back to him. "Didn't spill a drop."

"You're right, it is a good job." Elliot stretched his legs out and took a long drink. "And they pay very well." He laughed as he remembered the incident from the day before. "You'll like this, though. I found a note in my desk drawer that said 'Leave. You don't belong here.' Printed in red, as if someone thought that made it look scary."

Jay raised his eyebrows. "Wow. That doesn't bother you?"

It didn't. For once in his life Elliot was certain. This job held the answers. The life he had built around him was an empty shell. Over the years the people who were once his parents had grown into the foster parents he now barely knew. They certainly didn't know him. He was no one. He had to find his real family; even if they were all dead he had to find out who they were. He had to find out who he was. "I would kill to keep this job."

CHAPTER FOUR

Elliot yawned as he rummaged through the papers in his in-tray. Where had he put those notes? He slid open his bottom drawer then slammed it shut again. There was something in there. A dark mass in the gloom of the drawer, and two black, glaring eyes.

He swallowed and waited for his heartbeat to slow. It didn't. What the hell was in there? He told himself he was safe – he was in an office surrounded by people. He swallowed again. With a clammy hand he inched open the drawer, and a putrid smell tickled his nose. Another inch and he saw sticky, bloodied feathers. Another inch and twig-like, slick white bone. Another inch and he was looking into those glassy, venomous eyes again.

It was a huge dead bird, laid on top of the paperwork in his drawer. The smell of rotten meat was enough to make him gag. Was it a blackbird? It looked to have been ripped apart by a predator. The shredded, raw mess of it didn't make sense among the sterile white walls and plastic chairs of the office; the image didn't match the sound of the whirring printers and trilling phones. For a moment all Elliot could think about was that someone must have deliberately positioned the half-eaten head so the eyes would greet him when he opened the drawer.

"Are you available at eleven o'clock?"

Elliot jumped at Arthan's voice, slammed the drawer shut for the second time and swivelled his chair to face him. "Er, yes. Yes, I'm free."

"Good." As always, Arthan had squeezed his chubby young body into a starchy Victorian suit, and as always it made him look odd, like a teenager in costume for a nineteenth-century play. He was frowning his way through a fist of paperwork while he spoke, as if he was too busy to spare the time to make eye contact. "One of my clients is coming to meet me. I think you would benefit from observing our session – it will give you some context for your report."

It took Elliot a few seconds to piece together what this was about, and then he remembered. Arthan had asked him to prepare a report on possible services they could provide to clients using Sean's, Kim's and Gordon's powers. He mentally checked the dates and realised it was already overdue. He had spent hours researching the different types of sorcery, certain he would find some clue to help him understand his link with these sorcerers, but he hadn't, and he hadn't written a single word of the report. He forced a smile, his head still filled with those staring, listless black eyes. "That would be great. Thanks."

Arthan was already walking away. "Come to my office twenty minutes beforehand. Do not be late."

* * *

Elliot could feel his mind drifting again. He was inching open the drawer once more, to find that dark-feathered corpse, that inhuman stare. Whoever had left the bird there must be the same person who had left the note telling him to leave. It couldn't be Gordon – he was far too timid for this. Sean? Kim? Arthan? It didn't make sense for it to be Arthan; if he regretted recruiting Elliot, he would just fire him. Elliot knew it was useless to dwell – that was likely what his tormentor wanted. Someone had decided they didn't like him, but he couldn't let himself be distracted. He had to keep this job. He tried to focus on what was happening.

There wasn't a lot to focus on. Arthan and the client were sitting facing each other on two chairs in the centre of the empty meeting room, and hadn't moved for over half an hour.

Their eyes were closed, and they were leaning so far forward they looked like a pair of drunks who had slumped onto each other in sleep. The scene was given a comical twist by Arthan's gentle grip of the client's hands and the vacant, slack expression on the client's face just about visible behind Arthan's back. The client himself was an old man with feather-white hair displayed in a quiff above his puckered face. His suit and skin were both wrinkled and loose, his ears large, his skin spotted with brown. In every way he was a contrast to the plump, pink, tightly suited Arthan. Occasionally a shudder passed over them. Elliot wondered whether he still needed to be here. He had been told to sit in the corner and watch, but so far nothing had happened. There wasn't even a window to distract him, just four bare white walls, a thin, bristly grey carpet and two comatose men.

"I am going to remove you from future training sessions."

For the second time that morning Elliot jumped. Arthan remained slumped and unmoving, his back to Elliot, but his voice was controlled and alert, as loud as a gunshot in the silence of the room. Arthan's words sank in like stones. The training sessions allowed Elliot to spend time with the new sorcerers and learn more about their powers. He had been hoping he would hear some clue to the identity of his real parents. "But Briggs said—"

"Call him Belas, Elliot."

"OK." Elliot paused. "Is that his real name?"

"Belas is his sorcerer name." Arthan's voice sounded as grim as if someone had been murdered. "And he was once happy with it. He has since decided the name Ben Briggs would be more appealing to his customers, which is apparently a more important consideration than either tradition or integrity. You will find that Belas and I have quite different outlooks on life."

Elliot thought they were probably more similar than Arthan realised. "Yes, well—"

Arthan's back interrupted him. "Regardless of what Belas thinks, there is no benefit to you being trained as a sorcerer, because you cannot do sorcery. You will spend time on research instead, to support those who can do sorcery. Where is my report?"

"It's going well." Elliot couldn't think what else to say.

"It's late."

An uneasy pause followed. Elliot wondered whether he should apologise or reassure Arthan that he would finish the report soon. He opted for silence.

Arthan's voice barked again. "Why is it late?"

Elliot groped for a sensible answer, and found none. "I'm sorry."

The only movement in the scene before him was a bead of sweat that broke free and rolled down the client's creased face. The man's trance must have been deep because his face showed no reaction to their conversation. Elliot wondered what the expression on Arthan's face was; his back gave nothing away.

"Mr Pearson came to me looking for help." Arthan's clipped tone suggested Elliot's apology hadn't reached a sympathetic ear. "He is a successful businessman who would like to continue his success, but over the years he has lost the mental agility of his youth. Each month I look into Mr Pearson's mind, and I make it more efficient. Humans only use a fraction of their brainpower. Sorcerers use a significantly larger fraction, if they are skilled in the Yellow Elements. My mind, for example, is more efficient than yours. I can think more quickly."

"Of course." Maybe Arthan would be more amenable if Elliot accepted his boasts. This was a good opportunity to press him for information. "I have a question, actually – would it be possible for me to have access to the archives?"

"No."

It was the answer Elliot had expected. Arthan knew something about Elliot and the new sorcerers, something he was hiding. Elliot had already guessed the secret might be in a book in the archives.

"Using the Yellow Element, I can Control Mr Pearson's mind," Arthan's hunched back droned. "I first connect my mind with his, and see his thoughts, his instincts, his memories. I can examine the processing speed of his logical and analytical functions, and I can improve them. I can focus his thoughts upon the memories he will find most useful, I can tell his mind to prioritise certain activities, I can adjust the processes to optimise them." There was a pause as a shudder passed through Mr Pearson's body and was echoed in Arthan's. "Ask Holly for any books you need. If they are confidential she can ask me for approval. Are there any particular texts you wish to view?"

"*The Elements of Sorcery*?"

"No. Any others?"

Elliot had seen references to that book everywhere. Apparently it was the most important book written about sorcery, but clearly it contained something Arthan didn't want him to know. He considered the other gaps in his reading. "I haven't found any books on Grey sorcery."

"Why do you need to know about Grey sorcery? Your report is on commercial uses for Red, Orange and Blue Controls."

"It would be useful background."

Arthan's back snorted. "There have been two Grey sorcerers in our history. One lives in isolation pretending he is not a sorcerer, and his predecessor was a murderer. Neither has made any contribution to the study of sorcery that you need to be aware of."

"A murderer?" Elliot hadn't heard anything about a sorcerer murderer before.

"Yes, Elliot. Viros was a serial killer." Arthan spat the word *Viros*. "Grey sorcery gives the power to change one's shape. Viros abused this ability to disguise himself as innocent people so that his killings would be blamed on others. It is likely that he killed more people than any other serial killer in history, but because he never wore the same face for long we will never know how many men, women and children he slaughtered. When he was finally caught and killed, every sorcerer rejoiced, delighted that they would never have to hear his name spoken again. Does that satisfy your curiosity?"

Arthan's withering tone was no doubt intended to embarrass Elliot into silence, but Elliot had lost his voice the moment

Arthan started talking. A sick familiarity, a chilling memory, had gripped him.

"I am now examining Mr Pearson's recent thoughts," Arthan continued, sounding pleased with Elliot's silence. "Some are useful and should be encouraged, others may need to be suppressed. Remember, as always, the effect of our sorcery is limited – the weight of reality pulls against it. Do not convince yourself of the fantasy that sorcerers can do anything. We are restrained by our power, we are restrained by the difficulty of the Control, we are restrained by our own skill and knowledge, we are restrained by the laws of nature that we so often try to overcome. Sorcery, like so much in life, is never easy."

A pinch in his hands made Elliot realise he was clenching the sides of his chair. He let go and tried to concentrate on Arthan's words.

"Mr Pearson has been dreaming frequently, but peacefully, so there is no real harm or distraction there. I will suggest to him that I implant some dream scenarios, as training for work events."

Elliot's thoughts drifted again, unable to swim against a dark and icy current. He had been dreaming too. Bad dreams.

CHAPTER FIVE

*E*lliot prised each shoe off his foot with the other toe. Stretching back into the cushioned embrace of the armchair, he let his eyelids fall shut and reached out for a slice of beef from the tin plate balanced next to him, questing with his fingers. His hand walked across a cool slice, grasped it and folded it into his mouth. It tasted of heaven. He chewed, gulped down the meat, then dragged his sleeve across his mouth. He favoured country inns like this one: the food was usually fresh, there were plenty of strong horses and the local villagers kept themselves to themselves. The world was very nearly in perfect order, if it wasn't for the chill. The large room had grown colder as the afternoon dawdled on; he could hear the draughts whispering through the window shutters and guttering the candles. He would have to call that girl to come and start the fire soon. Not yet, though – he was just a little too comfortable to move. Maybe she would arrive of her own accord to check on him.

The door banged open and Elliot opened his eyes. Could this be her, summoned as if by magic? No. A red-faced, thick-set man marched into the room, wearing a bulky overcoat as though he had just arrived from the street. He brandished a crumpled sheet of paper.

"You, sir, are a fraud!"

It appeared unlikely that this fellow would light the fire for him. Elliot's cold toes would have to wait a little longer. As his heavy eyelids closed again he saw the man's eyes bulging even wider.

"Attend my words! You may have fooled my daughter, but I am no fool! You are a criminal, I know it!" Eyes still closed, Elliot tore a pinch

39

of bread from the plate and tossed it into his mouth. He hoped the man would lose interest in him and leave, but the yelling continued. "You have not paid a penny in rent, you thief! You have drunk nearly half our ale, by the look of the storeroom. You have somehow managed to wind Anne around your finger; she is bringing you food from dusk till dawn. You shall be gone by nightfall. You shall!"

Elliot cracked his eyes open to find the man had advanced into the room and now stood directly over his chair. He sighed. "Who might you be?"

"I am the keeper of this inn! I am the man whose services you have stolen!"

The innkeeper's face was turning a little purple. It seemed he was not going to disappear of his own accord. Elliot opened his eyes fully and summoned a polite smile. "You are the innkeeper? A pleasure to meet you. Where have you been this last month, my good man?"

As Elliot tossed another morsel of bread mouthwards, the man made spluttering noises that sounded something like a kettle making its first preparations to boil. "It is none of your concern where I take my business! What is your concern is that I return home to find you here stealing my rooms, my food and my ale!"

Elliot affected a pained expression. "But good sir, my trade has been welcome here before. Your wonderful daughter has agreed to delay my invoice, noting my previous impeccable record of fee payments."

"Aha! But you are not who you pretend to be! Your resemblance to Doctor Goodsmith is striking, I can see, but you are an imposter. You scoundrel! This letter awaited me on my return this morning." The innkeeper thrust the crumpled sheet of paper into Elliot's hand, and he straightened it out. It was written in a neat, scholarly hand. Scanning the page, Elliot gathered it was a letter to the innkeeper from a gentleman who had recently arrived in the city and was looking for a room to rent. He could guess the name at the bottom before he had read it. Dr Frederick Goodsmith.

When Elliot looked up he found the innkeeper glaring at him. "What do you say to that? Nothing? Well what of this then! Anne told me Doctor Goodsmith was here already, so I could not understand this letter. I took it on myself to visit the lodging where the letter had arrived from, and I found the doctor was indeed there! He told me he had been robbed some six weeks before by an odd foreign man, who had engaged him in conversation in a tavern. The doctor said he had told this foreign man of my inn, and how he rested here occasionally when he was in town. That very night the man made off with the doctor's possessions when he fell asleep. That foreign rogue must be your accomplice, and the doctor's clothes and jewellery must be the ones you wear now!"

Elliot toyed with the silver ring on his finger. It looked like this ruse had run its course. "I will miss living this doctor. His wealth and reputation open a lot of doors." He didn't look back up at the innkeeper.

There was a strangled shout, then silence, and Elliot could feel it was happening. It always happened like this. The innkeeper had opened his mouth to shout, but his jaw had been clamped shut. Elliot had clamped it shut. He was the only one who could allow the man's mouth to open again, and he knew that he wouldn't allow it.

He hadn't needed to even tighten a muscle to summon his power. It had leapt into him, coursing through his body like a river. He heard the door to the room swing shut and he knew that he was the one who had shut it. He didn't need to look at the innkeeper to see his thoughts as plainly as his face. The man must have been awakening from his shock, because Elliot sensed him deciding to swing a wild punch.

Elliot continued turning his ring, watching the light ripple over it. The man's case was hopeless; he could never prevail. Elliot's Premonition would have warned him of the punch even had he not watched the innkeeper's frantic mind resolve to throw it. His reactions were heightened to a degree that would have allowed him to rise to his feet and strike the innkeeper several times while the man's fist was still travelling through the air. Had the innkeeper's punch even connected, Elliot knew he would not have felt it or suffered any injury. There was nothing that could happen other than what always happened.

Elliot's power propelled the innkeeper backwards and upwards off his feet. He looked up at him. The stout fellow flew a little way into the air and then dangled there, hovering in mid-air, flailing like he was drowning.

Elliot began to undress, while the unseen hands of his power pulled the clothes off the innkeeper. The man's coat was tugged off, his waistcoat unbuttoned, his shoes and breeches freed from his legs and his heavy shirt yanked off over his red face. The clothes flew across the room to Elliot's waiting arms. He dressed in them, the innkeeper's outfit hanging on him like a scarecrow's rags. Elliot commanded his body to change.

He felt his bones move like butter, twisting and changing, his skin stretching and his stomach inflating to fill the large shirt. He felt his face twist and spread, his nose flatten and his brows dip to match the burly innkeeper's image. His feet swelled inside the shoes and his skin deepened to the innkeeper's oily tones. A few scars appeared on his arms, his hair grew a little, and it was done. Elliot could see himself in the room's grimy mirror. He was now the innkeeper. He turned to the floating man and gave a silent command for the mouth to loosen.

"What is your name?" Elliot asked.

The innkeeper could not help answering, although the tone of his voice was dead and unnatural. "Henry Beckerill." Then he gained control for a moment. "What are you? What kind of fiend are you!"

Elliot winced. Silence fell, although the innkeeper's mouth kept moving, as if he was now shrieking behind thick glass. In years past Elliot might have stood here for a while, looking at the man, thinking. Weighing it all up, going round in circles, testing this path and that. But the years of thinking were long behind him and he no longer could spot the join between the moments, the stitching of one action to the next. It was all smoothed down by time, a worn and flowing path that took him from this moment to that moment. He had already summoned his power and applied it to the innkeeper; he had already turned back towards his chair.

When he sat down he felt the heat rising behind him, warming his back, and heard the crackling of the flames, the greedy suck and growl of the fire. It was something like the cosy hearth he had been wishing for, but he knew the burning would not last long. He glanced back a little too soon, and the man was still there in the blue-white flames, blackish, cracked skin and eyes widened to eggs. Elliot looked away again, and noticed that the doctor's ring was still on his bulging fingers; he had forgotten to remove it. He twisted it off and set it on the table. The doctor's time was past. Elliot was somebody new.

A smell of bitter, roasting meat had filled the room, and it now turned smoky and dry. Finally Elliot heard a crumbling sound behind him, and he knew it was done. He gave himself a smile, testing the feel of the innkeeper's weighty jowls. A heavy body was hard work, but he would soon grow accustomed to it. He heaved himself to his feet and turned to where the man had been floating, and where there was now a black mound of ash on the floor. He spread it out and swept it under the rug with his foot. The burnt smell was lingering, so he flung the windows open to the noisy street and grimaced as the warmth escaped into the air outside.

He had just eased back into the armchair when a knock came at the door. After a polite pause, the innkeeper's daughter entered and smiled at the sight of Elliot. "Oh, there you are, Father! There are some men here for you — they said you sent for them, something about a thief in the inn? What is it about?"

Elliot returned her smile in what he hoped was a fatherly fashion. "It is nothing. A misunderstanding, I shall go down and tell them. Don't worry, sweetheart. Now be a good girl and get the fire started."

CHAPTER SIX

Elliot staggered to the table with another oversized volume, the shuffle of his steps the only sound in the bare room. He heaved the book onto the tabletop and himself into the flimsy chair. A thin sigh escaped him. The plastic crate of books by the door to the archives was nearly empty, but it had taken him most of the day to trawl his way through it. Holly would fetch him another crate tomorrow, just as she had every day this week. He had no idea how many more books there were in there. He glared at the locked door to the archives, imagining the long, shadowy shelves beyond enclosing their dusty secrets.

He should be writing Arthan's report. He had read so much about the Blue, Orange and Red Elements that he knew their Controls intimately, but finding ways to use those Controls in services to customers was proving a challenge. His only idea with any potential was for Blue Control: to provide a weather-manipulation service. Using Blue Control, Kim could guarantee the weather would hold for a client's special event. Elliot imagined large sporting competitions would pay well for guaranteed sunshine. But he couldn't think of any sensible use for Orange and Red. Gordon could move things, which didn't seem like a service people would pay for, other than maybe elderly people with bad backs. Sean's Red speed and strength seemed like something the police would find useful, but then Elliot had his doubts Sean would be any use against an armed criminal.

He would start the report next week. For now he was too consumed by his search for the secret that must lie in these books. He felt it, like a pulsing beat in his brain, an itch inside that he couldn't scratch. There was something here, some hidden piece of information that would tell him who he was. What if he could do some of this sorcery? It seemed impossible, but then it should be impossible for the others too. Was he one of them?

All the evidence suggested he wasn't. No matter how many times he tried, he couldn't do sorcery, and he knew he should give up. But each time he decided to stop, he found himself wondering if this next book could be the one.

Records in Sorcery: Volume IV. He flipped through the pages to the index by Control and scanned the list of Controls that were becoming familiar to him. Animal Contact, Animal Possession, Air Movement... He finally spotted one he hadn't tried before. Far Sight. He turned to the page number shown and read the description of the Control. *The sorcerer can extend his field of vision beyond his body, to see around corners, through solid objects, and over great distances. Orange Control, discovered by Whitelock.*

With no real hope of success, Elliot laid the book down and attempted to compose himself. Not that he knew if composing himself was the right way to approach this. No one could tell him how to learn sorcery. Sean had said that if Elliot had an Innate Control he would be able to cast it without thinking – it would be as natural as breathing.

He stared forward and tried to extend his sight out in front of him and leave his head behind. He stared until his eyes felt like they were about to fall out of his head, but the wall stubbornly remained where it was, a few feet away, and refused to come closer. He tried to bend his sight around the edge of the table, commanding the room to bend around him, but his disobedient vision slid across the surface without a hint of cornering. He told himself it didn't matter; he had to carry on trying. He held a piece of paper up to his eyes and held *Records in Sorcery: Volume IV* behind it. He bored his eyes into the white sheet, pushing his vision through the paper. Incredibly, a ghostly image of the book swam into sight. He felt a shiver run through him, and he stared even harder… He could almost make out the words on the page… Then he dropped the paper and sighed. He was seeing the outline of a book through a thin sheet of paper held beneath a sixty-watt lightbulb. This wasn't sorcery.

As the failed experiments continued and the books piled higher, the pulsing in his mind became a pounding in his temples. He would have to go back to the doctor; these headaches were getting worse. He resolved to attempt the Controls in the next book and then stop for the day. He attempted Heat, Mind Search, Shape-shift and Weaken before the headache finally broke in the now familiar way. It was sudden and violent, like someone had slashed his right eyeball apart. It lasted for a second only, and he was left panting and shivering, with that usual burning taste in his throat.

When he lifted his head a moment later, as always he felt a new energy surging inside. Maybe he didn't need a doctor. He closed the book with a thump, swallowed the last of his drink, slung the can in the bin and headed for the stairs, unable to keep the bounce from his step. So he wasn't a sorcerer – so what? He would find out who he was, somehow. The door swung open as he approached and Holly stepped through, a file tucked under her arm, her hair tied back loosely. Elliot felt his heartbeat quicken as it often did when Holly was around. He had noticed the parting of her lips and the curve of her breasts too often to deny the way his thoughts were developing. He held the door for her and flashed what he felt was a compelling grin.

"Hi, Holly."

To his surprise, she flashed an even bigger smile back. The smile transformed her – she had always been *interesting*, but this smile… It made her beautiful. It was like a sunrise. Elliot was still staring when she leant forward and planted a firm kiss on his lips. Time slowed and his eyes sank into hers for that moment of contact, her perfume enveloping him, the edge of her lower lip clinging to his as though it was glued there, then peeling off as she drew away. Those dancing green eyes blinked at him above that sunrise smile, the blink as lazy as a yawn in Elliot's slow-motion world. Then the film of life sped up once more and Holly bounced back on her heels and swept past his open mouth towards the archives. She shot him a hungry look over her shoulder as she went.

"Hi," she said.

Unsteady on his feet, a whirlpool in his stomach, Elliot tumbled out through the door and stumbled up the stairs.

* * *

Holly trotted down the steps to the lower-ground floor, flicking through the file she carried as she went. Would they have any books on improving arithmetic through sorcery? Probably not, but Arthan wanted to check, so she would check.

Her mind wandered as she descended, drifting back to the previous night, losing herself in Arthan's arms. It had been so long since they had spent an evening together like that. She had even felt some glimmer of that old feeling she thought she had lost, like she was floating through life and everything else was below her and didn't matter.

She reached the foot of the stairs, tucked the file under her arm and plunged through the door onto the lower-ground floor to come face to face with none other than Arthan. It was unusual for him to be down here, as if he had appeared to answer her daydreams. He was wearing a badly fitted suit and was gazing at her with an unexpected intensity; she felt his eyes flash down past her neck before returning to lock with hers.

"Hi, Holly." He smiled.

The floating feeling inside burst into a broad grin she couldn't hold back. She leant forward and dropped a kiss on his lips, then whisked past, remembering his look. She glanced over her shoulder at his open-mouthed stare. How sweet.

"Hi," she called back.

Elliot couldn't contain a smile as he climbed the stairs. He didn't know why Holly had given him that kiss, but he didn't care. If she wanted to have secret kisses downstairs he would make sure he was down there more often. With each step he felt his suit trousers digging into his waist, and noticed that one of his shirt buttons was coming loose.

He stepped into the toilets to rearrange his clothing. When he approached the mirror the smile fell from his lips, and he understood why she had kissed him.

Arthan's round eyes stared back at him out of Arthan's milky smooth face, complete with plump cheeks and shiny, slicked-back hair. His mouth fell open, and so did Arthan's in the mirror. His hand rose and touched the face in the glass. A cold shiver stole over him, and then Arthan's face twitched and writhed and melted back into his own. He stared at himself. Sweat was starting to roll down his forehead, his chest heaving with rapid, desperate breaths.

He was a sorcerer. A shape-shifter.

PART FOUR
AFTERMATH

The day of Kim's death

CHAPTER SEVEN

The phone dropped from Holly's fingers with a clatter. Rupert's words ran on a loop in her ears. *I saw who killed Kim. It was Sean, and he's going to kill you next.*

She spun around, but she was still alone in Kim's bedroom. Alone with the corpse, and the blood, and the head. She squeezed her eyes shut as if it would all go away, but it was still there. The stubby neck, the bent legs, the blotchy head staring at her, screaming at her, begging her for help. *Sean killed Kim, and he's going to kill you next.* She opened her eyes again, careful not to look at the mess on the bed, but regardless of where she looked her head hummed with a violence that painted everything in gore. The white ceiling looked like the bleached skin of a corpse, the brown carpet looked like a stain of congealed blood. *Sean's going to kill you next.* It was impossible; it couldn't be Sean – he would never hurt Kim. But then she didn't believe any of the sorcerers were capable of this, and if Arthan was right then she was wrong about one of them.

She summoned power and raised a breeze to chase off the rotten odour of death. She tried to think logically, like Arthan would. Sean was in the next room, separated by mere walls and doors. If he wanted to kill her, he would kill her. They were alone and she couldn't stop a Red sorcerer. He was a weaker sorcerer than her, but she was Blue – what use would she be against an Innate Red? She was so tired.

She almost ran for the door, but stopped herself. She couldn't be weak. She couldn't be a timid Blue sorcerer today. She had chosen to do this.

She still didn't quite know why she told Arthan she would investigate the murder. It was like a switch had flipped inside her and her pounding heart had been replaced by an iron weight. She had felt so sure, for an instant, that she must do this, and that she could. She tried to revive that feeling, to find the switch that had since flipped back and left her feeling like a fragile shell once more.

She had been thinking of her parents, and that had prompted her to volunteer, even though what happened to her parents was different. They weren't murdered, not really. Her father used to speak about that boy, Tomar, all the time, although she had no real reason to avenge him, some faceless boy she had never met. Maybe it would help, to solve this murder and feel like she had done something for Kim, even though she barely knew her. She could pour the blood of this murder into that gnawn-out hole she still felt inside; maybe it would fill it.

She drew a breath, held it, then let it slide out. *Think, Holly.* What did she really know? Rupert said Sean was the killer, but that didn't make it true. She knew Premonition could be unreliable, especially for a young sorcerer like Rupert. But he was an Innate Green, and that counted for a lot.

She decided there was no shame in getting out of the flat; it was the sensible thing to do. She had some information that told her Sean might be a threat, so she had to be careful. She would call the others to come and help her once she was outside, and then they could all come back and subdue Sean together. She hurried to the bedroom door without stopping to get her bag, swung it open and froze. Sean was standing outside.

He stood hunched in the doorway to his bedroom, staring at her. Something about the way he held himself always suggested strength, the visible sign of his Red sorcery, but today he was enormous. His shirt strained at his heaving chest, his brutish arms hung like sandbags from his shoulders. Holly shrank back into Kim's room. She knew his emotion fed his Red strength, but which emotion was it that had made him grow this strong? Grief? Anger? Bloodlust? She couldn't read him. His face was an ugly mask, his skin drained almost as pale as his curls, veins standing out like worms on his temples, his eyes two sunken red scars.

He is going to kill you next. Holly steeled herself. "Hello, Sean."

"Do you know who did this?" His voice was a deep growl.

Her heartbeat quickened. He might have overheard her conversation with Rupert. Although if he had, surely he would have already killed her. Perhaps he suspected that she knew something and he was testing her. She shook her head.

He stared at her a few moments more, then strode across the hallway to the open door that led out of the flat. He was leaving. She was safe. All she had to do was let him go, but she found herself summoning power. A stirring of wind pushed the front door shut with a click.

"Sean. I'm sorry, I can't let you go."

He turned those narrow, bloodshot eyes on her again. She wished she hadn't spoken.

"What?" He took a step closer.

"You need to rest, and I need to talk to you."

After a moment, he laughed, a cracked sound that held no humour. "I am a suspect?" His eyes bulged, and he took another step closer. She could smell the reek of his sweat. "Why?"

"No reason," Holly replied, a little too quickly.

"Then take me off the list." Sean turned back for the door. "And do not follow me. I never want to see you people again." He put a meaty hand on the handle. "Come near me and you will pay with your life."

Without thinking, Holly summoned a splash of molten iron into existence around the lock mechanism in the door, then cooled it. She heard Sean grunt in surprise as the iron solidified and welded the lock in place. There was a quiet moment while he stood with his back to her, looking at the door handle. Then he came at her.

In a leap his thick hands were clamped on her soft arms, his red face breathing in hers. One of her bones snapped in his grip, and she gasped. As the pain arced through her she tried to numb it with her power, but he moved her so fast she couldn't focus. She was hoisted into the air and flung, the room spun past, then her back folded around something solid and she heard another loud snap. The room went black.

It must have only been a second later that she opened her eyes to see him standing over her. Through bright, spinning dots she saw him glare down at her where she lay twisted on the floor. She noticed her left knee facing the wrong way and knew that her leg was broken along with her right arm. She tasted salty blood in her mouth. Had Kim looked up at Sean like this from her bedside? Had her limbs twitched like this before he removed her head?

"That is your last warning." Sean turned away with a scowl. "Do not follow me." He strode to the door and with one huge arm wrenched the lock and handle clean out of the wall. The sound made her wince, a deep, splintering crack. With his other hand he punched through a hinge and ripped the remains of the door to one side, then bounded through the demolished doorway without looking back.

CHAPTER EIGHT

Just another boring day. Danielle stifled a burp, accelerated around the corner and slapped down the lever to silence the insistent clicking indicator. She rummaged through the sweet wrappers in the plastic compartment by her side, keeping one eye on the road. She found the cigarette packet and hauled it out in triumph, only to be greeted by an empty box. She swore, then again, but it didn't make her feel better. Scott had been taking her fags again. She swore for a third time, this time including Scott's name, and she felt a little better. The car rattled like a box of nails as she yanked the wheel around to turn into the next street, then gave a whining scream as she stamped the accelerator pedal to the floor. She decided she wouldn't buy anything for Scott at the supermarket; he could go shopping himself. She would buy what she needed and use Scott's beer money to replace the cigarettes he'd stolen. They didn't have enough money for the amount he drank anyway. She was planning the argument she would have with him later when a disturbance rippled the air and a storm burst alive inside her head. Her grip on the wheel loosened as her mind reeled with buzzing static and burning pinpricks, her vision swam, and for a moment she forgot where she was, while strange and unsettling sensations rustled through her body.

A second later her sight returned and she saw another driver's open-mouthed face hurtling towards her. She screamed and twisted the wheel to the left, bringing her car back inside the lane, and heard the other car's horn sounding as it receded in the rearview mirror.

Danielle kept her foot on the pedal and clung to the steering wheel with shaking hands. She couldn't piece together what had just happened. The buzzing in her head had lessened, but the echoes of it still bounced in her skull. She put a hand to her forehead and felt a throbbing heat. She must be ill. It was Scott's fault – if he brought home more money she wouldn't have been drinking such cheap vodka last night.

She slammed the accelerator back down and tried to shake the ache out of her head. Supermarket, cigarettes, sofa. That was what she needed. Scott would have to do the housework today.

Danielle hated the supermarket. It was a sweaty, writhing pit of babbling families and hobbling old ladies, too busy, too loud and too many people in her way. She elbowed past a mother and her two greasy-haired daughters who were blocking the aisle. Following the strange headache in the car, a rhythmic pressure had been building behind her eyes. She would have to buy some painkillers, which meant even less money for the rest of the shopping. She glared at the sign above her head and her vision blurred. She squinted at the letters until they swam clear. Fish. Nothing for her here. She detested fish.

She found some bargains in the discount aisle and picked up some cigarettes. What else did she need to buy for dinner? Chips, of course.

Just then the headache struck again like a hammer. Several pounding blows to her vision knocked the aisle out of focus, and her legs buckled. She clutched the white plastic shelf beside her and managed to keep her balance, but it took a few seconds for her legs to stop shaking.

Danielle scowled at the concerned faces around her and wished they would stop staring. She hated shopping. What had she been about to look for? She gritted her teeth against the crushing pressure from her head, but her blurred vision remained, along with a fizzing sound in her ears. She could almost remember what she needed to buy – something for dinner – but the weight pressing on her mind clouded her thoughts. She had thought of it only a second before – what was it? As she clutched for the memory, the tide rose up inside, and with a sudden snap a belt of pressure slipped from her mind, a lick of flame burst from the shelf beside her and her vision cleared like a curtain parting. She blinked. Chips, that was it.

She frowned at the cereal packet on the shelf next to her. The whiff of smoke and the charred corner of the packet told her that the flame must have been real. She rubbed her eyes, unable to remember what had just happened and how the packet could have caught alight.

It wasn't worth worrying about it. The pressure in her head had subsided now, but she was definitely ill. She would get the shopping done as fast as possible and then she could have a smoke. Chips.

* * *

By the time she reached the chips aisle her headache had returned. She reached into the freezer for a bag of crinkle-cuts, but all the products were swimming before her eyes. Her right hand stumbled over sharp ice but couldn't find the packet, and her left hand shot to her forehead as the headache tightened like a vice.

"Can I help you?"

She whirled, but could only see a blurred pillar of lime green where the speaker must be standing. One of those shop assistant morons. The boredom in his voice made it clear he didn't really want to help her. As she swayed towards him the green pillar wavered and moved backwards.

"Are you OK?"

The assistant's voice was faint beneath the buzzing in her ears. She clenched her teeth and strained to pull the dirty smudges of colour into focus, to push the fog away from her mind. She had to focus on the shopping, she had to get the chips. Crinkle-cut chips.

"Crinkle-cut," she said, staggering towards the assistant. Through the blurred haze she thought she saw him step away again, and a wave of heat blazed through her. How dare he step away.

"Crinkle-cut!" she said. The pressure burned in her mind, but it was changing now – it was turning, twisting, roaring in her ears, finding a way out. Everything was melting. She couldn't see the assistant; all shapes were joining into one buzzing, soupy blur.

"What?" It was the assistant's voice, barely audible under the deafening thunder.

Something snapped and Danielle felt the pent-up heat vent from her. It was an instant release, the pressure rushing from her brain like air from a balloon. She felt some sort of current leap from her through the air, and violent, bright hues flared in the murky pool in front of her eyes.

Her vision cleared, the world suddenly silent and still, and she saw the crackling fire covering the assistant's arms and chest. The shoppers around them stood open-mouthed. A chill rippled over her, dousing the heat she had felt a second before, though something was still rushing from her, hungry and fast. The assistant howled in pain and tumbled backwards into the freezer, steam rising from the frozen food. As screams rose around her and shoppers fled in all directions, Danielle looked down and watched the stream of fire erupt from her trembling hands.

CHAPTER NINE

Gordon could barely place one foot in front of the other. London's streets had become a place of nightmares: hard faces leering, horns blaring, dead eyes and deep shadows on all sides. It was safest to keep staring at the patched, stained pavement. He watched his own thin legs tremble as he walked, felt the wind numbing his lips and listened to his heart hammering in his ears. The end was coming.

He still couldn't believe what Marrin had told him. Kim had been murdered. It was impossible, too bizarre to be true. He glanced up ahead to Marrin's broad, swaying back, and trotted closer. The thought of getting left alone in this nightmare was a chilling one.

Gordon had felt his throat go dry when Marrin approached him in the office, before he had even known what she was going to say. He hadn't been sure who she was, but when he realised she was the strange Purple sorcerer who had been teaching Ian Purple Controls, he knew it was going to be bad news. Ian said she lived in an ancient cottage with no lights or heating and never went outside. When she'd delivered her message, Gordon had tried to convince himself she was joking, but she didn't look like one to joke. Her scratchy cardigan and shawl, her stringy grey hair scraped into a tight bun, her thick round glasses, the deep creases under her eyes, it was all deadly serious.

So it must be true. There was a murderer loose, a sorcerer murderer. Marrin had said that it might be Sean, and they had to go and help Arthan to stop him. *It might be Sean.* Just to hear those words made Gordon's head spin. How would they stop him? What could Gordon do? He knew the answers; he felt them with certainty like dull kicks in his stomach. There was nothing they could do; they were all going to be killed. His life was over. The world was painted in shades of shadow and black, the veil was already drawn across his eyes, his funeral was in procession, and he was too frozen stiff to even cry. He was dead.

He almost stumbled into Marrin's back, which had come to an abrupt halt. She frowned as she peered down at him, her eyes bulging through her glasses. Then Gordon nearly jumped when he noticed someone standing in front of them. But they were safe, for now – it was Arthan.

At this point Arthan would usually be the one who would take control of this nightmare, but Gordon noticed immediately that his boss wasn't his usual self. He wore the expected spotless pressed suit, but his plump cheeks were flushed and his normally smartly combed hair was matted on his forehead.

"What took you so long?" Arthan said.

"Had to heal the girl, then pick up the boy." Marrin's voice sounded like something being dragged through gravel.

Arthan glared at Gordon, who shrank behind Marrin. "Do we really need him?"

"You wanted help."

"Hello." Gordon barely heard his own whisper. Seeing Arthan like this made him feel even colder. Arthan always knew what to do; he always had the answers. If Arthan himself wasn't coping, their situation must be even more dire than Gordon had thought.

"Enough talk." Arthan grimaced and threw a glance over his shoulder at the busy street. "I have traced Sean to a public house back there. We must hurry – you two have delayed us too much already."

Swallowing, Gordon peered in the direction Arthan had

looked, to where his death awaited him. He should run – there was still time to run. Further down the street, past the lit shop windows and the milling shoppers, Gordon could see a sign jutting high from the wall that bore a painting of a bell. That must be the pub, and Sean must be inside. Gordon shivered and shuffled even closer to Marrin.

"You could have gone in on your own," Marrin said.

"Sean is dangerous! He attacked Holly!" Arthan paused, his frown fading. For a moment he looked lost, as young as his body. "How is she?"

Marrin shrugged. "I healed her."

Arthan grunted. "Good."

Much too soon, they started marching towards the pub. It was time to die. Gordon dragged his feet along behind them, trying to follow what they were saying but unable to concentrate. Every whisper of the wind felt like the brush of a murderer's fingers along his neck, every growl of a car engine sounded like the guttural roar of a madman. He wondered if Arthan and Marrin were scared too. Arthan didn't seem scared; his eyes had narrowed to nothing but venomous slits. Marrin gave no sign of what she was thinking. Her mouth was a taut line, her face was expressionless. She was a person carved from rock.

They stopped outside the pub, and Arthan put his finger to his lips and pointed at the murky window. Gordon felt his stomach clench when he saw Sean sitting at the bar among the drinkers, his vast back facing the window. Even from this distance he looked enormous.

"I will have to subdue Sean's emotions." Arthan grimaced. "And he may also need controlling physically. Gordon, can you restrain him if necessary?"

What? Gordon tried to say no, but he couldn't form any words.

Arthan nodded, seeming to see a response in Gordon's face. "Good. Marrin, you will provide assistance as required."

That was it then. Gordon was going to be flung into Sean's hands and torn limb from limb. His stomach churned as he imagined his approaching final breaths. Pulverised by a

Red sorcerer, ripped to bloody strips. There was no escape. Marrin wouldn't be able to provide any assistance. She was an old Purple sorcerer, a healer; she couldn't protect them against Sean.

But he clutched her dress all the same. She didn't look at him, just answered Arthan in her grating monotone. "I will help."

* * *

"Sean."

Gordon could barely hear Arthan's murmur over the chattering of the drinkers that filled the pub. Sean didn't move. He sat only a few feet from Gordon, a giant among the low wooden beams, his blond head bowed over the bar as if he was praying. Arthan whispered his name again, looking more than ever like a child beside Sean's bulk, but the Red sorcerer still didn't move. Gordon tensed as he noticed Arthan lay a hand on Sean's huge shoulder.

"Get lost," Sean said, without turning. A few heads turned in their direction, then returned to their conversations. How could these people not realise the danger among them? Gordon couldn't tear his gaze from the innocent-looking curls on the back of Sean's head. He could smell his own sweat mixing with the aroma of beer. If Sean turned and attacked now, Gordon wouldn't even have a chance to run. He found himself shrinking backwards but was held in place by a solid hand on his shoulder.

"Calm, Gordon." Marrin's voice was made of iron, an anchor in the storm. Gordon tried to slow his breathing. He was going to die; there was nothing he could do but accept it.

Arthan glanced back at Gordon and Marrin, then Gordon heard him speak to Sean again, his voice as smooth as silk. "You must come with us."

Sean spun round, sending glasses clattering along the bar, and Gordon cowered backwards. Sean's face was a raw red shock, his eyes blotchy, his lip curled in anger. Somehow, in that moment Gordon was reminded of Kim's gentle features, and an old, bad, stirring feeling resurfaced. Sickened, he pushed it aside. He didn't want to feel like that any more, not now of all times, not ever again. It was wrong.

"Must I?" Sean sneered at Arthan. "Because a snotty boy like you wants me back in his club?"

Arthan's frame stiffened, but his reply betrayed no emotion. "Come with us."

Sean's voice dropped to a deadly whisper. "Leave me alone." Suddenly Sean's bloodshot eyes were fixed straight at Gordon. The world stopped moving. Like a distant echo Gordon felt Marrin's hand on his shoulder again, but this time it held no comfort; Sean's eyes speared him, he couldn't move, he couldn't feel, he couldn't look away. Sean must know about his wrong feelings. Gordon's time had come; Sean was going to kill him. He was dead.

Arthan stepped in the way of Sean's gaze and Gordon almost collapsed as he was set free from those eyes. "Let go of it," Gordon heard Arthan say. "Come with us."

There was the scrape of a chair as Sean rose to his feet. Sean was a clear foot taller than Arthan, and so that livid red face, that murderous glare, was visible again over Arthan's head. Gordon held his breath. Arthan took a step backwards and Sean advanced, his vast chest gathering and expanding with long, rumbling breaths. They were so close Gordon could smell the stench of beer on Sean's breath as he hissed at Arthan, "Leave me alone or I will break you like I broke your girlfriend."

Then everything happened quickly. There was a high-pitched scream, like a small girl's, and it took Gordon a second to realise it had come from Arthan. A fist flew at Sean's face, and by the time Gordon had realised the fist also belonged to Arthan, Sean had hurled the Yellow sorcerer aside like a wooden doll. Gordon watched wide-eyed as Arthan's limp body sailed past. In front of him crouched Sean, his long arms dangling, his hackles raised, his red eyes burning. Gordon heard a smack as Arthan's head hit the stone floor to his right, and out of the corner of his eye he saw Marrin rush to Arthan's side and lay a hand on his head. Gordon was alone.

It was the end. It was time for him to throw himself at

Sean like Arthan had and be ripped apart. There was no choice – he had to do as Arthan had instructed, he had to try and restrain Sean. But he didn't move. Sean glared in the direction he had thrown Arthan, then back at Gordon, but Gordon still didn't move. His skinny limbs had become heavy, as if made of stone, and his thoughts moved like mud. What had taken hold of him? There were screams around him, pale faces jostling to escape. He couldn't move. He knew he should be summoning power, his final futile act, reaching out with his Orange Control to stop Sean escaping. Why wasn't he? He just stared as Sean strode past him towards the door of the pub.

It was over, and he was alive. Arthan still lay slumped on the floor, Marrin still crouched over him, but at the moment Sean placed his hand on the door handle, Marrin looked up from her healing. She waved a hand and Sean stumbled in mid-stride then collapsed to the floor in an unconscious heap.

A buzz of chatter spread around the watching crowd. Gordon turned to find Arthan regaining his feet, his suit ripped and stained, looking shaken but unharmed. Gordon let out a long, ragged breath. His legs were shivering as though it was cold, but sweat was running down his forehead.

He had never felt so glad to be alive.

* * *

Gordon peered around Marrin's stomach at Sean's lifeless, milky eyes, which had been so deadly just minutes before. Arthan and Marrin had hauled the huge Red sorcerer into a taxi, and now they were driving back towards the office with Sean, Marrin and Gordon all wedged onto the back seat. Sean didn't look so big now. His legs were folded against the door, his head bumping on the window as the car sped along, his mouth lolling open.

"What did you do to him?" Gordon asked.

Marrin lowered her impassive, bug-eyed gaze towards him. "I put him to sleep. He will wake in a few hours."

Of course. Purple sorcery controlled other people's bodies. There was no reason it should only be used for healing. Gordon looked again for some sign of emotion under Marrin's stony face. There was none. How did she control herself so completely? Gordon watched his own hand trembling, then clasped his thigh to stop it. "Why did Arthan punch Sean?"

Marrin seemed to consider this for the first time. "He was angry."

Gordon peeked at Sean's still form again. "But why did he punch him? Why didn't he use sorcery?"

Marrin grunted. "Being a sorcerer of mind magic doesn't stop you acting stupid."

Gordon's eyes widened. How could she speak of Arthan that way? Fortunately Arthan didn't seem to be listening; he was sitting in front beside the driver, staring out of the window.

"I couldn't move in there. Sean must have cast a Control on me."

"No, Gordon." Marrin's eyes twinkled for a moment, and Gordon saw an unexpected softness there. "You were just scared."

Gordon shook his head mutely.

"Being scared is useful, Gordon. It is only by feeling emotion that we learn to control it."

Gordon himself now stared at nothing through the window, thinking about how frozen he had become in the pub. There must have been some sorcery to it, although he couldn't deny that he had been scared. He was always scared. He wished he could block his emotions out like Marrin did, bottle them up along with the bad feelings he shouldn't have felt.

The memory of Kim's face rose like an insistent ghost, her silent voice calling him, her bright eyes watching him. He shut her out, feeling sick. It was wrong. He promised himself that from now on, he would control himself. He would shut everything out, his nightmares and his dreams and his hopes and his joys too. He would shut his heart off from the world and let it wither in some stale place inside him. Then he wouldn't have those wrong feelings, and he wouldn't be scared any more.

CHAPTER TEN

Naomi sat shivering at her desk, staring at her lifeless black computer screen.

All the others had gone. Briggs had told her to go home too, but she couldn't move, she couldn't think straight. How long had she been sitting here trying to make herself feel normal? Kim. The name buzzed around her head, a fly she couldn't swat away.

Briggs had told her the news in his usual way. He used phrases like "difficult times" and "we'll pull together", but it all meant nothing. He spoke words of comfort like he was reading them from a book.

Kim. She was the only one Naomi had really liked. At one of their training sessions Kim had stopped Rupert and Ian from killing a spider; Naomi had adored her for that. Naomi had even wondered if Kim might become her friend, but now she was dead.

Naomi wished she could stand up to them like Kim about the spider. If Naomi had been recruited by Arthan and not Briggs, it all would have been different. She would have been working with Kim every day, and she imagined she could even tolerate the men at Arthan Associates; Gordon, Sean and Elliot all seemed quiet enough to be bearable. In comparison, Briggs & Co was a zoo. Rupert and Ian were adults, even if Rupert's body had stopped ageing when he was a teenager, and

Briggs was over a hundred years old, but all three of them acted like schoolboys. Naomi couldn't stomach much more of their jeering and chortling at each other's dirty jokes. As soon as she learnt how to control her power she would leave.

The blare of her ringing telephone made her jump from her chair. Her heart thumped. She turned her back on the ringing and sloped away through the empty desks. She knew what would make her feel better.

Naomi caught a glimpse of her reflection in a window and hurried past. She loathed the sight of herself. Fat and ugly. She dropped her head to let her hair hang in a lank dark curtain in front of her face. She wished she could hide away from the world. She wore lumpy black jumpers and thick black trousers in desperate hope her bulk might blend into the shadows. She could imagine what people must think when they looked at her. Low brow, squinty eyes and greasy skin. Fat, ugly pig. She didn't match Briggs's slick, trendy office. He had tried to make her wear designer clothes, to cloak her gross body with a feminine disguise. She had worn the outfit for one day, her skin bulging from the gaps like trussed meat. Ian's and Rupert's smothered cackles reared in her memory and she shoved them back down.

She took a corridor to the right and pushed through an unmarked door. The smell hit her the second she entered the room. No more fresh paint and disinfectant, just the warm, earthy aroma of nature's beautiful creatures. She was with them again.

Her heart swelled and she drew power for her Innate Green Control as she weaved across the room between the scattered boxes. Briggs still kept his things in here despite his promise to let Naomi have the whole room, but at least he hadn't tried to move her friends out. Having them here was the only request she had ever made of Briggs, and this room was the only place in the building where she could find some peace away from the three schoolboys. She reached the far wall, where three large plastic cages sat side by side on the carpet, and flopped down before them with a grin.

She peeked into the smallest cage. A tiny white mouse

peeked back at her from a red-roofed house. The mouse sniffed, then emerged onto the sawdust. "Hello, Boris," she whispered.

Boris twitched his whiskers, and with her Green Control she felt his little brain thinking. Communicating with animals was the only Control Naomi could manage without miscasting, much to Briggs's disappointment. He thought that the prediction sorcery that Rupert specialised in was a far more valuable Green Control than Naomi's animal abilities.

Boris had been asleep for a while and was now hungry. She pushed a thought towards him that his food was at the end of the cage. She felt Boris's gratitude humming from his mind as he scampered across to it. She blew him a kiss.

She looked in the next cage for Clive the lizard, who scrambled out from behind a mossy rock to greet her with a flash of his tongue. She answered him with a giggle and reached a finger in to stroke his smooth head.

In the last cage Jenny had already slithered out and sat bunched on her fat coils awaiting her turn. The python tilted her head in response to Naomi's greeting. Naomi summoned a little more power, slipped into direct mind contact and felt the snake's thoughts mingle with her own.

-You are so clever, Jenny. You speak to me so clearly now.

-*I like it. It is happy to speak.*

Jenny showed Naomi her memories, as Naomi had taught her. She had been sleeping most of the day, but had noticed Briggs in the room earlier that morning, whispering urgently on his mobile phone. Naomi stored this information away for future reference.

There was a noise behind her, and she broke off her mental link to the snake then turned to find a thin figure peering in through the doorway. Holly. What was she doing here?

"Is now a good time?"

At the sound of Holly's voice, Boris and Clive scuttled out of sight, and even Jenny slithered back behind her log. Naomi scowled. A good time for what? It was never a good time to interrupt her when she was with her friends. But her retort evaporated in her throat when she noticed what Holly was dangling without due care and attention from her right hand. A plastic cat box.

Naomi nodded. "Yes, come in."

The plastic box bumped against Holly's leg as she limped across the room. Naomi winced at each jolt.

Holly hobbled to a stop. "Don't worry, I'm fine," she said, misreading Naomi's concern. "Just had a little fall earlier." Holly rested the box on the floor, and a pair of large wet eyes appeared between the white plastic bars. Without waiting for an invitation, Naomi flipped the catches and opened the small door, and a cat padded out of the box to greet her.

She was gorgeous. Her fur was a thick, sleek chocolate, her paws dabbed with grey, her eyes innocent white circles. She was perfect.

"This is Kim's cat. I thought maybe you could look after her, at least for a while?"

Naomi nodded as she stroked the cat's velvety ears. What a wonderful thing to happen on such a terrible day. A new friend for Boris, Clive and Jenny. She looked deep into the cat's eyes. *I will look after you forever.*

"Her name's Rosie."

Naomi nodded again but could not afford to pay Holly any more attention; it was time to devote herself to Rosie. She started compiling a mental list of all the supplies she would need to take care of her. By the time she had finished, she noticed that Holly had gone, and settled into a more comfortable position, heaving a long breath out. She was alone with her animals again.

Rosie purred as Naomi picked her up and sent a wordless message of love into her sweet little cat mind. She told Rosie there was no need to be frightened, everything would be fine. Rosie rumbled contentedly at these warm waves of comfort, and rubbed her pink nose against her new friend's chin. Naomi giggled, and their minds slipped together.

Rosie was thinking of Kim. Looking through the window of the cat's memory, Naomi watched as if she was there, as if they were one, and she was Rosie. Kim was bending down from far above to feed her, tickling her cheek in that tender way that made Rosie feel special. Kim was smoothing her fur as she drifted into sleep. Kim was—The image clouded as an enquiring thought pressed Naomi's consciousness. Rosie was asking her a question, although it was shaped in emotions rather than words. She would need practice to communicate properly with Naomi's mind, but this time her meaning was clear.

Naomi's heart twisted in knots as she explained to Rosie in large, clear thoughts that Kim was gone and wouldn't be coming back. The cat's response was confusion. Naomi told Rosie someone bad had taken Kim away forever. Rosie sniffed and licked her paw. Eventually she responded. *Who?*

-I don't know, someone bad.

After a pause, another of Rosie's memories rose like a dream before Naomi's mind. It was daytime, after the morning feed. All was still. She was lounging on the cold wooden floor in Kim and Sean's flat, her paws stretched out, her stomach too full for her to bother pursuing the various scents meandering across her nose. The door opened and a strange human entered. Naomi watched the memory through Rosie's round eyes, as Rosie had watched from the hallway floor. Naomi's heart froze when she recognised the intruder's face. *The murderer. It's the murderer.* Unable to tear herself from the memory, Naomi watched the view swing away as Rosie sprang to her feet and scampered away from the intruder. Seeking more familiar company, she trotted into Kim's room. From Rosie's viewpoint near the floor, Naomi could see Kim sitting at her bedside table, a ring-bound file open in front of her. When Rosie hopped onto her favourite chair and began circling to lie down, Naomi saw the murderer enter the room carrying a long, gleaming sword. Naomi stopped breathing. Kim spun around, saw the sword, then her eyes widened and her mouth fell open as the murderer advanced. Naomi willed herself to look away but couldn't. With piercing screams echoing in her ears, Naomi watched, transfixed, as Kim was slaughtered.

CHAPTER ELEVEN

The supermarket car park was littered with cars, fire engines and ambulances, like discarded toys. Alarms flashed and sirens blared. Herds of onlookers clustered by the glass doors where ragged bands of shoppers streamed out, chased by plumes of smoke. The air hummed with shimmering heat and a smell like bonfire night. Above it all stood the supermarket itself: a squat, blackened fort, thick, dirty clouds billowing from its windows, its once bright and inviting welcome sign now a grim, burnt wooden board.

Rupert grinned. This was cool.

The sickness of prophecy still burned in his throat, but he felt infinitely better than he had two hours ago. It seemed the immediate danger had passed. Arthan had gone to retrieve Sean, who apparently hadn't caused Holly any permanent injury. Once Arthan had Sean captive they would all be safe… although that laboured breathing still rasped in Rupert's ears, the reek of congealing blood still filled his nostrils and he kept seeing Holly's blank face whiten as Sean squeezed the life from her thin frame.

Briggs stood next to Ian and Rupert and surveyed the scene with them, his beady eyes flicking over the carnage. He looked as polished as ever, his suit spotless, his thick chestnut hair slicked back from his creased, tanned face.

"Right then, chaps." Briggs rubbed his hands together.

"The quicker we get this sorted, the quicker we can go home. What are we looking at?"

"I reckon it's a supermarket, boss," Rupert said, before Ian could say it first. Ian chuckled. It was good to see his friend laugh; Rupert hadn't seen even a hint of a smile on Ian's broad, solemn face since the news of Kim's death had arrived earlier. Rupert knew Ian had a tendency to let life get him down, and today it was more important than ever for Rupert to lift him out of his misery.

Briggs nodded. "It is a supermarket. You're a bright lad, Rupert. What does your glorious intellect suggest we do next?"

"Shopping?"

Rupert's boss wrinkled his nose. "Probably not, I'd say, given all the fire. But let's go and have a look round anyway."

Briggs removed his suit jacket, eyeing the ash and dirt around them. Rupert smiled, knowing how much Briggs hated getting his clothes dirty. *Image is everything, boys.* But Rupert removed his jacket too; it was nearly brand new, after all. He glanced at Ian, who watched them but didn't move. "Don't be ashamed of revealing your beer gut, Ian, you're among friends! We'll tell you if any buttons pop."

Ian's response was a glare. He seemed to be getting more and more touchy these days, especially about his expanding waistline. It was unfortunate that Ian's body hadn't stopped ageing yet, as youth helped to keep the weight off. It probably didn't help that Ian spent all his time with Rupert. Of the two of them, Ian would always be the fatter, plainer one, but Rupert refused to feel guilty for being handsome. He took care to retain his slim figure, and regularly spent money on haircuts and clothes to make the most of his looks. Ian insisted on wearing cheap, misshapen suits that made him look older than even Briggs; he clearly had a complex about being unattractive. Rupert often tried to help him make light of his appearance, but it was no use; he was always so sensitive.

They made their way across the cluttered car park, weaving between abandoned cars, skirting the piles of burnt debris, and finally arrived at the large glass entrance doors. Rupert found himself in the lead and had to force his way through the tightly packed crowd, receiving more than a few scowls and mutters along the way. The sliding mechanism on the glass doors had either broken or been switched off, so they stood unmoving, a few feet apart. Rupert slipped through the gap, finally leaving the scrutiny of the crowd behind him.

Inside, he found the lighting wasn't working either. The supermarket was as dark as a cave, and hot. The rustle and pop of flames could be heard in the distance. Smoke clung around them, obscuring Rupert's vision and stinging his eyes, but between the dark clouds he could see that the aisles, floor and walls were strewn with burnt and broken packets, ash-smeared tins and jars. It was like a war zone, or at least what Rupert imagined a war zone would be like.

He crept forward, no longer sure if Ian and Briggs were behind him. In the darkness his thoughts wandered, inexorably, back to the prophecy. The shadows shaped themselves into rippling arms that closed around a pale neck; the flames that flickered here and there were bloody spittle shaken from bluing lips. He shivered despite the heat. Sean had always seemed so normal, if a little quiet, but Rupert could not deny what he had seen, what he had felt with every resisting fibre of his body. Sean had killed Kim, and he was going to try and kill Holly too. Prophecy could never be denied, and could never quite be forgotten. His heart started beating faster. From the shadows his old nightmares clutched at him once more. He saw the stained white hospital bed and the bony, fleshless arm, heard the slow drip of a tap and caught the bitter stink of urine. He swallowed, steeled himself and headed for the hazy brightness in the distance where the light would leave less room for visions.

He was making his way down a darkened aisle strewn with crushed cereal boxes, the air growing hotter with every step, when he felt a familiar twist in his guts. His Green Control. He spun and yelled into the gloom, "Ian! Move!"

Through the smoke he saw Ian skitter sideways as a six-foot-high shelving unit peeled away from the wall and crashed to the floor where he had just been, throwing up a cloud of ash and scattering boxes around them. Briggs looked on while Ian regained his breath.

"Thanks," Ian said.

It was a rare chance to savour being the hero, but Rupert couldn't resist the opportunity. "Ben! Watch out!"

With a cry Briggs threw himself to the ground. After a second he peered up from the floor wide-eyed, looking something like a frightened rabbit. Nothing happened.

Both Ian and Rupert were giggling by the time Briggs clambered to his feet, brushing ash off his suit.

"Not funny." Briggs gave Rupert a dark look. "Not funny at all." He stalked ahead with a scowl, and Ian adopted a serious expression and hurried after him.

Rupert rolled his eyes. Could no one take a joke any more?

* * *

"This is cool." Rupert drank in the bizarre scene in front of him. They were in an open space beside the frozen-food aisle, although the food was no longer frozen; murky brown water swam over the floor with charred boxes and blackened plastic slumped here and there in the pools. Spread in a wide circle, twenty or thirty police officers and firefighters stood with abandoned fire hoses snaking across the floor around them, and in the centre of the circle blazed a pillar of fire.

The fire was the source of the brightness Rupert had noticed earlier, and it was giving off a heat that stung his nose and cheeks. It was a huge, fierce red arm of crackling, hungry flames that reached all the way to the distant ceiling; it looked as though it had burned a hole all the way through the roof, and it seemed to be gushing out of a squat, scruffy woman who stood at its base, scowling.

"It seems we have found the Host," Briggs said.

The Host. She was the sorcerer created in Kim's place when Sean had brought the sword down hard, his huge hands clenched around the handle, the blade vibrating as it struck, the wet thunk of metal into flesh. Rupert shook his head clear and tried to concentrate on his surroundings.

A number of the police and firefighters nodded greetings as Briggs, Rupert and Ian joined the circle.

"Thanks for coming so quick, Ben." The speaker was a stocky policeman with a rosy sweat who stood next to them in the circle. "I figured she's one of yours."

Briggs nodded. "She certainly is. What have we missed so far?"

The policeman shrugged. "Fire and more fire. It just pours out of her. We managed to persuade her to stop waving her arms about and point the fire upwards, but it won't stop burning."

Rupert peered at the blazing woman. She herself seemed unaffected by the heat of the flames – her clothes and body were unscathed. The fire was issuing from her outstretched hands, which she held aloft, into the scorching column above her.

"What's your problem, speccy?" the woman said. Rupert blinked, taken aback.

"She's got a mouth on her," the policeman said to Rupert.

Rupert found himself adjusting his glasses. He hadn't realised they were so obvious; the designer frames were supposed to blend in with the shape of his face, according to the lady who had sold them to him. Maybe it was time to go back to wearing contacts.

Briggs finished a whispered conversation with another policeman then led Ian and Rupert a couple of paces inside the circle, where it was even hotter. Rupert felt moisture forming at his temples. "It's all under control, boys." Briggs kept his voice low, his beady eyes on the flaming woman. "The shoppers have all been evacuated. All we need to do is extinguish the Host's fire, then our work is done. Piece of cake."

"How are we going to do it?" Ian asked.

Briggs sighed. "I'm not sure." He flicked ash from his trousers with a grimace. "I always end up with the worst jobs."

Rupert glanced at the woman again, quick enough so she wouldn't notice. She looked like bad news, even if she hadn't been on fire. She wore a faded pink tracksuit with a shiny black jacket, and large silver hoop earrings that hung almost to her shoulders. She looked like one of those women who trudged prams past Rupert's house towards the council estate in the next street. An unsavoury character, his father would say. Foster father, Rupert corrected himself. He still couldn't get used to the idea he was adopted.

"Can't we just pour water over her?" Ian said.

"You're gonna what?" the woman said, apparently not quite out of earshot.

Rupert noticed Ian flinch, and smirked. "Go on, Ian, she likes you!"

"You lot had better tell me what's going on! I've had enough of this!"

Briggs frowned, ignoring the woman. "Sorcerer's fire is difficult to quench, especially when it's a blaze like this. I expect the fire crew have already tried their best." He thought for a moment. "We need her to stop casting the Control. The tricky thing is, she won't know how she started casting it, let alone how to stop."

"We could teach her," Ian said.

Rupert laughed. "I don't think she's in the mood for a lesson."

"I'm going to count to ten!" the woman yelled.

Briggs nodded. "Yes, a lesson would take too long." He tapped his chin. "The Control is probably being channelled by her emotion – if we could calm her down it might lessen the fire."

"We could sing lullabies to her," said Rupert with a grin.

The others laughed, but the woman noticed, and her voice became a scream. "Why am I on fire?"

Rupert looked in the other direction. Ian coughed, trying to cover his laughter.

Briggs turned to her with a loud sigh. "Madam, we are trying to find a way to put you out. Please keep it down."

She lowered her arm from the air and thrust an accusing finger in Briggs's direction. "You stupid—"

Rupert never heard the end of the insult, as it was drowned

in the roar of a huge gout of flame that shot through the air towards them from the woman's finger. Rupert's Premonition hadn't warned him this time; he was too late to even shout a warning. Briggs dived out of the way and collided with Rupert, who found himself toppling to the floor as the fire crackled past his shoulder. There was a loud scream behind him, and he heard people bellowing "Hands up!" over the thunder of the rushing fire. By the time he lifted his head the woman had pointed her hands at the ceiling once more, and the tower of fire was back in place. The screaming continued behind him, and he turned to find Ian dancing on the spot, batting at his clothes. He was on fire; his legs, his body and his head were all drowned under seething, dancing flames.

Briggs began waving his hands in a fluid pattern, presumably casting some Control on Ian to try and quench the fire, but it was all Rupert could do to stifle a giggle at the sight of Ian's bizarre jig. The jerky dance slowed as the flames subsided, until Ian eventually dropped to his knees, coughing hoarsely.

He looked a state. His clothes were charred black, his sleeves tattered, his usually fair hair a blackened nest. Rupert grinned. "You dance much better when you're on fire, Ian."

Ian's head snapped up towards him, and Rupert took an instinctive step back. An ugly, raw burn crawled from Ian's left eye down his cheek to his burnt lips and spread onto his bright red neck. "How does my face look, Rupert? Any jokes about that?"

Rupert recoiled. "Relax, mate, use Red Control. Just heal yourself."

"Probably not," Briggs muttered beside him, panting with the effort of his sorcery. "It's sorcerer's fire."

"You see, Rupert?" Ian was on his feet, his burnt face twisted in taut creases. It was an ugly sight up close. "Not everything is a joke!"

Then, without warning, Ian swung his fist and punched Rupert hard on the chin. The shock of the impact on his jaw sent Rupert sprawling backwards to land in a heap on the grimy floor, the cold tiles hitting the back of his head with a smack.

Looking up at the high ceiling, his thoughts ran in confused circles. His jaw throbbed like the bite of Sean's sword, like the ache in his head, like the tightening around Holly's neck. Why did Ian hit him – why not hit Briggs, why not hit the flaming woman, why not hit Sean? His foster father's drawn face looked down at him through the curling smoke, with that empty, broken, questioning expression. *Why, Rupert? Why did you take her from me?* The smoke coiled into a hooped silver earring, then a pair of designer glasses, then a plastic tube leading into a fleshless arm. Why did everyone blame him? Why did everyone take life so seriously? The mess on this floor was going to ruin his suit trousers.

He realised it had gone quiet. He turned his head towards the flaming woman just in time to see the pillar of fire vanish as she collapsed to the floor in a dead faint.

CHAPTER TWELVE

Danielle blinked open her eyes. There was a bright light. She remembered fire, a scalding heat and a rushing, rattling emptying from within.

She couldn't see properly; her eyes wouldn't focus.

She decided she must be dead. Great. That was the last thing she needed.

A vague silhouette moved into view and a woman's voice sounded. "You're not dead. You've just had a very traumatic experience."

The voice was strange – it had a musical sound to it, a whisper of song. A traumatic experience. Danielle's memories of the supermarket emerged from her cloudy mind and she thrashed her hands out of the bedsheets, expecting to see the flames still pouring out and hear again the screams and crackle of flesh. She realised at last that her hands were as they had been all her life: creased pink skin, and nothing more. She glared at the silhouette to see if it was laughing at her. She scowled. "You're one of them, aren't you."

The hazy lines were resolving into normal vision. She was in a small white bare room, lit by a shaft of warm light from a window to her left. It was almost silent, although she thought she heard faint music in the distance. There was a slight scent of roses. The silhouette became a young woman's face, pale and delicate with round eyes and tumbling blond, almost white, hair. The woman was sitting next to the bed Danielle lay in, gazing at her, as still as stone.

"Are you deaf?" Danielle snapped.

Danielle noticed a shimmer of annoyance pass over the woman's face before it returned to an expressionless marble facade.

"I did not answer you because I do not understand the question."

Danielle barked a laugh. She struggled to prop herself up on the pillows, and discovered that every muscle ached. "I don't understand either. I don't understand why fire started coming out of me when I went shopping." She scanned the room, looking for clues to where she was. "But that posh idiot and the two boys, they knew what was happening. And they're your mates. Aren't they."

"My name is Elizan," the woman began, in the manner of someone starting a long speech.

"Do I look like I care?" Danielle drew some satisfaction from the woman's blink. If there was one thing Danielle hated, it was stuck-up cows like this one who thought they were better than her. "Tell me where I am and why I'm here, before I slap it out of you."

Now the woman did more than blink. She shrank backwards in her chair so fast she almost fell. Danielle guessed the woman wasn't threatened very often, and made a mental note of this. Wherever Danielle was, it was likely she was going to have to look out for herself, and she would need every weapon she had. If it came to a physical contest, Danielle had the weight advantage and no doubt the advantage in experience too. She had been in enough fights to know that she could throw a hard enough punch to knock over this skinny tart. The woman looked like the sort who spent all day plucking her eyebrows and waxing her legs in the hope of catching the eye of some rich man. That gold dress she was wearing was the stupidest thing Danielle had ever seen. Who did she think she was, the Queen?

"You are in my home." The woman seemed to have

regained her composure, and her blue eyes had turned icy. Her voice still had that song-like, sparkling quality, but now it held something more ominous too, an echo of strength that penetrated to Danielle's stomach. "A sorcerer has been murdered, and her power passed to you. I have been controlling the surges of power within you, so that they will not harm you or others. Your mind cannot bear the weight of sorcery without help. Without me you will die, and would probably have died already." The woman stood, her golden gown shimmering like water. To Danielle's surprise she saw tears glistening in the woman's eyes. "You had better pay me some respect, or I shall leave you to your fate."

With that the woman stalked out. Danielle busied herself arranging her sheets and plumping her pillow. She was pleased to find that the stupid cow's tantrum hadn't bothered her. It was clearly a trick, a way of getting Danielle to lower her guard. What had she said her name was? Elizan. That was clearly fake. The whole thing was fake, all that rubbish about sorcerers. What a headcase, storming out of the room like that. Danielle hadn't said anything wrong; she had just been straight with the woman. She didn't know what the hell was going on or where she was, but she knew that she felt very tired, and there was no way she was losing sleep over some weirdo in a golden dress. So she settled back down to try to get back to sleep and put all thoughts of Elizan out of her mind.

CHAPTER THIRTEEN

Holly pressed the button and heard the doorbell ring beyond the door. She stepped closer and peered through the pebbled glass, and her white face rippled back, her reddened eyes huge like a clown's. The sky was a grim grey and black above her, the night sharp. It was her blackness, she knew, her dark day. A shadow approached behind the glass, and she almost whimpered in relief. She needed to lean on someone.

The door opened and he was there, the same as ever. The same coal-black scruffy hair, the same untucked shirt and big brown eyes. She fell across the threshold into his arms.

"Hello," Elliot whispered into her hair.

* * *

She sat down and stretched her aching leg out onto Elliot's faded, loose-skinned sofa. It felt as luxurious as a plump feather bed. After the deathly tidiness of Kim's flat, it was a welcome change to be surrounded by the warmth of living mess: the bulging lid of the bin, the trainers slung in the corner, the water stain on the glass of orange cordial he had given her. It smelt of home. Elliot rested the glass on the unoccupied corner of a table, then pulled a chair up beside her and sat down.

"Do you want to talk about it?" There was a current of emotion in his voice.

She didn't want to talk about it; she just wanted to be held in his long arms and feel his breath on her neck.

"No," she said, but heard herself continuing. "It was so horrible. She was just lying there, as if she'd fallen over, but—"

Without her head. She couldn't say the words. After a moment's silence Elliot patted her arm and got to his feet. "Come on, I'll get you something to eat."

But she couldn't get up. Not until she'd told someone about the horror she'd seen. Elliot sat back down, took her hand in his, and it all flowed out.

"So Marrin healed you?" he asked when she had finished talking. "Does it still hurt?"

"Not much." It wasn't true. Her leg burned with every step, and her arm was a throbbing weight. Marrin had mended the breaks and sealed her scratches and cuts, but Holly still felt broken. She had showered and washed her hair and changed her clothes, trying to clean away the violence, but Sean's attack had left deeper marks than that. She could still see him coming at her, still hear the snap as her bones broke. She winced, and tried to think of something else. "Marrin was nice to me, in her way. She doesn't talk much, but I think she's not used to people. Apparently she lives on her own. She had to go and help Arthan find Sean, but before she left she examined the body." She stumbled to a halt at the thought, and the word *body* came out of her as a whisper. She took a deep breath and continued, willing away the tears, blocking out the memories. "Marrin said Kim was drained of power, that she must have used sorcery before she died. Whatever she did, it didn't work. There was no sign that the murderer had any difficulty. Both her legs and arms were broken, her whole body beaten and bleeding, and" – a vision of Kim's pasty-white severed head invaded her mind – "you know the rest."

Frowning, Elliot considered this. "So the murderer must have been a sorcerer? Someone with high enough Resistance that Kim's sorcery couldn't stop them."

"I think so." Holly wished there was room for doubt. It would be so much easier to deal with this if the killer was a stranger. But the killer was someone she knew and she had to cope with it, no matter how hard it was. She thought about her parents, let herself focus on the memory of their faces. She was doing this for them.

After Marrin healed her she had put all thoughts of her encounter with Sean and Rupert's prophecy from her mind and examined Kim's flat, but she had found nothing useful. There was no obvious sign of forced entry; nothing was upset or overturned. There were none of the clues that the detectives on television found so easily.

She couldn't rule any sorcerer out; any one of them could have broken in and taken Kim by surprise – locks didn't stop sorcerers. There were so many ways to break in, so many ways to kill. Holly had tried to think it through step by step, imagining that it was a hypothetical question and it hadn't actually happened. She didn't know of any application of sorcery that could behead someone with a thought. Purple Control could harm a victim's body, but surely not in such a bizarre way. A physical weapon had probably been used, a sharp-edged weapon. Although, perhaps a sorcerer with strength enhanced by Red Control could do that much damage with a blunter object. She shuddered.

"What are the police doing about it?"

She shook her head, feeling almost too tired to reply. "I don't know, probably nothing. Arthan spoke to them."

Elliot's hand slipped from hers as he leant back into his chair, his head tilting as he thought. He did this often, as if he disappeared somewhere else for a while, his mind floating out of his body. The news that the murderer was a sorcerer didn't seem to have disturbed him as much as her. Perhaps she was naïve to never expect something like this to happen. She watched him, and wondered if he had forgotten she was still there and still needed him. She knew it was wrong of her to need him; she knew she should be strong, but maybe she just wasn't. Maybe she really was the timid young girl everyone thought she was. Just like Kim, just another weak Blue sorcerer to be crushed by those with power.

Elliot turned his thoughtful gaze back to her, his eyes

returning to the room. "What are you going to do next?" he asked.

She gave a small shrug. "I don't know. I'm supposed to question people."

"Maybe you should ask everyone the same questions. It will show up any inconsistencies in their answers."

He was acting as though they were figuring out a puzzle in a book, as though no one had been killed. She wished she could do that.

There was something else she had to say. She knew if she didn't tell him he would wonder why when he found out from someone else. She tried to adopt a neutral tone. "Marrin said Kim was pregnant."

It took him a few seconds to reply. "Are you sure?"

"Marrin was sure."

"Do you think it could have something to do with the murder?"

Holly didn't say anything. She couldn't, in case her secret tumbled out. *I'm pregnant too, Elliot. And the baby might be yours.*

She had known for a week, but continued to pretend to herself it wasn't true. It couldn't be true. It was impossible. She had been so careful, so convinced this would never happen.

It seemed so long ago that Elliot had surprised her with his feelings. She hadn't seen it coming, and hadn't expected her own reaction. *We can't do this.* She had rehearsed the speech so many times, but the words never came. She hadn't rejected him, but she hadn't accepted him. And Arthan, somehow she had managed to smile at him, kiss him, carry on living with him and carry on betraying him. It was as if she floated in separate bubbles with each of them unaware of the other. A mess. And now she carried a baby and didn't even know which father it belonged to. She croaked a sob, and Elliot stroked her hand.

"It's OK, Holly. It'll be OK."

She closed her eyes and wished he was right. She wished it would all disappear and she could open her eyes and be someone else, someone who didn't have problems.

"What about Rupert's prophecy?"

She swallowed and opened her eyes. "Arthan doesn't believe it. He said Green Control is useless at predicting events more than a few minutes ahead. Something about unstable outcomes."

Elliot nodded but didn't reply. She could see in the flicker of his frown what he was thinking. *That's what you want to believe, Holly.* And she could tell by his silence the prophecy worried him.

She didn't feel any better for having told Elliot about the murder; she just felt empty. The world passed through her like a sieve, all the life drained away, and she was left with nothing but dry, powdery facts. She wished it was still yesterday, a normal day.

Her hand wandered unconsciously to her stomach. She kept thinking about the prophecy, despite her dismissal of it to Elliot. Arthan was right: prophecies were unreliable; her own research in the past had shown that. Little was known about how prophecies worked, what triggered them, what caused a particular future event to grip a Green sorcerer like a vivid, living dream. There was also very little evidence to suggest they worked and that there would be any truth in Rupert's gasping, chilling predictions. But Holly had told Arthan and Elliot only part of the prophecy. She could still hear Rupert's voice on the end of the phone line, his words murmuring in her ears like a hideous, morbid song. *It was Sean*, he'd said. *He's going to kill you next*, he'd said.

And your baby.

How did Rupert know about her baby? No one knew about the baby. She shivered and huddled closer to Elliot. Sean's mad, reddened eyes danced before her. She smelt his sweat, heard his growl and felt his meaty hands on her as her bones went snap.

If the prophecy had shown Rupert she was pregnant, what else had it got right?

PART FIVE
SECRECY

Two years before Kim's death

CHAPTER FOURTEEN

An unfamiliar reflection peered back at Elliot from the window. A middle-aged man, broad-nosed and heavy-browed, with thinning hair tinged with silver. A stranger to Elliot, a convenient mask. But he was a son to someone, perhaps a husband too, or a father. The expression on the man's face was shrouded in shadows, his image painted in grey splashes of half-light. Elliot's head pounded, lending an aching rhythm to the darkness. He shivered in the night's chill, and the man shivered too.

Elliot punched through the glass and the man's face shattered with a crack that reverberated in the silence. He noticed the blood dripping on the windowpane before he realised how deeply he had cut himself: his hand was riddled with seeping red lines where stinging needles of glass were sunk into his skin. He grimaced, before remembering he no longer needed to suffer such inconveniences. Drawing on his power in that now familiar way, he let his hand melt away to nothing but a stump of a wrist, and the glass chips fell tinkling to the pavement. He restored his hand, flexed his fingers and clambered through the jagged gap. Though it wasn't Elliot's hand he restored; it was the broad-nosed man's hand. And it wasn't Elliot's blood left as evidence on the windowpane.

He crept through the dim office in the shafts of pale moonlight, a faceless ghost in the quiet tomb of computers and piled paperwork. He swept past his own desk without a sideways look, ignoring his growing headache, and made for the stairs.

It was darker in the stairwell, so he flipped a light switch on. He tried not to listen for sounds of anyone else in the building and tried not to imagine being caught. After all, if someone noticed a light and investigated, it wasn't Elliot they would find here. He told himself again that what he was doing was justified. When he was a child morality had been so simple: don't do bad things; do good things. Now he was an adult he had learnt ways to rationalise the bad things he did. He tried to stop holding his breath. He was safe, he was disguised, and it was worth the risk. Tonight could be the night he found out who he was.

When he placed his hand on the handle of the door to the archives, the pain in his head burst open. He clutched his face as he tumbled to the floor, the crack of his jaw striking the stone floor a welcome distraction from the blades of agony searing his right eye. But as he writhed in the throes of the invisible knives, throat burning, he began to smile, because he knew it was nearly over, and he had come to relish the feeling that always followed.

Seconds later he was grinning as he swept through the door to the archives. He was someone else after the pain left him, someone who didn't worry, someone who didn't care, and he was that person for longer and longer each time. What was he becoming?

The rows of bookcases rose either side as he strode further into forbidden territory. Declared off-limits to all new sorcerers by Arthan, the archives were as dull as Elliot had expected: nothing more than a dusty, cluttered library, but it was a library that could be of use to him. The air was thick, the smell of old paper almost bringing back some distant, forgotten memory. He trailed the broad-nosed man's fingers along the sleeping book spines, humming a tune that he knew by heart but couldn't name. Whatever he was becoming, it was an improvement. He could do anything, go anywhere, be anyone. No one could keep secrets from him any more. He walked deeper into the darkness, closer to the truth. Tonight would be the night he found out who he was.

Reaching the section he needed, he scanned the titles, lips moving as he read the faded words. There it was. He yanked the book from the shelf, slid a nearby chair beneath him and opened the cover.

It was the book everyone talked about: *The Elements of Sorcery*, by Whitelock. Apparently the foundation of all research into sorcery, it was the masterwork of the earliest known sorcerer, the most important book in the history of sorcery, the ultimate authority on casting techniques. Blah, blah, blah.

Elliot scowled at the book. It didn't live up to expectations. It looked genuinely old, the hard grey cover connected to the rest by a few frayed threads, the yellowed pages thick and brittle, but it was thin and the words were written by hand in an inky scrawl that allowed only a few sentences to a page. How many secrets could this little book really hold? Elliot frowned, shrugged, opened the cover and began to read.

ELEMENTS OF SORCERY
Introduction
And so here I sit, to write my final farewell to this world, and to the worlds that have passed and those that are yet to pass without me. As my gift in leaving this earthly place, I will make permanent record upon these pages of my studies in sorcery, in fervent hope that, studying further upon this foundation I lay here, future generations of sorcerers should progress my work. It is now the year 1685 and, truly, I can scarce believe it; my long life winds behind me like a rope I have lost the end to. It is time and right. I am writing behind the false name of Whitelock, a somewhat foolish and hastily assumed title I hope you will forgive, which I have worn to keep my secrecy. You will allow this indulgence and trust in my reason, dear reader, when I sincerely assure you it would not be safe to act otherwise.

It was a less than exciting start. Elliot hoped Whitelock would have something interesting to say soon. He skipped to the next section.

It seems proper to bring out some details of how I came to sorcery, or how it came, rather, to me: the combination of circumstance out of which my life as a sorcerer unfolded.

I discovered

There were some pages missing here. Had someone removed them? Elliot examined the brittle page joins, then read from the start of the next available page.

if a sorcerer dies or is born.

Should two sorcerers bear a child, it will be a sorcerer too, and power will be drawn into it from another sorcerer.

What was this? Elliot re-read the sentence, sitting up in his chair. If he was to believe this statement was true and applied to all children of sorcerers, then it seemed sorcery was hereditary. *Power will be drawn into it from another sorcerer.* He read on.

Although it may chance to be so, the child's power need not draw from the parents of the child, and thus the colour of the child's sorcery need not follow its parents', although the colour of the Element will match the sorcerer it is drawn from. However, the Grey Element of power is different and stands apart from the rest: it only travels by blood. A Grey child can only be born if it has a Grey parent.

Elliot breathed the words in like a drug. *A Grey parent.* His true parents must be sorcerers, and one was Grey like him. He leant closer to the pages, racing over the words.

I must also note here that the Element colours are significant in their affinity to other similar colours. A sorcerer will be by his very nature, or perhaps by the nature of that sorcery within him, more skilled and more familiar when drawing on those Elements with a colour closer to his own. Thus a Red sorcerer will find more simple the mastery of Orange and Purple sorcery than Yellow and Blue, but by the same measure will find Green more difficult than any of these. Once again, Grey sorcery does not follow this general rule; no sorcerers other than Greys themselves will be capable of Grey sorcery.

Wherever a sorcerer child's power comes from, it will leave in its wake a sorcerer who has lost his power; and this sorcerer will find himself unequipped to survive. When the mind has learnt to accept sorcery's power it cannot survive hence without it; I, as you must, find this a horrible consequence, but it is unavoidable: sorcery's forces must be obeyed. The sorcerer who loses power will die when the baby is born. I name this morbid prospect Fading.

Elliot drummed his fingers on the chair arm as he read the scrawled words again. Fading. That must be it. That was the secret that Arthan didn't want them to know. Every time a sorcerer is born, another dies.

The implications filtered through his mind, the faces of his fellow young sorcerers passing before him. Eight of them, including him. All born in the same year, all sorcerers. They each must have had sorcerer parents. And eight sorcerers must have died in their place. Did one of his own parents die when he was born, drained of power by their own son?

He searched the page for more details, but there were only a few words of the introduction left before more missing pages:

Should a sorcerer be caused to die by another agent than Fading, the power of that sorcerer would be loosed and would need to settle in a Host; it would travel as an insubstantial force to seek a new lodging, the mind of a human. If this human, the Host, is an adult, there are likely to be complications

Elliot stretched himself out to think. Arthan and the other older sorcerers had kept Fading a secret from the new sorcerers, perhaps because they were worried about the danger. Any one of the older sorcerers could be killed by the arrival of a sorcerer baby. But then Fading was a threat to any sorcerer. If two sorcerers had children, he might die. He toyed with this thought for a second before discarding it; there was nothing he could do about it anyway.

The most important conclusion was that he was one step closer to his true identity: he was a sorcerer and his real parents were too. He would find out who they were; someone must know – Arthan must know. That smug, babyish face hid a lot of secrets, Elliot was sure of it, and now that Elliot was discovering his powers nothing would stop him finding out. He smiled in the gloom.

He whistled as he strolled out of the archives, the door swinging shut behind him with a bang. He mounted the steps two at a time, strode through the empty office, flung a leg through the broken window while avoiding the jagged glass, hauled himself through to the other side, then froze. An old man stood beside him on the pavement, an open-mouthed statue with a black briefcase dangling from his hand, staring at Elliot and the shattered window.

Elliot leapt at him without thinking. If the break-in was traced back to Elliot, his time at Arthan Associates would be over. He couldn't risk the old man calling the police. He took him by the collar and struck him across the face with the back of his hand. The man collapsed to the pavement like crumpling paper, blood spilling from his mouth, his slender arms buckling under his fall.

Elliot stared at his own raised fist, then unclenched it. His certainty began to shrink and curl, the pain in his head echoing like a distant voice, his worries returning in a chilling wave, the sense of lightness he had felt draining away. What was he doing?

He backed away from the old man, who writhed on the floor clutching his bloody face, his whimpering loud in the still night. Elliot looked at the man's briefcase so he didn't have to look at the man. It lay open on the pavement, its innards spilt across the concrete. Elliot shivered, his stomach filled with a dread cold. Why had he attacked him? Elliot was disguised: there was no risk of being caught. And how would he have stopped the old man saying anything? He looked at his shadowed hands, remembering his own clenched white fist. What had he been about to do?

The night hummed with blackness. Elliot turned away from the whimpering man and his broken briefcase and slipped into the shadows.

CHAPTER FIFTEEN

"Your friend knows about us, doesn't he?"

Holly's voice yanked Elliot back from the gate of sleep. She was curled on the bed beside him, her knee tucked over his thigh, her left arm trailing across his chest. She looked beautiful, her skin turned milky white and silver in the moonlight from the window, like a black-and-white photograph.

Elliot yawned, his eyes heavy. "Jay? Of course he does. He saw us come home together."

He found it strange to see Holly at work every day and not to go to her and hold her. When they met in the evening and their lips touched it was a release of that unnatural separation, an inevitable magnetic collision that propelled them back home and through the door to land here in his bedroom, entwined and naked among the shadows and silhouettes of his books and clothes, their grey bodies interchangeable in the bleached gloom.

"Not me and you – I mean he knows about *us*, the sorcerers."

Elliot blinked, his sleep shattered. How had she found out?

"His Resistance is weak even for a human," she continued. "I could tell you had told him about sorcery without even trying to sense his thoughts."

It was a statement there was no use denying, so Elliot just stared at the ceiling. *Not only that, Jay knows I'm a sorcerer*, he thought. He was lucky Holly hadn't picked that up from Jay's mind too. Or maybe she had and she was testing him, waiting to see if he would tell her.

It hadn't been long after Elliot had discovered his sorcery that Jay had walked in on him changing shape. It had taken him an hour to calm his friend down. That now seemed like a long time ago, and Jay seemed to have accepted it, taken it in his stride like he did with everything else. He was endlessly concocting ways of using Elliot's sorcery to make them both rich, although his schemes were usually illegal. Jay always guffawed when Elliot pointed this out, leaving him unsure whether his friend had been serious.

"You should have reported that a human found out." Holly's expression was hidden from Elliot by her pale hair layered on his chest. "His memory will need erasing."

The edge to her tone surprised him as much as her words. Perhaps he had made a big mistake telling Jay. For a moment he felt guilty, then tossed this aside when the true injustice of his position came back into focus. Holly had no right to lecture him about having secrets. The only reason they were forced to sneak out of work separately was that Holly didn't have the courage to end her relationship with Arthan. Not to mention the information about Fading that she, Arthan and Belas were hiding from Elliot and all the new sorcerers.

He could feel his jaw clench as his thoughts marched down familiar paths. What did she see in Arthan anyway? A self-important bore in a teenager's body. He had no idea what had first driven her to him; it could have been loneliness. Holly said they had been together for a long time, although Elliot could only guess how many years or decades that meant. Time meant something different to sorcerers; their long lives made them relaxed about timescales, indifferent to urgency. Maybe after all that time Holly was so familiar with Arthan's company she couldn't break the habit of seeing him, despite his obvious flaws.

It still rankled Elliot that his first kiss with Holly had happened when he was disguised as Arthan. After that brief taste of her Elliot had pursued her relentlessly, his crush verging on an obsession that drove him after her despite his nerves, that owned his heart despite the risks. She had soon given in and kissed him in his own skin. She had meant it; she had wanted him by then, he knew that. But it didn't stop that first kiss staining his memory of their romance. When she had brushed her lips against his, her eyes closing, her breath warm on his face, it hadn't been him she was kissing. She had kissed Arthan.

Holly stirred, perhaps noticing his tension. "Are you OK?"

"I was just thinking about the other sorcerers being orphans," Elliot said, hearing the sharpness creeping into his own tone. If she could lie to him about sorcerer families and Fading, then he would make her realise what she was doing by keeping this truth to herself. "They must wonder about their family like I do."

Holly was silent and still beside him.

"It's horrible," Elliot said. "To live your life knowing nothing about your real parents."

"I know something," Holly said in a small voice.

Elliot's next words evaporated. That was a surprise. He had thought it would take more than a gentle prod to make her spill her secrets. The silence stretched, Holly didn't move, and Elliot began to wonder if he had imagined her speaking.

Eventually she spoke again, in a barely audible whisper. "Twenty years ago seven sorcerers were born." He saw her fingers tightening around the bed sheets, felt her tensing almost imperceptibly. "They were septuplets, four brothers and three sisters. Their parents were called Verrin and Haris." After a pause he heard a ragged sigh. "You know them better as Sean, Ian, Gordon, Rupert, Kim, Naomi and Olivia."

"They are septuplets?" Elliot's surprise was genuine. He had guessed some of the young sorcerers were siblings after finding out sorcery travelled by blood; it was too much of a stretch to believe seven different sorcerer families each had children at the same time. Sean and Kim knew they were twins already, and the others behaved much like bickering brothers and sisters, but he hadn't expected them all to have the same parents.

"Multiple births are common among sorcerers."

She stopped talking. Perhaps that was all she was prepared to say. Elliot was about to prompt her when he heard her sob. He sat up and pulled her towards him. In the dim light he saw silvery tears rolling down her white cheeks, and he heard the rain pattering in echo on the window behind him, her Blue sorcery spilling her mood into the clouds. He held her as she wept into his shoulder.

"Verrin and Haris hid them." Holly's voice was a croak. "Other sorcerers wanted them… gone, so they hid them. Foster families, no one knew where. It was how we found them later, how we recruited them – we wrote to those who were orphans and born at the right time."

"I got one of those letters." Elliot's family was still the missing piece. Holly had said there were only seven children, but then she didn't know about Elliot's sorcery. Should he tell her he was a sorcerer too?

"So did many others. Your date of birth roughly matched and you were an orphan, which made you a possibility." She glanced up at him for only a second. "We had to interview a lot of humans to find those seven."

Could Elliot be an eighth child of Verrin's, unknown to the other sorcerers? It was more than a possibility, and Holly must see that too, even without knowing about the power that he had discovered in himself. Elliot had the Resistance of a sorcerer and was born at the right time to be part of the Verrin brood. No doubt it was the reason Holly was so controlled when they were alone in bed; she must worry that he might be a sorcerer. If they had a child together, a new sorcerer would be born, and someone would Fade.

Holly was regaining her composure. She unwound herself from his embrace and sat back on the bed, her hands idly picking at the sheets. The pattering of rain slowed to a gentle tapping. Her eyes were shadowed by the dim glow from the window, but Elliot could see the pain in them. His sorcery coiled like a snake in his stomach. It was a secret he wouldn't tell her yet; he would hear what she had to say first.

"You know there are thirteen sorcerers," Holly said, her head down.

Elliot nodded.

"Well, there have always been thirteen. Ever since Whitelock."

Elliot tried to imagine what he would say if this was news to him. "What do you mean?"

"Sorcerers do not age like humans. One of our current thirteen is Elizan, who was one of the original First Casters who followed Whitelock. Before that we have no record, but Elizan has lived for around three hundred years. Judging by her we may have the capacity to live forever. But there is a reason we don't." She closed her eyes. "Fading. Whenever a sorcerer child is born, an existing sorcerer Fades."

Elliot waited, his secret burrowing further inside him as hers tumbled out. He knew he wouldn't tell her about his sorcery, despite the pain he was causing her, despite his surprise that she had opened up to him so easily. Some dark instinct told him not to tell her, and he obeyed.

When she opened her eyes again, tears were chasing down her face. "We knew Verrin had been pregnant, we knew she had hidden the babies, but we didn't know how many. When we were called with the news about Ollas and Dorar, we acted as though we were sad but secretly we were relieved, as we had escaped. But ten minutes after hanging up the phone, Dad sat down and said he felt tired." Her voice dropped to a dead tone, a chilling monotone that made Elliot think she had spoken these words hundreds of times. "He looked so pale, like his blood was being drained away. Then his hands curled up and I noticed his skin was thin, like paper. I screamed as he shrivelled into the chair, and turned to Mum, but she was already curled on the floor into a brittle shell. It took longer for the kettle to boil than for them to become objects. For most of that day I tried to persuade myself it hadn't happened. Then all I could do was cry. I didn't care about the other five who died, though I knew them all well. Some of the other sorcerers said it was good that Verrin and Haris were among the dead, but I didn't care. I just wanted my mum and dad." She looked up at Elliot, but her vacant eyes didn't meet his. "I watched them shrivel up and die."

Elliot swallowed, and silence yawned again. He considered offering sympathy, decided it was too weak a gesture, and then said it anyway. "I'm sorry."

"It's OK," she said, her voice mechanical. "It was a long time ago."

Did she hate the Verrin children, Elliot wondered. He thought he would, in her place. Her parents had died so that two of the children could live. She must look at Sean, Kim and Gordon every day at the office and see her parents' murderers. He couldn't believe that Verrin and Haris could make that choice and knowingly cause death in order to have children. Surely a current life was worth more than a potential future life.

"I'm sorry you weren't told." Holly sniffed, wiping tears from her pale, freckled cheeks. "I'm sorry the other sorcerers haven't been told. Arthan says he will tell them, but I don't know when." Her face was half in shadow, her voice half in whisper. "I hate secrets."

Elliot wanted to say "me too" and hug her, but it felt like just one more lie on top of all the others: his sorcery, his confiding in Jay, his break-in to the office, the old man's whimpering as he writhed on the floor, the dead bird in his drawer that he had never confronted anyone about. And his dreams. So vivid they felt like a memory.

As he sank into reflection Holly kept whispering, her voice a ghostly rhythm. "My father wasn't even a sorcerer, not to start with." She laughed unexpectedly, a cold sound. "He wouldn't have lived long enough to meet my mother if he hadn't been nearby when that boy's power was loosed." Elliot drifted in her murmuring, her memories wafting around the room. "Father always talked about that boy. His name was Tomar."

Her words curled around Elliot like fingers of smoke, the shadowed faces in his dreams billowing from the darkness. *His name was Tomar.*

CHAPTER SIXTEEN

*T*he horse's hooves pounded the dirt with a breathless drumbeat. Elliot watched the ground rush by beneath him, then raised his head to the wind and laughed as his hat was whipped away to tumble to the track behind him. He had spent too long lingering in the smoke of the city; he had almost forgotten what it felt like to breathe clean air. He pushed his mind onto the horse's, driving its legs, flattening its will, tearing its muscles. He knew the beast didn't have much strength left; it had already begun foaming at the mouth. Elliot could travel faster himself, but while the horse lived he may as well use it. Horses were supposed to enjoy running.

The problem with the city was all the people in it. Out here he could finally relax, his only company the brown-and-gold sea of wheat sailing by, the azure dome of the sky above painted with cotton clouds, and the track before him, leading to – wait! A gleam of light caught his eye. He squinted. It was a rider, just in sight before the road curved three miles or so ahead. Elliot crowed. What luck! He would happily abide a small intrusion on his peaceful day in exchange for a new horse. No doubt the rider would be keen to hand it over.

He urged his stolen steed into a final surge, a sprint to send it to its death, but the horse's body could no longer contend with the commands Elliot planted in its mind. One of the creature's legs buckled with a loud snap, and Elliot clicked his tongue. Life was full of disappointments. He floated out of the saddle to alight on the track in front of the animal, broke off his link with its mind and let it collapse to an untidy pile of jerking limbs.

He gazed ahead at the oncoming rider. Something felt odd. He reached with Green Control towards the figure, probing and testing. Yes, that was it – Resistance! It was a sorcerer.

He fired his sight out on an invisible dart and the rider rushed closer, growing into a sharp, focused image. A young-looking male in a dusty shirt and coat, fair hair that was almost white, gritted teeth, scratchy beard, earnest eyes. Elliot didn't recognise him; he must be a new one. One of Gasar's children, no doubt. It was too much of a stretch to believe this could really be a chance encounter; the boy must be looking for him. Elliot's mind wandered to his stomach as the rider approached. It had been hours since he ate that farmer's bacon and bread, and he could now feel a murmuring of appetite. He would have to seek out another farm after relieving this young sorcerer of his animal.

Soon the rider was close enough for Elliot to see that it really was a fine horse. Athletic and well muscled in the shoulder, it had an excellent-looking gait. Elliot grinned. "Why thank you, my boy! I just finished off my previous beast, and here you come bringing me a fresh one!"

The young sorcerer didn't answer but rode closer. He reined in his horse a hundred yards away and settled in his saddle awkwardly, like he was sitting on a pin. His eyes widened at the sight of the dead horse at Elliot's feet, but his fierce stare was soon fixed back on Elliot himself.

Elliot sensed hot emotion rising from the boy without needing to search his mind. It was too tempting not to tease him a little. "Pipe up, boy! Wipe the snot from your nose and introduce yourself!"

Still no response came, so Elliot decided to make his own investigations. He flung his power across the distance between them, shattering a Yellow shield the boy had erected in his mind against this course of action, and delved into his memory. Ah, the Red one. Tomar. Elliot browsed the young mind. It was wild, bursting with ambitions and emotions, much like a human's. But that was to be expected – this boy was barely fifty years old, a baby in his crib.

Young Tomar broke his silence, his cheeks flushed. "Get out of my head, you monster!"

Elliot sighed. He found that he was being called "monster" more and more often. The boy must know who he was, despite his latest disguise as a rangy farmhand he'd encountered on his flight from London. It didn't matter; the farmhand was getting tiresome already, so Elliot would happily change faces. He never found much favour with wearing the bodies of the poor; their clothes were always so damned itchy.

"Get out of my head!"

The boy's voice was comically high-pitched, like an outraged mouse, but with effort Elliot kept a straight face and gave the red-faced youth a nod, withdrawing from his mind. "Don't mind me." He noticed that the boy chose to keep a great distance from him. Elliot had to raise his voice to make sure it carried the distance. "What is the name of that wonderful creature beneath you?"

"You will not distract me." Tomar seemed to be gathering his resolve now as he swept into what was clearly a pre-prepared speech. "My name is Tomar," he squeaked. "You do not know me, but I know who you are. You are Viros. I know what you are. Your evil has haunted this country for too many years. I shall not allow it to continue. The others of our circle beg me to use caution, and would have you left alive in vain hope you will find a reason to change. But I know you have no reason. You are not nearly a man of reason. You are—"

"How long is this going to go on for? I do have appointments today." This wasn't true, but Elliot felt it was a witty line.

Having his speech cut short seemed to anger Tomar more than anything else. "Silence! You die today!"

"But my appointments…"

"Your only appointment is with death!"

Elliot couldn't suppress a giggle at this. Tomar continued to redden, his face now almost as bright as a tomato.

"There really is no need to be so agitated." Elliot peered at the boy. He wondered what drove him. "Why should you concern yourself with my business?"

Tomar's eyes blazed. "Do you even remember a little girl named Molly Fellows?"

"Ah." Elliot nodded, although he didn't remember. "You knew this girl?"

When Tomar replied his squeaky voice was trembling. "She was the sweetest child in the world, my friend's only daughter and the joy of her family. Do you not think about the lives that you ruin?"

"Hmm." Elliot turned to look at the fields. These conversations always went the same way. It was going to happen again, just like it always *did. He could hear Tomar continuing, but he looked out over the wheat and thought about the world instead.*

It continued. Despite all of the rest, despite the towns growing, the books written, the angry people like Tomar talking and talking about justice and monsters and murder, the sunlight spread over the fields every morning just like every one before. He found that some days he could just sit and watch the world, suppress the call of his stomach and sit cross-legged on the ground all day long, watching the sun crawl up into the sky and then dawdle back down at dusk.

A movement drawing his attention, Elliot looked up to see the boy jerking his reins. Then the boy and his horse were charging towards him. The conversation was over now, and so this was what happened next.

Elliot set his mind to the present, drew his power up around himself and watched Tomar approach. As he neared, the young sorcerer swung a long knife from the inside of his coat, his Innate Red abilities obvious. The knife moved so fast it was a sparkling blur.

Elliot vanished, his body disintegrating into air, and floated in a million pieces on the wind as the knife sliced between him. Tomar charged past, then turned and glared at the empty air where Elliot had been.

"They told me you would do this," the boy called to the vacant road. "You cannot hide forever."

"You are right." Elliot heard his voice echo in the wind. "I know." He reasserted his body and materialised upon the road once more as the rangy farmhand. Tomar's eyes narrowed and he gave a grim smile. His horse whinnied and the boy charged again.

Again Elliot waited. This time, as the knife flashed down Elliot stepped around it and snatched the handle. Tomar was quick, his Red abilities lending him speed, but he was not as quick as Elliot. The knife was in Elliot's hand and struck Tomar's side before the boy could blink. The blade cut through Tomar's coat and shirt but jarred at contact with his skin, sending vibrations up Elliot's arm. Tomar was rolled from his horse by the force of the blow and skidded across the stony track, but he seemed unharmed. Elliot leapt on him and thrust the knife again, moving the air around himself to speed his movements, and again the blade pierced cloth but couldn't breach the barrier of Tomar's flesh. Elliot rose and stepped back, considering. Tomar drew another knife as he regained his feet, but it spun from his hand with a burst of Elliot's Orange Control before he could use it.

Despite being unhorsed and losing his weapon, Tomar's glare was steady, his jaw clenched, his voice a hiss. "Your steel cannot harm me."

So it seemed. Elliot nodded agreement and tossed the knife aside. He wiped his hands on his shirt while Tomar scowled, the sun throwing deep shadows on his face. "It will be another way then."

He punched his power at the boy's mind. Tomar had seen his intention and tipped his own power into a mental shield to save himself, but Elliot brushed it aside like a cobweb. He entered the boy's mind once more.

Elliot sensed Tomar's thoughts turn to escape, so he cut the cords tying the boy's body to his mind. Tomar went slack and tumbled to the floor, sending up a puff of dust. Silence fell again. Tomar's voice was lost and his eyes were glassy, but he was alive.

Elliot regarded him, slung on the ground like a sack of potatoes. He had never killed a sorcerer before.

Perching on the carcass of his previous, now dead horse, Elliot shifted back into his own familiar shape. He liked to wear his own body occasionally, although the feel of his own bones brought back both comforting and disturbing memories. His hand rose instinctively to rub his right eye socket but he stopped himself. He took a deep breath of the countryside air. The wheat fields stretched out around him in a swaying carpet, the sunlight streamed through the gauzy clouds, and there was no soul in sight but the two horses and the two men. Two collapsed, two healthy.

He thought for a moment, then spoke to the open air. "We have to see what happens now, Tomar. You might still live, I think. Although you are chasing me. So we have to see." Elliot stood again and began walking a wide circle around Tomar's still body. "What will you do, Tomar? Will you leave me be?" He stopped for a moment. He could hear the boy rage and thrash inside his lifeless shell. "If you hadn't met this… girl you mentioned, you wouldn't be concerned. Just imagine, Tomar." Elliot watched the wheat sway, so peacefully. "Imagine you hadn't."

Elliot listened, but there was no answer in his mind, the only sound the rustle of the wheat. He shook his head. It continued.

He reached into Tomar's head with Purple Control and twisted the paths in his brain, wrenching the boy's life in his hands and squeezing out its breath like he was wringing out a wet shirt. It was soon done. Elliot could sense the loosed sorcery surging into the air, seeking a Host. He *wondered where it would alight, which lucky human it would occupy.*

He snapped his fingers. His new horse came trotting at his bidding, and Elliot swung himself into the saddle and clamped his will over the horse's mind. Before that meeting he had been enjoying a ride. He took a lungful of fresh country air, trotted past the dead boy and horse and galloped away down the track.

There was nothing quite like a good ride in the country.

CHAPTER SEVENTEEN

Y ou wanted to see me?"
Arthan didn't look up. "Elliot. Come in and shut the door."

Whatever they were about to discuss, it must be confidential. Elliot found his way across the floor with difficulty; Arthan's office was even more chaotic than usual. Piles of files and papers crowded the chairs, floor and windowsill, like mounds of fallen leaves. The only window, half hidden behind stacks of folders, looked as though it had been shut for some time, and provided no breeze to chase off the smell of stale cigar smoke. Arthan perched in the middle of the chaos like a shiny peacock, poring over the papers on his desk, his pressed suit and gleaming hair impossibly neat in the surrounding mess. He didn't acknowledge Elliot's approach. The only sound with the door closed was the scratching of Arthan's pen.

After Elliot had been sat down for what felt like several minutes, Arthan put aside his papers and leant back into his leather chair with a squeak. With an eye on Elliot he clamped a cigar in his teenage lips and lit it. "I'd like to discuss something that has recently come to my attention."

With sudden nausea, Elliot realised what Arthan was going to say next.

"I know you are a sorcerer, Elliot."

Elliot's first instinct was to escape. His hands tightened on the chair, his muscles tensed, and he almost bolted for the door.

"Calm down." Arthan blinked, which meant he was using sorcery, probably trying to subdue Elliot's panic with Yellow Control. It seemed to have no effect – Elliot imagined the sorcery had bounced harmlessly from the wall of his Resistance – but he forced himself to calm down anyway. He had to think fast.

His secret was out. What would happen now? He had been safe when Arthan hadn't known about his sorcery, hidden and invisible. Now he was suddenly exposed, flushed out in the open beneath the glare of Arthan's piercing eyes. If Arthan knew about this, what else did he know? Did he know about Elliot and Holly?

If he did, Arthan was giving nothing away. He watched the smoke uncoil from his cigar. "Would you like to say anything at this point?" he asked the thinning swirls.

Elliot didn't want to, but he had to find out what else Arthan knew. "How did you find out?"

Arthan screwed his face up as if he smelt something unpleasant. "Your friend Jay has very weak Resistance. I don't make a habit of invading the privacy of every human I stumble across, but…" Arthan tapped his cigar on the china ashtray, frowning. "There was no barrier. I entered his thoughts without realising, and I couldn't help noticing why he was here. It was lunchtime – you weren't around."

Elliot's insides were icy cold. Jay had come to the office. Why hadn't he mentioned this?

"Your friend had come to talk to you about your next shopping trip."

Elliot tried to disguise his reaction but couldn't. He gaped, limp-jawed, into Arthan's hard gaze.

"How long have you been stealing, Elliot?"

With these words the final pieces of Elliot's warm cocoon of secrets crumbled away. If there was anything Arthan didn't know, it could only be because he had chosen not to read it from Jay's mind, which seemed unlikely. The game was over. He would certainly be fired. His chance to find out about himself, to find out what it meant to be a sorcerer, to find his family, was gone. His time with Holly was over. His new life was over.

"Elliot?"

"It has been a few months now," Elliot heard himself mumble to the table.

"And you use sorcery to disguise yourself, so you cannot be caught?"

His head still down, Elliot nodded. "I shape-shift into a stranger."

"The perfect alibi."

Elliot looked up at Arthan then wished he hadn't. The flinty eyes in that young face knew what he had done; they called him scum. They said, *You have been sleeping with my girlfriend, and I will see you suffer for it.* Arthan didn't need an excuse to take his revenge. Elliot had revealed sorcery to a human, but far worse was that he had used his powers for theft, for his own gain at the expense of others. Arthan's familiar words sounded in his ears. *We are a chosen few. A chosen few with power. We must use this power responsibly to help our fellow creatures.*

"Show me how you produce the money."

Arthan must have read this part from Jay's mind too, so there was no need to ask Elliot to demonstrate, but perhaps Arthan was enjoying drawing this out. Elliot slipped a hand into his suit pocket and then let the surface of his fingers stretch, deform and spread. His skin separated from his hand in one smooth, crisp rectangular sheet. Elliot drew his hand out again and slapped it on the table, with a fifty-pound note underneath.

The only reaction from Arthan was the rising of his eyebrows. He put his cigar aside, plucked the note from the desk and rustled it between his pinched fingers. "This is part of you?"

Elliot nodded, wondering when Arthan would get to the point. What was his punishment going to be? His fingers twitched self-consciously as he realised Arthan was staring at them.

Arthan examined the fifty-pound note. "Your fingers don't look any different. Do you create the extra material, as a Blue

Control would?"

"No, I just… respread myself."

"What does the human do?"

"Nothing. Jay just stays out of the way. He helps me decide what to, um, buy."

While Arthan pursed his lips and considered this, Elliot realised that Arthan was going to make this last as long as he let him. He stopped gripping the seat, straightened his back and lifted his head. He had to accept the consequences like a man. He braced himself to keep his emotions in check, to resist crying and begging for his job and his life back. "OK. What happens now?"

"It's a clever scheme."

"Sorry?"

Arthan handed him back the fifty-pound note. "Presumably you can easily recall the money to you once you've paid."

Elliot accepted the note dumbly. He coughed to clear his throat, and tried to keep his voice steady. "I've been turning it into air once it's in the shop till – or restaurant till, or… wherever." Elliot couldn't bring himself to list out loud the places he had used the fake money. Shops, restaurants, hotels, cinemas, theatres, football stadiums, airports… "Then I float it out through the gap in the till drawer to join my body again."

"It turns into air?" Arthan frowned. "It disappears?"

"Well, it doesn't go anywhere." Elliot couldn't find the words to describe how it felt to have part of his body detached and dispersed somewhere in the air, or explain that he could feel that part was still his own but in some way it was no longer him at all. "It's still there, just invisible."

Arthan's voice dropped to a whisper. "Can you make your whole body invisible?"

Invisible. Just hearing the word made Elliot want to disappear right now. Yes, he could do it, and he did it often. He vanished to hide from people he didn't want to talk to, or just to avoid being disturbed. He liked to walk invisibly through public places, listening to the conversations people had when they thought they were alone. Sometimes the things he heard were embarrassing, sometimes mundane, sometimes incriminating, sometimes sexual. It was a sense of security he had never felt before, the ultimate safety of complete anonymity. He was a ghost, not a person, just an imagined breath on the wind, a half-felt shifting of the air. And it hadn't been long before public places weren't his only haunt. He started following people into their homes without even considering if it was wrong.

When Elliot was invisible no one could hurt him, stop him or even look at him. He was beyond the reaches of society, untouchable and invincible. He floated on the wind through half-open windows, into keyholes, under cracks beneath doors. He watched people in their private lives, almost forgetting that he was sometimes a person like them too, that he had a visible life somewhere, just another normal nobody trudging predictable footprints through the mud of life. He wondered what would happen if he forgot to go back to his real life and just drifted away unseen on the breeze, a ghost forever. Would he eventually lose himself so much that he ceased to even exist?

"You can!" Arthan's eyes were wide, his face alive in a way that Elliot had never seen. It made him look even younger than usual. "Invisibility is said to be the most difficult Control of the Grey Element! It has been disputed whether it is even possible! It's – that's incredible!" Arthan trailed off into silence, cleared his throat, and his face settled back into its severe mask. He picked up his cigar again and leant back in his chair, puffing. After a few smoky wreaths had reached the ceiling, he gave Elliot a frown. "You will cancel all future shopping trips."

Elliot nodded. "Of course."

"You will email me a list of all purchases you have made illegally. We will need to reimburse the retailers involved."

A list of all purchases? It would be difficult to remember them all. He nodded, wondering what Arthan meant by "reimburse". Elliot didn't have any real money to pay everything back. He was pretty sure Jay didn't either.

"Can you use other Controls apart from shape-shifting?"

"Not as easily."

"Have you abused those Controls too?"

Elliot flinched at the choice of words. He supposed he deserved it. He shook his head.

Arthan puffed on his cigar, his eyes narrowing on Elliot as if he was an unwelcome stain on the chair. "You haven't started that report I asked you to do."

It was a statement, not a question. Elliot supposed it was best to get all his misdemeanours out in the open at once. "No. I've done a lot of reading though."

"Don't start it." Arthan stubbed his cigar out. "Your recent actions force me to conclude you are unsuitable for your current role. I need to take action, Elliot."

In a heartbeat Elliot's world caved in again. He had thought for a brief, glorious moment he was going to escape with his hopes and dreams intact, with Holly, with his new life and with the knowledge of who he really was still within reach at the tips of his outstretched fingers. But now it was over.

He swallowed. "What are you going to do?"

Arthan's lips twitched in a way that, by his standards, might conceivably have been a smile. "I'm going to teach you how to use your power."

PART SIX
INVESTIGATION

A few days after Kim's death

CHAPTER EIGHTEEN

Holly began straightening her jacket, then stopped. She didn't want to appear nervous. She resisted looking up again at the yawning gape of the intricately painted ceiling far above, but she couldn't resist feeling as conspicuously unwelcome as an insect on a newly polished floor. A faint whispering of music called to her through distant half-open shutters. *Get out, Holly. Get out.*

She was fulfilling a long-held dream: visiting Rushworth Hall to speak with the most powerful sorcerer alive. But her dreams had always been unspecific: why would the great Elizan invite a young, unimportant sorcerer to her magnificent home? The answer was today's bitter reality: Holly had invited herself here to interview her idol as a suspected murderer. She was an intruder in this peaceful place, dragging the ugly accusation of murder behind her like a filthy stain smeared across the creamy marble floor. Every crystal chandelier bristled at her presumption, every carved wooden door shielded their long corridors from her prying, unworthy eyes.

She thought she felt her baby moving, and flinched. That was stupid – it was too early to feel anything – but she still couldn't help wondering if it was noticeable. Could others see some difference in her, some clue to betray her secret? She knew how the other sorcerers would react: without thought, without doubt, they would make her end the pregnancy. But she didn't want to think about doing that. *It's OK*, she told herself for the thousandth time. *Elliot isn't a sorcerer, so the baby won't be and no one will Fade.* But she worried all the same. After all, she would be a mother. A mother to someone who would grow old and die while Holly didn't age a day.

How could she and Elliot have been so reckless? How many times had she told herself she wouldn't make the mistake so many other sorcerers had made, that her parents had made, that Verrin and Haris had made. Children were for humans, not sorcerers. There were too many problems – there was Arthan, there was Elliot, there was too much to cope with. She felt her heart beating faster and her head getting hot. *Focus on the interview, Holly, focus on today.* She swallowed, and clutched the chair. *Just get through another day.*

She would be facing Elizan soon, and she would need to be ready. She had to find that iron certainty inside herself again; she had to be someone different. She thought of her parents, their laughing faces turning grey and tired. She thought of that boy, Tomar. He was killed like Kim, leaving Holly's father in the wake of the bloodshed. A life should not be taken like that, and Holly couldn't let herself be the weak girl who did nothing but stand by and cry. For once she would be the one in charge, not the one trailing Arthan's heels and jumping at his commands. *You will have to be strong*, Arthan had said. And if Elizan was the murderer then Holly would have to… what? Her focus faltered, her forced confidence shrinking like a balloon letting down. She imagined how Elizan would laugh inside when she met the skinny ginger girl who intended to interview her. How could Holly hope to determine the guilt of someone this powerful? It was a farce.

With sudden clarity, Holly realised she was wasting her time. She got up to leave just as a white-suited man appeared at her elbow.

"Elizan will see you now."

* * *

She's so beautiful, Holly thought, then blushed when Elizan smiled. She could not afford to think so loudly in the presence of the most powerful Yellow sorcerer who had ever lived.

"Please do not fret," Elizan said. "I could read your thoughts if I wished, but I find such behaviour impolite. I will not intrude on your mind. However, I am afraid I cannot help reading your body language – you are nervous. Please relax."

Elizan's voice was as exquisite as her appearance. Each word rang a pure note, each sentence played a song. Something in the great lady's smile put Holly at ease, and she found herself wondering why she had been so flustered.

Elizan was composed in a cushioned white chair, her sun-gold gown spilling over the marble floor, while Holly sat opposite her with her notepad on her knees. Another white-suited man had furnished a delicate table beside them with frosty glasses of lemonade. The glass sparkled in the dusty light that drifted in from the gardens along with barely heard murmurs of music and a wandering fragrance of roses. The high-ceilinged room and all the furniture within it was sculpted in white and gold, every drape and curtain breathed in harmony, and at the centre of it all was Elizan. Her face was hard and yet feminine, her long hair like tumbled white silk. She looked young, although Holly knew she wasn't. She had the bearing of a queen.

Holly met those wise, sparkling blue eyes and asked her questions. Had Elizan known Kim? No, but she knew of her. Where was Elizan on the night of the murder? Here at Rushworth. Why did Elizan imagine Kim was killed? She didn't know.

Elizan didn't seem to mind the questioning. The same encouraging smile never left her lips, her attention never wandered. Holly listened to every beautiful word and made her notes, turning over the answers in her mind, looking for something useful. She knew that it was very likely she would learn nothing, even if, unthinkable as it was, Elizan had been involved in Kim's murder. The lady in front of her would not have needed to be at Kim's flat to commit the murder; she could command the minds and actions of others at her whim, and she would not be caught out by simple questions. Even if Holly were to find out anything Elizan did not want her to know, Elizan could be rid of her with a wave of her golden-robed hand. But Holly had no other course of action available than to ask her questions and hope for the best. She told herself it was a research project just like any other back at the office. Research was her speciality; she never tired of the painstaking hours of reading in the archives that Arthan found so tedious. Accumulate data, analyse it, spot anomalies, identify trends. Construct theories, test them, draw conclusions.

The conclusion she hoped to come to, although she had no idea how she would, was to be certain of Elizan's innocence. Not just because she wanted to believe it, but because it would solve everything. If Elizan's innocence could be proven, then it would mean she could be trusted, and Holly could ask her to read the minds of the other sorcerers to find the murderer. She was the most powerful sorcerer by a distance, and an Innate Yellow, so none of the others would be able to Resist her reading their thoughts. Not even Arthan could hide something from Elizan if she turned the force of her sorcery on his mind. It was the only plan Holly had, but it hinged on proving Elizan's innocence, and Holly had no idea how she would do that.

Then she felt something odd happen.

Elizan was sitting in the same poised way she had throughout the interview. Holly asked her how often she made contact with other sorcerers, and Elizan replied that she didn't speak very much to anyone any more. Holly wondered if she would provide more details, but Elizan lapsed into silence. Holly glanced at her notes, and as she looked back up the light streaming into the room dropped, as if veiled by a sudden cloud, and she blinked. She shifted in her seat, feeling as though someone had given her a gentle push. She reached for her lemonade to cover her awkwardness, and noticed just before she sipped that the glass was smeared. Elizan's warm smile remained while Holly sipped and replaced her glass, and the interview continued. On some half-conscious level Holly noticed it all, but the jigsaw pieces were upside down and back to front, and wouldn't assemble just yet.

It wasn't until after the interview, as she watched a white-suited man carry away their glasses, that Holly realised the smear on the glass was the mark made by her lipstick.

And it wasn't until she was following the white-suited man back out of the marble entrance hall that she remembered that the glass had been full. It had been her first sip.

And it wasn't until she was walking away from Rushworth Hall, up the long gravel drive, that she pieced together the full glass, the smear, the sudden cloud and the gentle push. The jigsaw slotted into place.

Elizan had erased part of her memory.

Had Holly stumbled across an awkward question for Elizan to answer? Perhaps the great lady had revealed something to Holly she hadn't intended to. Holly must have sipped from her lemonade during the incriminating section of the interview, and so a white-suited man had been asked to top up her glass before her memory was to be erased, leaving no evidence of those first sips except the tell-tale smear. Then Holly's memory had been tampered with by Elizan, a suitable period snipped out of her mind and the ends taped together. It would have been impossible to know that the period of time had ever occurred were it not for the darkening of the sky, the smear and the slight change in Holly's seating position causing the "push". It was a simple trick for the world's greatest sorcerer. It seemed proof to Holly that Elizan *hadn't* been reading her mind, at least not deeply, because she couldn't have realised Holly had noticed the smear, and the light, and the push. Otherwise she would have erased those memories too. Holly only escaped with the information because her thought process was slow enough that she did not piece it together straight away. If she had, the revelation would have been written clearly over her face, if not her mind, and Elizan would never have let her slip away with the knowledge intact.

She stepped across the threshold onto the street outside, and a white-suited man swung the iron gates shut behind her.

She shivered at the drop in temperature and found her thoughts darkening with the purple sky, the close pressure returning to her temples.

Her plan had failed. She had not proved Elizan's innocence, so she could not rely on her to read the other sorcerers' minds truthfully. She had discovered something from the interview but had no idea how to act on it. She was left with no answers, but yet another question. Hidden in that erased memory, what had Elizan revealed?

CHAPTER NINETEEN

Sorry?"

Marrin looked up from her book to see who had spoken, but there was only one person she knew who could introduce himself by apologising. He cowered in the doorway.

"Hello, Gordon. Come in."

She put her book down and waited while he slunk into the kitchen, skirting the used mugs and teaspoons as if they might bite him. It was incredible that the boy seemed scared even in the building where he worked every day. It must be exhausting to be so terrified all the time.

He wedged himself between the sink and the window, and Marrin tutted. To even call the room a kitchen was ridiculous. It was an alcove with a sink and a kettle and a stale stench of coffee that Arthan had grudgingly made available for his employees to squeeze themselves into when they needed a break. Somehow two plastic chairs had been forced inside years ago and were now a permanent fixture. Marrin suspected the lack of space was a deliberate ploy of Arthan's so that his staff took less breaks and did more work. It certainly wasn't a large enough room for Gordon to be shy about sitting close to her.

"Come here." She pointed the chair next to her. "I don't want you standing there staring down at me."

He didn't speak but did as he was told, without ever coming close to making eye contact. She winced at the sight of his matchstick legs, visible beneath his flapping trouser cuffs. He was so thin he might snap. She wondered why he was here; he usually sat at his desk the whole day long.

Not accustomed to finding herself the most talkative person in a room, it took Marrin a few seconds to break the silence. "What are you working on at the moment, Gordon?"

"I didn't do it."

Marrin frowned. "What do you mean?"

"Please believe me. I know you all think I did it."

Gordon's head was bowed, his wide, watery eyes clamped to a spot on the floor between them. She waited for him to say something else, noticing his bony knuckles were white where they gripped the plastic seat, but he said nothing.

"Why would we think that?"

His eyes flicked up at her, then back to the floor, like an animal in a trap. "What?"

Marrin wondered what he was hiding. "I don't think you killed Kim."

Now he looked more terrified than ever. His chair creaked as he bent to get up, but Marrin laid a firm hand on his leg. He froze.

"Gordon, tell me what is going on." Finally, the boy looked up at her. Marrin had never been one for clever words, but she knew how to get respect. Direct eye contact and a tone of voice that allowed no excuses.

Gordon shook his head mutely, but she held his gaze.

"I... liked her."

It was barely a whisper, but Marrin had been ready to catch it. She opened her mouth to ask who he meant, when a glistening tear escaped Gordon's wet eyes and silenced her. She thought hard. "It's normal to have feelings for people, Gordon." She knew that wasn't the right thing to say. She was being too logical, too blunt; she needed to tiptoe around the issue. But she didn't know how to; all she knew how to do was charge ahead.

"It's not normal to fall in love with your sister."

It took a moment to register. He didn't mean Olivia, or

128

Naomi. He *liked* her, in the past tense. Kim.

The poor boy. She should say something to reassure him, something wise and kind. She was still wondering what to say when he spoke again.

"I didn't know she was my sister," he murmured. "When I found out I stopped my feelings."

Marrin snorted. His words triggered memories of people she had made herself forget. Distant, fog-shrouded places of warmth and laughter, creased smiles and bright eyes rising from time, huddled round the smoky, spitting fire in her old brick hearth so many half-forgotten years ago. "That never works, Gordon. You can't stop your feelings, you just get used to feeling them." She sighed, pulling her mind from the ash of yesterday to the boy beside her. Something about Gordon's hollow stare made her dwell. She patted his arm and he flinched at her touch. "Why on earth did you think this made you a suspect?" He shook his head again, and she chuckled. "As if you are a murderer, Gordon. Did you think everyone knows about your feelings for Kim—"

"I don't have them any more."

"Well, I won't tell anyone. And if anyone suspects you I will put them straight."

His scrawny shoulders seemed to loosen a little. "Thank you."

She smiled, the lines of her mouth feeling rusty and disused. When did she ever smile these days? Life was too bleak.

"You're never scared." Gordon's saucer eyes suddenly latched on to her, his face a skull behind stretched white skin. "How do you do it?"

"A lot of practice," she told him. But beneath her skin she felt the lie. She was scared too, scared of the thin crack in the rock of her armour being levered apart by this boy. She had been shut away alone too long; she couldn't let the painful world back in to disturb the warm memories packed away beneath cold, settled dust. She didn't want to start to feel again.

They sat and stared at the wall. In the office beyond, Marrin could hear the clacking of keys and murmuring of work voices, the sounds of life traipsing by. Being back in a workplace after so long had been a shock, a wrench away from her decades of daily routine, but she could see the routine that people clung to here held the same comforts as hers. The steady, repetitive embrace of days marched out one after another, the steps of a slow and dismal dance that people walked through with a familiarity that let their minds close up and switch off, never questioning the future beyond an assured expectation that the next day would be the same.

She glanced at her book open in her lap. An inviting escape. Did social etiquette allow her to start reading again while Gordon sat here? She had little idea of what was expected these days. "Do you feel better now?"

Gordon rocked in his seat, his bony fingers trembling as he kneaded them. He didn't answer.

Her eyes narrowed. There was something else. "What is it?" She let her voice harden to a steel that commanded an answer. "Tell me."

Her words seemed to decide something in him and he drew his head up to meet her gaze. He still looked as fragile as a leaf, but there was a purpose pulling his shoulders back and setting his jaw, and there was no trembling in his voice when he spoke. "It's about Elliot."

CHAPTER TWENTY

H ow long is this going to take?"

Such ceaseless questions! Elizan ignored the woman and continued her examination of the Host's mind. She was forced to guard her thoughts while their minds were linked; it would be too easy for the Host to overhear something she shouldn't. At least the woman hadn't threatened her today; perhaps there was hope that Elizan's scolding had left an impression on her.

"What are you doing?"

Elizan broke off the mind link, not trusting herself to conceal her irritation, and found herself back in the small white room beside the Host's bed. Why did this woman unsettle her so much? She rested her hands in her lap and regarded the Host lying there watching her in turn, slumped on the pillow like a plump bag of sand, her lips twisted in a sour pout. Elizan took a deliberate breath before responding. "I am trying to ascertain how your mind has responded to the influx of sorcery. If there are any uncontrolled surges of power I will need to subdue them."

Unexpectedly, the Host thrust out her hand from the bed sheets. Elizan flinched.

"You're Elizan, aren't you? I'm Danielle."

Elizan nodded but ignored Danielle's hand. "Pleased to meet you." She decided there was no benefit in befriending this woman; she had already proven herself to be of unpleasant character. The sooner Elizan could send her on her way, the better. "We had best press on."

She plunged back in, the room vanishing once more as she slipped into the world of the Host's mind. It was an ethereal, otherworldly and yet all too familiar environment. Elizan hadn't seen solid walls other than those of her own treasured Rushworth in so long, but she wandered the rooms and palaces of other people's minds every day. She felt safe in here, nested inside the protective shells of cocooning realities: inside her home, inside this room, inside the woman's mind, inside her own.

In a detached way she recognised that it was strange that this world of thought was more reassuring to her than the physical world, considering that in here nothing was solid or certain, and the only images that swam before her were born of the shifting half-shadows of imagination. It felt like a partial blindness: her sight was not rendered useless while she was mind-linking; she could identify the threads and knots of thought before her and find the parts of the mind she needed, but these things were only glimpsed as something in peripheral vision, and when she tried to turn her head to look, the objects danced out of focus again.

Who was to say that the physical world was any more real than the imagination, that the ability to see and touch a thing was the means by which to validate its reality? The true medium to experience the mental world was not sight but emotion. She could reach out and touch every bubble of curiosity, every gust of doubt, every wisp of joy, every tremor of fear. It was a tactile landscape of feeling, and one that felt as real to Elizan as any other.

But the mental world was not always a pleasant one. In this instance the landscape was the emotion of the Host, and the woman's personality crawled on her. Elizan was immersed in the greasy pool of the Host's cynicism, swimming in the soup of her distrust. Elizan hurried her mental self along, as she could already feel the woman's poisonous outlook diluting her own objectivity. It was best to avoid being drawn too deeply into a Host's mind.

-Can you hear me in there?

It was the Host. The woman must have deduced that she could speak to Elizan using the mind link.

-Yes. I can hear your thoughts if you project them clearly.

A stronger voice spoke.

-Is this better?

Elizan ignored the question and continued gliding through the crevices and caves of thought, alert for any sign of sorcery. The woman was undeniably learning fast, but there was no need to bolster her already amply inflated ego.

She sensed power nearby. She homed in on it and opened her mind to embrace the sorcery and quell the currents of power that would be writhing within.

-What's that?

Elizan frowned.

-What is what?

-You have something weird inside you. Inside your mind.

What was the woman prattling about?

-No, I do not.

-You do. The Host's mind voice was insistent, as grating as her physical voice.

Despite the idiotic nature of the claim, Elizan couldn't ignore a horrible suspicion that the Host might have noticed something important. Over the years Elizan had learnt to trust such instincts; they were usually natural manifestations of passive Green Control, her sorcery telling her that something was about to happen. She took a breath and burrowed under the Host's consciousness. The tide of the woman's deepest thoughts closed over her head like quicksand, and she was immersed in Danielle, the woman's thoughts mingling with Elizan's own, her feelings seeping through Elizan's veins. Elizan strove to keep her head clear.

-Show me.

-It's right there.

Elizan felt her mental focus being steered around by

133

Danielle's guiding presence. She felt Danielle watching her own mind, as if she was not herself any more, and she saw what Danielle saw.

It was true. The woman was right. There was something there.

Elizan turned cold; she wanted to scream. It was impossible, but it was right there in front of her. There was a strange presence nestled in Elizan's own thoughts, an intruder deep within her mind. How had she not seen it? How could it be there without her knowledge? It wasn't a sorcerer remotely observing her through the lens of a Yellow Control; the thing was actually inside her. It was as if some hideous parasite had not only picked the locks and scaled the walls of her home and sanctuary but had crept though the hallways to her room and invaded her soul itself, settling like a cancer deep inside.

She withdrew from Danielle's mind with a painful jerk and stood up, her chair clattering to the floor behind her. Before Danielle's feelings drained from her she felt her shock reverberating through the woman, and when she looked across the bed, Danielle was as pale as the sheets.

"What is it?" The woman's voice had lost its edge, revealing an unexpected wavering tone. "Why are you so scared of it?"

"I'm not scared." Elizan's thoughts raced. *Slow down. Settle.* She had to examine that thing; she had to determine what it was, how long it had been nesting there and what it knew.

She retrieved her chair and sat down again, drawing a deep breath to steady herself, then extended her power towards the Host's mind once more, ignoring the woman's questioning look. Their minds met and mingled, her consciousness seeping through the net of the Host's outer thoughts, and they were linked again, in the tunnels of the Host's mind. Elizan felt a strong urge to detach herself, to turn and run from the room, away from the disturbing, violating presence she had found. But she couldn't run from the thing, *because it was inside her own mind.* She swallowed and dived deeper, back into the Host's inner consciousness.

Clamping her own thoughts in a vice, she felt the disorientation again as she saw, felt and thought through Danielle's sight, feelings and thoughts. This sort of deep-consciousness linking was dangerous; it was too easy to forget which thoughts were your own and which were the other person's, and if you held the link too long you started to wonder whether you were the woman in here or the woman sitting out there linking her mind with yours. Elizan shook herself mentally, asserting her personality, willing her identity onto her own consciousness. She spoke to Danielle.

-Show me again.

She felt Danielle's reply as if she had spoken it herself.

-I'll show you. But why can't you see it?

Elizan didn't want to admit that she didn't have an answer to this. This parasite in her mind wasn't like anything she had seen before; it wasn't the probing nose of a Yellow Control – it was more… permanent than that. It nestled deep inside, and she had the unsettling feeling it had been there for a very long time. But even more disturbing was her own blindness; she had been oblivious to its presence until now, and she couldn't comprehend why.

The Host's mental voice cut off her thoughts.

-It is like a spot on your face. You need me to hold the mirror.

Elizan tried to conceal her surprise. Had the Host heard what she was thinking? Either way, it was a remarkably insightful, if inelegant, description of the thing. A spot on her face. She couldn't see it because it was part of her, and she was looking out at the world, not standing out there looking at herself. For a second she wondered why Elizan spent so long pondering such simple things, then with a start realised her sense of identity was slipping.

-We must not linger like this. Where is it?

-There.

Elizan let her mental focus be steered by Danielle's will, and she was faced with it again, a small, repugnant boil in the folds of her mind. With her breath held in her body somewhere, she reached out a questing sense towards it.

The sensation was nothing like she had expected. It was

like feeling a hand touch hers, then realising it was her own. Almost automatically, she slipped into the thing's consciousness, as she would delve through her own thoughts. There was no resistance, and she stumbled inside it, faced with its inner workings as though she had swung the back of a clock open.

It is not part of me, and yet it acts like it is. I can control it.

The thing's pulsing sentience was laid bare to her, a tangle of vivid emotions that was the web of its personality, a ragged grey stream that was its thoughts, but before she could focus on the thing itself, she noticed the thin line trailing from it.

With growing horror she realised what she was seeing. The thing was sitting here, deep in her own mind, watching her thoughts as they formed, and a delicate, invisible strand of sorcery had been tied to it and spooled out to… where? The line grew faint as it left her consciousness; she couldn't see where it ended. Who would invade her mind like this? She realised the answer at the same time as she recognised the cold, lazy, malevolent personality that surrounded her, leaking from the thing like pus from a wound.

It was him.

Without wasting a second to think, she summoned vast amounts of power, gathering her Yellow Control for a mental battle with an equal, one who had spent as long as she had with sorcery swimming in his veins, growing stronger every year. One who was powerful enough to kill her if he attacked with his full strength.

But nothing happened. She pushed her sorcery against the intruder and felt only a glimmer of thought and a trickle of power Resist her. She enveloped it easily; it was a simple creature submerged in her tide of power, unable to Resist her. *So it wasn't him?* She paused, confused, then stripped the creature of its senses. She left it unharmed but unable to see any more of her thoughts, and left the trailing link intact for her to investigate further. Maybe she would be able to find out where it led.

-It's like a spy camera, isn't it? Danielle's mental voice no longer wavered; it just sounded curious. Elizan wished she could share her detachment and dispel the numbing terror that gripped her.

-It can listen to your thoughts and see through your mind, but it's not a full person – it's just an invisible, tiny creature that has been turned into a spy camera.

Elizan conceded that this was an accurate assessment of the situation.

-Yes. It seems it is a spy someone has implanted in me. But strangely, I can control it using Yellow sorcery as though it's part of me.

Danielle's response was immediate, as though her statement was obvious.

-Your sorcery works as though the spy is part of you because the spy has been in you for so long.

Elizan broke the mind link and was back in the room, blinking in the light. She stared at Danielle. "That's it. That's why it's so weak – it's not him. It was once but it's changed – it's an offshoot, a part of him and yet not. I knew I recognised him! The boundaries of self are blurred by his Grey Control… He has injected some of himself into my mind, and over time that part has stopped entirely being him, and has started to become indistinguishable from me."

"Yeah." Danielle picked her nose. "You said 'him'. You know who did this?"

"No," Elizan lied, though she knew she couldn't keep the details from Danielle for long. Not if she wanted to examine the spy further using Danielle's mind as the portal.

"Suit yourself." Danielle shrugged. "The spy is still linked to whoever it came from though, isn't it. Some magic link."

Elizan nodded, almost to herself. "Grey sorcery can split the physical body but retains a non-physical bond between the parts of the sorcerer. That must be the reason for the spy's dual nature – the bond leaves the spy with an intrinsic connection to its creator, but the physical integration means my sorcery can act on it as though it were my own body."

"Yeah, some magic link."

How long has he been watching me? Elizan took a deep breath and let it slide out. The chilling impact of what she had discovered was fading as she realised what she had to do, grim iron will laying a thickening veneer over the chaos. The spy was, for now, in her grip, and it might be possible to use the link to do her own spying. If the spy's creator was who she thought it was then this was an opportunity that couldn't be missed. "I have to investigate the spy's memories."

Danielle pulled herself up to her elbows, pausing to scratch an itch. "Well, as fun as that sounds, I have to go."

Elizan shook her head. "You must not leave yet. I need you here so I can examine the spy."

Danielle barked a laugh, making her silver hoop earrings dance. Surprisingly nimble for one who looked so ungainly, she sat up and swung her stout legs out of the bed. "Find another slave."

"Your power isn't fully settled yet."

"I'll risk it."

"I saved your life."

"So you tell me." Danielle's squinty eyes were dark with challenge. "I bet I would have been fine without your help."

Elizan felt her own jaw clench. "There is too much at stake for these games. I believe that creature inside my mind is linked to… someone dangerous. If I can read his memories through the link then I may be able to gain some advantage. We could save lives. Are you so selfish that this means nothing to you?"

To her shock and shame, Elizan heard her own voice tremble and felt tears hot in her eyes. The years cascaded from her and she was a little girl again, loud words hammering her down, cruel hands clutching her. She grappled for control, desperate not to show weakness to this woman. How many hundreds of years must she live before she could rely on her courage? She folded her hands deliberately, drawing her usual pose around herself like a steel shield. She was Elizan. She finally fixed her gaze back on the Host.

Danielle stared at her for a long, venomous moment, then blew out a noisy breath and rolled her eyes. "You're a do-good-er so I have to be one too?" She collapsed back onto the bed, causing a loud creak. "Where is this dangerous person?"

"I don't know."

"Are you going to go and find him?"

Elizan's throat tightened, her skin crawling at the woman's words. She tried to conceal her reaction. "No."

There was a brief silence.

Danielle scowled up at Elizan from the bed. "What are you waiting for? Let's read some memories."

It was difficult to say for certain in the low light, but the woman's hard eyes seemed to soften for a second, reminding Elizan of that wavering moment that had surprised her. Their deep mind-linking had clearly left some residue of the woman's emotion on her, which was now manifesting itself falsely as sympathy for the woman. The mind was a curious machine. Elizan nodded, took a deep breath and prepared to link minds again. The Host was unimportant; she needed to focus on the task in hand. She would be confronted with his memories in there; she would feel them and live them as though she were him, wandering in his footsteps, laughing with him, thinking with him. She shuddered. Danielle would see it all too. Her darkest secret. But there was no avoiding it – she had to investigate this creature and the memories it held while she had the opportunity. There was no saying how much time she had – who knew when the link from the spy might break?

"Thank you for staying," Elizan said on impulse, her resolve to be cold with this woman seemingly overrun by the after-effects of the mind link. "When you see his memories, please don't judge me too harshly."

Before Danielle had a chance to reply, Elizan wove their minds together again, and the room vanished.

CHAPTER TWENTY-ONE

The scar traced a puckered, raw *S* across his face, from his left ear where it nestled in his thick blond hair, along his cheekbone, skirting under his broad nose and curling his lip, down to his jaw where it grasped his neck and pulled his skin taut like clutched sheets. Holly couldn't stop looking at it.

"I was working all day. Here in the meeting room."

Holly nodded and bent over her notes to record Ian's answer, although for a moment she couldn't even recall what she'd asked him. It was all becoming a blur: the investigation, the grave faces looking at her as though she was now someone important, their hoarsely intoned answers to her delicately posed questions. It was all a buzzing swarm of noise. A noise from which she had to tease some thread of coherent insight, when she was herself barely coherent, sleepwalking through each day.

All of her colleagues, and the other sorcerers in Briggs & Co, had sat here before her in this square grey room. She had asked them all the same questions, recorded their answers and waited for the clue that was surely to land in her lap, a telling inconsistency in someone's story that would neatly unmask the killer. She was still waiting. In the meantime, every second she spent here dragged her thoughts further down a darkening spiral, the life kicking out of her until she would eventually become a hollow shell. She had liked this room; it was a little-used part of the office, with little furniture or decoration other than the two uncomfortable metal chairs, perfect for quiet, uninterrupted work on a project. Now its bareness had been populated by each grim face she had asked for an alibi, the silence filled with their droning, melancholy answers. It was a place of death now.

"Can anyone else vouch for your whereabouts at that time?"

"Rupert and Briggs were with me. We left the office for lunch, but we all went together."

Hadn't Rupert said the three of them were somewhere else? Holly shuffled through the papers on the desk but couldn't find the right page.

"Why don't you ask me about my scar?"

Holly flinched at the coldness in Ian's tone. He was staring at her, his head tilted, his eyes a bloody pair of knives. She groped for some composure. "I'm sorry?"

"You like looking at my scar. Why don't you ask me where I got it?"

Holly swallowed, suddenly feeling alone, and very aware of the locked door and Ian's intense, staring closeness. "I heard what happened at the supermarket."

"Ask me anyway."

"Where did you get it?"

"When I became a bad person my face grew evil to match."

Holly tried to laugh, to turn his chilling statement into a joke by sheer force of will, but her mouth was too dry.

"People say appearances don't matter." Ian's stare was unmoving, his words cut out like blocks of ice. "But they do. Looking at someone tells you what they are. I was once a nice guy. That's just Ian, they said, he's harmless. But everyone knows now who I am, when they look at me and see this face." He traced a finger down the burnt river of milky, twisted flesh. "They know the scars go deeper than the surface. They know there is a blackened, burnt person inside.

"Ian was the guy everyone liked. Ian was the guy who had a normal family, one who loved him. Ian lived on a farm

142

and thought he'd be a farmer one day too. Then you and your friends told Ian it was all a lie and his family weren't really his family." He barked a mocking laugh, and Holly flinched. "The funny thing is, you people told me sorcerers are the ones who don't change, that they live forever and their bodies stop ageing so they get frozen in time like Arthan in his teenage body. But the only time I changed was when you took me from my life. That's when Ian got burned inside and out."

His stare had become a sneer, and he was leaning forward in his chair, pushing his scarred face closer. Holly imagined she could smell the fire that had burned him. His words rang around her, but the only one that reverberated was *family*, and she felt something harden in her heart.

"Did you kill Kim?" *Like you and your brothers and sisters killed my parents?*

"What?" For an instant Ian recoiled, then recovered his sneer. "No, I didn't."

Holly felt herself trembling, but she realised to her surprise she was angry, not scared. Angry at anyone with a family, no matter how they had found out about it. "Then shut up and answer my questions."

Ian looked at her as if he was wondering now who *she* was. Eventually, and to her surprise, he nodded.

She drew a shaky breath, processing her own words. Perhaps she was discovering her own old, invisible scar. She couldn't be the meek Blue sorcerer now, so perhaps someone else was taking over. She looked down at her notes but couldn't focus on them. Who was she looking for – a murderer, or herself?

She shook herself out of reflection. She had to put everything she was into the investigation now; there was no time for self-examination. She had no evidence, no leads, not even a hunch, but she had to keep doing something, anything, to exhaust herself.

Even as she readied her next question, she knew this interview was another dead end. She didn't have any evidence that Ian was the murderer, but she couldn't rule him out. She didn't believe that any of the sorcerers could be the murderer, and yet one of them had to be. Again she tried to draw conclusions from the mess in her head. Elizan had spoiled her original plan by erasing Holly's memory; now she couldn't be trusted to test anyone else, no matter how much Holly wanted to believe in her. Holly couldn't challenge Elizan directly; if Elizan wished to she could crush Holly like a fly. Who could she trust at all any more?

She secretly hoped the murderer was Paros. He was the one she knew the least; she had even spoken with Olivia Gale more than him. It would be easier to accept he was the killer than someone she had known and trusted for years.

She would interview Paros the next day. Other than Olivia, who still hadn't returned any of the calls Holly had made to her management team, Paros was her last interview. If she could only find something, some clue, when she spoke to him, it might all be over soon. She had blurted out to Arthan last night that she was going to ask Elliot to accompany her. Arthan's silence had left her trembling with the thought that he might have realised what was going on between her and Elliot, but he had eventually just nodded. In that moment, her heart beating fast, so close to it all coming out, Holly had sworn to herself that she would tell Elliot it was over. There was too much at risk. She couldn't bear the thought of losing Arthan; he had been there for so long. Within an hour she had discarded her own vow. It was impossible not to see Elliot; she couldn't stop herself thinking about him, despite Arthan, despite the murder, despite her pregnancy, despite all the problems she already had and the extra problems Elliot might cause. She couldn't give him up.

Ian was staring at her again. "Well?"

For a moment she was once more unwillingly transfixed by his scar. It didn't make him a bad person, but it made him look like a bad person, and that made everyone, including him, wonder if he was.

"Let me ask my own question then," Ian said, his eyes narrowing as he examined her. "How burnt are *you* inside?"

144

Holly cleared her throat, shuffled her notes and hurried on to her next question.

It was best not to even think about his.

CHAPTER TWENTY-TWO

Elliot's first impression of Paros was that of a man who didn't want to be seen. When his pale face eventually crept around from behind the door in answer to Holly's ring, he looked like he expected to find his worst fear before him. Was his desire to hide a shadow cast by his Grey sorcery? It was commonly believed that a sorcerer's personality was influenced by his Innate Element. Like Elliot, this man could become invisible, leaving the world and its problems to those who couldn't; Elliot knew himself how this experience could make being visible so much less appealing.

It was the perfect street for anonymity. Paros lived in a red-bricked semi-detached house with a manicured front garden, identical to every other red-bricked house huddled in this unassuming, leafy hideaway. The air felt a little charged and a damp fog hung on their shoulders, but the unsettling weather was no doubt brought here by Holly, brooding on the murder investigation. The street itself was as resolute and unchanging as the red bricks that made it.

Paros had already been told why they were there, but Holly told him again at the door. She described Elliot's role as "assisting" her with the interview. If Paros became hostile, which was likely to happen if he was the murderer, it might take all the assistance Elliot could provide just to keep them alive, but the thought didn't trouble him. It was one of those days when he felt such a sense of lightness that the troubles of everyday life seemed trivial. He was alive, and surely that was enough reason to be cheerful.

He had to hide this levity from Holly, who had barely spoken on their journey here. He could tell how deeply the murder was affecting her by her silences, her bleak stares and the way she laboured through each hour with such deliberate, controlled movements. Was it strange that he didn't feel the same distress? Kim was dead. People died. Everyone had to die sometime. Holly's news that Kim had been pregnant had troubled him, but he had now cast that disturbing detail on the pile with the rest of life's unwelcome facts that he could do nothing about.

Paros nodded politely through Holly's introduction and beckoned them inside. Elliot couldn't help rushing to the conclusion that this man wasn't dangerous. He was stooped, thin and balding. He looked like a man who chewed pencils in a bank and took an apple to work in his briefcase. His eyes were wide and pondering, his glances frequent and earnest. He wore loose beige trousers, the kind that Elliot thought of as old-man trousers, a faded blue woollen jumper and slippers. The only part of his clothing that didn't match the rest was a chunky gold bracelet hooped around his wrist.

They were shown into a cramped lounge smelling of stale tea, and took a seat on an ancient brown sofa while their host shuffled off to make drinks. The room was scattered with mahogany furniture that looked like it belonged in a museum. A thick dark carpet oozed under everything, smothering any light in its depths.

Paros returned and settled in the armchair opposite, and after Elliot had endured several tedious minutes of sipping and pleasantries Holly finally began the interview.

"Where were you between nine a.m. and one p.m. on twenty-seventh June?"

Elliot watched Paros curiously, his notepad and pen poised to record anything of interest. The murder investigation didn't consume him as it seemed to consume Holly, but he was intrigued to finally meet a Grey sorcerer in person.

Paros cleared his throat. "I was here, I think." His voice was hoarse and cracked, as if little used. "Yes. That was a Monday, so I was cleaning."

"Did anyone else see you? Can anyone confirm where you were?"

A shake of the head. "I live alone." A black cat wandered into the room and stretched, unconcerned by the newcomers. "Apart from Thomas."

Holly gave the animal an appraising look. "Did Thomas see you?"

Eyes wider than ever, Paros blinked. "Excuse me?"

"Did the cat see you here that day?"

"Oh. I think so. Why?"

"Can you keep him inside? I'll question him later." She ran an absent hand over the cat's fur. "Don't worry, I won't hurt him."

Before her next question, Holly leant across to whisper to Elliot, her scent billowing around him. "Kim had a cat. I should question it."

Elliot nodded and scrawled something in his notepad, his mind lost in imagining the touch of her pale skin, the caress of her moist lips.

There was a cough, and Elliot looked up to see Paros was flushed. "Of course, sorcery with animals. Yes, of course. Thomas would have seen me."

Holly gave Paros another of her intoxicating smiles, which seemed wasted on this man. "Do you have any experience of breaking and entering using sorcery?"

"Breaking and…?" Paros chuckled, a dry, croaky sound. "Oh, I've never done that, of course. But I would be able to, I imagine."

"What about restraining someone using sorcery?"

"Well. The same answer, I suppose. I've never wanted to, but I believe I could."

The interview was turning out less interesting than Elliot had hoped. With any luck they would be able to finish soon and get back to his flat. He made his notes and sipped his tea, glancing around the room. The tea was thin and insipid, as weak as this pale-faced sorcerer. There was no visible evidence that Paros was anything other than a normal human. He seemed to know very little about Kim or the other Verrin children, and claimed to have no idea why she was killed. He clearly led a very different lifestyle to the sorcerers Elliot knew, and judging by the answers he was giving, he rarely practised or had a need to use his power.

As he dwelt on this man's solitary existence, Elliot felt his mood darken, and his light-heartedness drifted away like a cloud, revealing a burning headache and a jagged pile of anxiety. Was this man's fate what awaited him, now that he had become a sorcerer? An old, empty man in an old, empty house, with no family and no wife. Paros had hinted that he had once had both, long ago, in his previous life before sorcery was thrust on him. Like Holly's father, Paros was a Host, the random recipient of power following the untimely death of a nearby sorcerer, snatched from his human life and gifted with a long and miserable existence. He didn't seem sad, Elliot decided, just resigned. How many human friends had Paros made, he wondered, only to watch them die? This was the life of a sorcerer, a narrow, colourless existence with no one to talk to but ghosts.

A sorcerer's untimely death... As so often these days, Elliot's thoughts strayed unwillingly to his dreams. Why couldn't he wake up and forget? Why did those raw visions spin bloodily before his eyes even now? He couldn't put all that violence aside; he couldn't live his life without flexing his hands and feeling throttled pulses slow in his tightening grip.

In the book about Viros's life that Holly had given him, he had read descriptions of events that matched those he experienced in his dreams in every detail. There was no way around the obvious conclusion – he was dreaming about Viros. He was dreaming *as* Viros. He felt cold when he awoke from the dreams, an uneasy familiarity always chilled him. In his dreams he was a murderer, a psychopath, and though he knew he wasn't himself, sometimes Viros's thoughts and feelings felt like they were his,

Viros's jokes made him smile. Shades of Viros's personality felt like his own, like echoes of his voice in an unfamiliar room. The Viros of his dreams resonated with something. Something dark within him.

"Elliot?"

"Yes?"

Holly and Paros were both looking at him.

"I said, did you have any questions for Paros?"

Elliot forced a smile back at Holly's frown, his headache now a thick hammering. "No, I have everything I need," he replied, shutting his notebook.

"Sorry, what was that?" Paros leant forward in his chair, his head cocked.

The sight of him struck Elliot as odd, and a moment later he realised why. Elderly people were often hard of hearing – but not elderly sorcerers. The level of ambient Red Control for a sorcerer as powerful as Paros should give him keener hearing than any human's. Elliot frowned, trying to think through his pounding headache, re-examining everything they had seen and heard since coming here.

"We're nearly finished," Holly said to Paros. "I just need to interview Thomas."

"Of course." Paros nodded several times, head bobbing like a turtle's, trembling to his feet. "I'll fetch him."

"Actually, I have one or two more questions for you," Elliot said. "Maybe Holly could fetch Thomas."

Holly frowned, her lips thinning, but she got up anyway and went to look for the cat. Paros sank back into his chair, wide-eyed.

Elliot's desire to leave early had vanished like smoke. This man was no murderer, but there was now a more important question to resolve. A question that Elliot's intuition told him might reveal something about his own origins. This Grey sorcerer was not what he seemed.

He smiled at Paros, but he knew he couldn't fake warmth like Holly could – his smile probably just looked sinister. Paros's hands twitched in his lap, and Elliot dropped the smile. "When did you last use sorcery?"

Paros's mouth flapped for a few seconds before any noise emerged. "I, er, I don't remember."

You don't remember? Or you never have? Paros was a man who wanted to be invisible. A man with no seeming interest or knowledge of sorcery. A man who didn't seem to use sorcery. He should have had a sorcerer's sharp mind, his power fuelling his brain, but he couldn't remember what he had done on the day Kim died, didn't realise that Holly would be able to speak to his cat and couldn't even hear what Elliot and Holly were saying. Paros was a man who wanted to be invisible, *but he wasn't a sorcerer.*

"Oh, I remember!" Paros hurried from his chair to the corner of the room and started shuffling through a box. Elliot waited. He couldn't explain how Paros might not be a sorcerer – how had he lived this long as a human? – but he felt sure he was right. Who was this pale, lonely man really? Why would a human pretend to be a sorcerer?

When Paros returned from the corner he was bearing a small, crumpled piece of paper. He pushed it into Elliot's hands then switched on the tiny black box television that perched on the sideboard.

"The 2.10 at Doncaster is just about to start." Paros motioned for Elliot to look at the piece of paper.

As the television blared on at full volume, Elliot looked at the names and numbers scribbled on the paper. About halfway down was a heading of *Doncaster, 2.10*, and underneath was written *Golden Boy 1st, Monday Morning 2nd, Archimedes 3rd, Pip Post 4th.*

"I like to use my Premonition on the horses, just for fun." Paros folded into his chair, his energy seeming to fade as fast as it had arrived. "Silly, I know."

The television's crackly, colourless picture was now showing the busy hubbub of a race track, presumably Doncaster. As the horses milled about on the starting line Holly returned with Thomas the cat in her arms.

"Time to go now, Elliot."

Paros looked delighted, but Elliot shook his head. He couldn't leave without finding out. "Not just yet, Paros is showing me something."

Holly lowered Thomas to the floor but remained in the doorway. "Is it important?"

"It won't take a minute."

Her frown deepened but she said nothing. While Paros squirmed in his seat, Elliot turned back to the screen.

Predicting the first four places of a horse race a few hours before the race seemed like it would be a difficult feat, and Elliot had to admit that this would be strong evidence that Paros really was a sorcerer. Although it remained to be seen whether Paros's predictions would be correct.

The three of them watched in silence as Paros's four named animals made a good start and his winner, Golden Boy, took an early lead. But two other horses he hadn't named moved into second and third place, and the next horse, Paros's predicted third place, Archimedes, was a long way behind the front three. Elliot noticed Paros's pale hands clutch his seat.

In the final stretch the horse in second place stumbled and fell, bringing the third-place horse down with it. Archimedes had to swerve to avoid the fallen horses, and Monday Morning overtook, then Archimedes recovered. A moment later the horses crossed the finishing line in the order Paros had predicted. Golden Boy, Monday Morning, Archimedes and Pip Post. Paros sighed and smiled, clapping his hands together. Golden Boy's jockey was celebrating. The *LIVE* logo was clear in the top-right corner – it was difficult to deny Paros had used sorcery. Elliot's head pounded. Why did he still feel suspicious?

"A clever trick," Holly said. "Do you make a lot of money from it?"

"I never put much on." Paros sounded almost apologetic. "It's just to keep my eye in, you know."

"Well, thank you for putting up with us. We'll be on our way now."

But Elliot didn't move. It all felt wrong; Paros had seemed so nervous. What did he have to worry about if he really was a sorcerer? There was something going on. Could another sorcerer covering for Paros have given him the sheet of predictions? Elliot tried to thread his aching thoughts together. How had he felt so relaxed just a few minutes before? The murder, the secrets, the distrust, his conviction that Paros was hiding something – it all weighed on him, suffocating him. "What about shape-shifting?"

"I'm sorry?" squeaked Paros.

"Elliot, let's go."

"You're a Grey sorcerer, so you must be able to shape-shift. I'd like to see that."

Jaw clenched against the pain in his head, Elliot ignored Holly's scowl and kept his eyes fixed on Paros.

Paros sighed. "Of course. Shape-shifting."

To Elliot's surprise, Paros then stood up and clasped his hands before him. Elliot had expected excuses, not an actual demonstration.

"My former farmhand," Paros said simply. Then he changed. He continued to wear the same plain clothes but his pale face twisted, shifted into something new. It was disturbing to watch him change shape, even though Elliot had seen many such changes, watching himself shape-shift in his bathroom mirror. The skin rolling and stretching like dough, the eyes clouding then blinking clear a different hue. In a few seconds it was done.

This, Elliot supposed, was the face of Paros's former farmhand. He was slighter than Paros, so the blue jumper hung off him in folds. The face was darker skinned, scarred, and the skin was weathered. The farmhand had a scratchy beard. It was difficult to tell in Paros's clothes, but Elliot thought he had lived and died long ago. The style of his hair and beard, maybe the scar, made him look as though he should live in a history book.

After giving Holly and Elliot the opportunity to take in the transformation, Paros changed back. Elliot caught the sound of a faint but audible click just before his body melted back to his usual shape. Paros unclasped his hands and sat down.

So he really was a sorcerer? Holly complimented Paros on

his demonstration, but Elliot lapsed into silence, dwelling on the noise he'd heard. Had he also heard a click when Paros had first changed into the farmhand? He thought now that he had. "Would you mind showing us again?"

"Elliot!" Holly's glare looked dangerous. "Haven't we harassed Paros enough?"

"Just one more time, Paros? If you don't mind?" It was hard to keep the tension from his voice. He was close to something, he felt it.

"Um, OK." Paros rose to give the performance again.

Elliot watched, and listened. Paros clasped his hands as before, and this time Elliot was certain. A click! Paros shifted into the farmhand. He didn't remain that way for long, perhaps unnerved by Elliot's stare. When he changed back Elliot heard the click again, then Paros was his pale self once more.

Holly began gathering her things to leave, but Elliot stared at Paros, and at the large gold bracelet on his wrist. It must be the bracelet. Elliot had thought it was strange when he saw it, such an ornate device on such a plain man, and he now recalled that every time he shape-shifted Paros had clasped his hands over it. The clicking must have come from the bracelet. It must be an Enchantment.

All Enchantments were supposedly destroyed, but Paros had got hold of one somehow; it was the only way a human could have carried out the shape-shifting. The demonstrations had been faked. The horse race had been impressive, but could be carried out by another Enchantment, or could have been set up in advance by another sorcerer. He didn't know how Paros had lived such a long time, but maybe that was achieved with an Enchantment too. Was that possible?

Elliot glanced at Holly. She was pointedly ignoring him. There was time for one more test.

He packed away his notebook while Holly made polite goodbyes, waiting for his moment. Before he turned for the door, he summoned a small amount of power. Without speaking he cast a Yellow Control, sending a probing presence towards Paros's mind. Then he said goodbye, shook Paros's hand and made his way to the door.

Elliot's thoughts raced as they returned to the anonymous street, his headache buzzing in the brightness. He had entered Paros's mind instantly. There should have been a barrier, a natural, ever-present and almost impregnable barrier, the Resistance of a sorcerer who was hundreds of years old, but there had been nothing. Elliot had swept into Paros's mind, and the man's thoughts had been wide open, exploding into Elliot's consciousness as if Paros had shouted at him: *I'm getting away with it. They're leaving.*

Elliot watched Paros disappear behind his door. *Getting away with it.* The murder? No. *Getting away with his disguise.* Elliot's hunch had been right. Paros wasn't a sorcerer.

"Well?" Holly had marched ahead to her car and now stood waiting with her hands on her hips. Her face was a carving of stone, her eyes like shards of green bottle glass. "Are you going to explain why you hijacked my interview? You think you can do a better job than me?"

Her fury surprised him, but Elliot didn't have time to dwell on it. She was under a lot of stress, and he had more important things to worry about. For a second, he considered telling her about Paros, but rejected the idea just as quickly. "Sorry."

She blew out a noisy breath and got into the car, slamming the door. Elliot took one last look at Paros's plain and silent door and decided he would return tomorrow. He had to read Paros's mind, to find out what was going on. Paros was a fake Grey sorcerer, and Elliot was a real one. Did Paros know the secret to Elliot's identity?

A man who wished he was invisible, couldn't become so but pretended he could. Elliot was going to have to find out who he really was.

CHAPTER TWENTY-THREE

Naomi crept through the office, shying away from the light slanting from the hall. She had been here often enough for the surroundings to be familiar, but in the fading evening light the shadows began to stretch, and as their grey fingers edged along the carpet towards her she felt her steps falter. She swallowed. *This doesn't feel right*, she thought, *but I have to do it*.

She headed towards the corridor at the far end of Arthan Associates. *Keep walking, keep walking*. She tried to keep her footsteps soft, conscious of her laboured breathing as she struggled along. She was terrified of walking into a desk and sending something clattering to the floor, but thankfully the few desks were dotted at wide intervals, leaving expanses of clear floor visible even in the dim light.

It was a shabbier building than Briggs & Co, paint peeling in places, a worn grey carpet stretched across the floor, but Naomi preferred it to Briggs's sterile offices. The lack of cleanliness had provided the opportunity for a spider to spin a web in the far corner of the room, and this alone gave her strength. She didn't have to see the spider to sense that he was there, to feel the innocent hum of his small mind. Animals were so much better than humans.

When she was halfway across the room she heard faint voices upstairs. She froze. She didn't move for a full minute, straining to hear over the sound of her heartbeat, counting the seconds. Someone was up there. Arthan?

She had to get moving again. She had to be quick. She listened for another thirty seconds, could hear nothing, and finally convinced herself to carry on. *I have to do this.*

When she reached the corridor she sought, she hurried down it, leaving the light switched off as she had at the entrance. *Stay hidden.*

Getting inside the building had been difficult enough. She had hoped her key card would still work at this time of the evening, but no such luck. She had strained to move the heavy steel bolt with Orange Control, hoping her adrenaline would feed her power and overcome her inexperience and weakness in the Element, but again no such luck. As usual an animal was her saviour. A starling sleeping nearby had been delighted to hear her voice inside its mind, and was more than happy to help her by finding his way inside the building through an air vent, fetching the metal ring of keys from the post room and bringing them back outside to her open hand. She was so proud of the little bird for his cleverness. How shocked Rupert and Ian would be if they knew she had broken into Arthan's office! They might not think her so pathetic now. She crept onwards. Now came the really difficult part.

At the end of the corridor she stopped, facing the door marked *FIRST AID*. She drew a deep breath, then entered.

* * *

Sean woke from yet another dream. The neat stump where his sister's head should have been was still imprinted on his eyes, but through it he saw Naomi creeping towards him. It was at times like this that he was thankful for his Red ability. His reactions were sufficiently heightened that in spite of the fog of sleep and drugs, he could have been out of bed and on top of the intruder before she realised he was awake. But it was Naomi – no need for violence here. Yet.

He flicked the bedside light on and Naomi blinked. She stopped.

"What are you doing here?" he said.

Naomi's eyes took a while to react to the sudden light. Sean had moved so fast, his arm flashing out in a blur to turn the light on. She had heard that Marrin had been sedating him here for two days, and now she realised why. He must be difficult to control when fully awake.

"What are you doing here?"

She stood petrified for a second, took two steps closer to the bed, then stopped again under the fierceness of his stare. Was she doing the right thing? Should she tell her secret to one of the others rather than Sean? Or keep it to herself? She took another deep breath.

"I know who killed Kim."

PART SEVEN
ESCAPE

A few days after Kim's death

CHAPTER TWENTY-FOUR

*H*e *banked on a gust of wind and stretched his wings to let the air ripple through his feathers. He rolled and dived in the giddy rush of flight, but as he spun around he kept an eye on the cart far below. From this height the countryside was a rosy-and-verdant-checked blanket flung over the hills, the cart a black ant crawling across its folds. A cloud drifted past and he plunged sideways through it, his vision filling with cotton wool tufts of white then clearing as he burst through the other side. He cawed, giving full throat to his bird voice. Today he should not be troubled by men's concerns — he was just another bird, a curious hawk turning lazy circles aloft.*

A shadow of feeling far below reminded him he was not entirely the hawk; he was split. He could feel a small part of himself down there, a Splinter, nestled in the mind of the driver but connected to him by an invisible thread of power. He had chosen not to give that smaller part of himself the power of sight; forming two separate shapes, each with independent vision, made him nauseous. He coasted on the playful currents, almost letting himself forget he had a task in hand. But it was almost time, and so he had to focus.

He had a plan. For once, he wasn't just drifting along with the current and poking away hazards with a stick when they floated near; he was at the helm and steering his own course. It was tiresome to go to these lengths to plot and anticipate, then once committed to it be so constrained by his own design, but maybe he would come to like it. Maybe these plans would become his new way of doing things. He applied Yellow Control to sharpen

163

his mind, and the world crystallised into icy facets: nothing but the Splinter, the cart, the riders and the plan.

The cart wound its steady way along the road, unaware of its observer high in the sky. Elliot could see the riders gaining on the cart, and with Red-enhanced sight he could even identify them. Elizan, Charen and Salas. Elizan in her usual robes of gold, her face a mask of concentration, her long hair whipping behind her in the wind. Charen in his ankle-length blue coat, frowning over his short grey beard. Salas following behind, still looking like a boy after all these years, his eyes intense beneath his violent brows. They were always so serious. *Life was too short to be serious. Elliot spotted a small infant bundled in cloth and secured to the back of Elizan's horse. The intended Grey Host, no doubt. So they did mean to kill him. Elliot grinned inside. Let them try.*

The three sorcerers below were riding fast, faster than horses could usually ride. Sorcery. Elliot couldn't hear any noise from the hooves; perhaps Charen was using the air to shield the noise somehow? In truth Elliot didn't really care; he had never been interested in theory. He angled his wings and began his descent. The plan was all that mattered. It was important that he had a good view of how things unfolded when it started.

He reached for that part of himself that was the Splinter, deep in the driver's mind. Elliot listened to the man's thoughts through the Splinter as though he crouched at the keyhole of the door to his brain, eavesdropping on his idle reverie. There wasn't much to listen to. The man was a dumb crop-sower, dreaming of his dinner, unaware of the sorcerer that dwelt in his mind, unaware of his impending messy death and unaware of the ornate silver ring with a purple stone that Elliot had squeezed onto his fat index finger not an hour earlier. The man slumped in his seat as if he was dead already, his hands anchoring the reins on his bloated stomach, his eyes drooping while the rickety horses plodded along in front of him and the rickety wooden cart bumped along beneath him.

All was set. The riders were closing in, the farmer was semi-comatose and Elliot was ready, both his bird shape and the crucial part of him lodged inside the farmer's brain. The bird and the Splinter. The angler and the bait.

The riders were within a mile now, and Elliot the bird dropped lower, although not too low. Charen and Elizan were well versed in Green sorcery; they could sense him if he flew too near. He kept his presence in the bird hidden, but in the farmer's mind he left the Splinter uncovered, like a jewel displayed on cloth. Its glinting power would be a beacon to Elizan as she raced towards it, reeling in her catch. Would she notice she had only caught one scale of the fish?

As the riders came charging up the final stretch of road to catch the dawdling cart, the Splinter of Elliot assumed control of the farmer's mind. His presence flooded the human's brain, he saw through his eyes, he heard through his ears, he felt through his skin. The farmer's consciousness struggled for a few grunting breaths then collapsed under the pressure. While Elliot still circled above, in the cart below he held the reins.

The horses were still shrouded in silence as they swept around the side of the cart to emerge into the view of the farmer, and the Splinter. Elliot heard nothing, but he felt them come.

The farmer's hands obeyed Elliot's commands and twisted the purple ring he wore. Salas was already using Orange Control to bind the farmer to his seat, and Elizan was already rendering him unconscious, but they were both too late. Power surged hungrily from the ring to fall upon the nearest target. Charen's mouth opened in surprise as the lash of power arced into him. Crimson spurted from his mouth and the other two turned in surprise. Salas was the first to react. He drew a long silver sword, and as Charen tumbled from the horse beside him he struck the motionless farmer's head from his shoulders.

Circling in his bird shape high above, Elliot watched as the spring of blood bubbled from the farmer's headless neck and the fat, simple head bounced to the ground. Without pause Elizan and Salas leapt from their horses, pulled the headless body from the cart and piled it with the head. They stood over the remains of the farmer, and the pile of flesh burst to life with raging Blue fire.

As the flesh burned Elliot felt the pain himself through the Splinter that was still secreted in the farmer's head. The crackling flames seared him, the white-hot heat making him gasp and his wings flex involuntarily. He felt himself stall in the air and almost dropped like a stone, but he sought for strength and stretched his wings wide, regaining his balance. Just a few more seconds. He concentrated on flying, on the wind, on his aching wings, on anything but the bright, hot agony of the fire. He thought he smelt his own burnt flesh just as the pain rose in a scalding wave over his mind, and he could no longer hold against the tide. Instinctively, unable *to stop himself, he called the Splinter back to him. It raced along the line of power that joined them, merging into his body as if it had always been there, and the pain of the flames blinked out as if it had never been. He bunched and stretched his muscles in relief. Had he held the contact long enough to convince them?*

Below him, the farmer's body was now a black mess of smoking ash splattered across the ground. Elliot soared in circles on the currents and watched the two sorcerers standing over the carnage. Elizan was staring at Charen's body. Elliot could see her and hear her speak as if she were next to him. A tear loosed itself from her eye and dribbled down her cheek. "Goodbye, Charen."

Elliot ignored the tears. They were just water. The important part was the plan. The important outcome was whether the plan worked.

Salas wiped his brow. "He's not dead." His voice sounded cracked, his resolve damaged. "How can he be dead?"

"Look at him." Elizan gestured at the dark pool around Charen's head. "It is done. We must find the Grey Host."

The other sorcerer shook his head. "How can he be dead?"

"The ring. It was an Enchantment. Viros collected them."

"It can't be!" Salas rounded on Elizan. "You destroyed all the Enchantments."

Elizan shook her head. "You have too much faith in me. I always knew there must have been more I never found." She sighed and remounted her horse. "Come, it is over – I promise you, the farmer was him."

The other sorcerer shook his head.

"Salas, we must find the Grey Host. I have not let the contact drop for a week – I have not slept since. It was him. Viros is dead."

Above, Elliot flapped at the air, a wild laughter growing inside. The plan, it seemed, was working.

Salas climbed into his saddle, his shoulders sagging. "A Grey Host?"

Elizan glanced at the baby that still rested on the back of Elizan's horse. "Yes. Charen's power entered the child. The Grey power will find another."

Elliot dipped a wing and banked around behind them, cawing, unable to contain his energy. Elizan and Salas were speaking unguardedly now, thinking him dead. Unbelievably, incredibly, he had done it!

"Can you locate the Host?" Salas asked.

166

"When we get close." Elizan raised her head to the air. "For now we just look for humans."

"This way then?"

Elizan nodded. "This way."

They spurred their horses on, Salas giving one more look back at the two corpses they left behind, and Elliot followed. He would make sure they found what they were looking for. As the horses below set off at an unnatural pace, Elliot decided his bird shape wasn't fast enough; he needed to get ahead of them. He let his hawk body melt into the air and shot forward, tunnelling along the wind, becoming the wind. He smiled internally, invisibly. The air was warm, the world was before him, and he was just a few minutes away from securing his peace from these people forever.

He shortly overtook the riders and spied a farm nearing in the distance. It must be Elizan's target; she would have sensed the humans there. He dropped between the stands of trees that had arrived below and sped through the branches, his body of wind splitting and twisting through and around the gnarled oaks.

The farm rushed closer. A small group of low stone buildings, fields rolling to a drooping fence. Elliot slowed to locate a target. Four humans. One female infant, one male child, one female adult, one male adult. Not the baby or the child – they would be expected to join sorcerer society, and that was too much hassle to either arrange or avoid. The adult male.

Elliot swept through the farm as a breeze, past the house and into the stable. The adult male was tending the horses. Elliot split a part of himself from his invisible body and tentatively probed the man's mind. The man started at the touch, his hand on a horse's flank, then shook himself, continued working, and Elliot was in control.

He grasped the man's mind and commanded it.

CHAPTER TWENTY-FIVE

Inky darkness roiled around the square of light. Sean pushed groping wet leaves away from his face and shifted his bare feet on the cold earth. The world scraped at him, brushed over him, whistled in his ear, eager to distract him from his purpose, but he locked his jaw and bolted his gaze to the figure in the bright window. Wearing only the T-shirt and shorts that he had been sleeping in, his legs and arms were exposed to the night's sharpness, but he didn't let his muscles shiver. A fire burned inside him that ruled every movement and every thought.

His senses were awakened, and hot Red power coursed along his veins. The scents of the garden wafted around him as vividly as coloured smoke, rose and lavender mingling with the smells of earth, brick, blood and the murderer. He could hear the long, deep thumps of his heartbeat like giant slowing footsteps. He didn't know why his heartbeat slowed at a time when a human's would quicken. It didn't matter.

In the corner of his vision he noticed a silky line of crimson on his forearm. He was bleeding. Without turning from the figure in the window he let power pour into the wound and knit together the flesh.

He had been watching his sister's murderer for almost an hour, his muscles as tense as wound iron springs, his focused mind an unflinching rock. He couldn't unclench his jaw.

He could swallow the distance between him and the

murderer in a breath. He could be through the window and inside the room in seconds, but he had chosen to wait, grinding his fury sharper.

His sister had been killed. He had to keep reminding himself of what had happened, or he would stop believing it. His sister had been killed, by a sorcerer.

It was time for justice.

He shot forward, leaping over the bushes and twigs. The trees were no longer visible against the blackness, at least to a human, but Sean's Red eyesight could pick out the obstacles. A truck roared on a nearby road, leaves whispered in a rising wind, but nothing else could be heard. He made no sound, and his eyes never left the figure at the window.

The window's light clicked out into blackness. An after-image of square gold hung in Sean's eyes as he leapt over a low fence, landed on springy ground and reached the sheer wall of the murderer's building.

He summoned more power, muttering a focusing chant, and sprang cat-like onto the face of the wall. He scaled the bricks fast, occasionally stabbing his fingers into the mortar for grip. In a heartbeat he was level with the recently lit window. In another heartbeat he had ripped the window open, stripping the catch. The murderer sat on the bed. In another heartbeat he was inside.

He screamed, without words. The murderer looked up, eyes wide.

* * *

Olivia looked up, eyes wide. It was the Red boy, Sean. As he lunged towards her, she rolled off the bed and was on her feet and facing him by the time he turned round. He wore only a stained T-shirt and football shorts, his feet bare.

"What are you doing here?"

His eyes narrowed to red slits, he stepped close and hurled a fist towards her. He was fast, nearly too fast to follow, but her Red sorcery was already reacting instinctively to the danger and channelled her response at equal speed. She ducked inside the punch and spun behind him. Her thin arms were up around his neck, and he was held.

"What are you doing here?" she said again.

Sean strained against her grip, grunting, but she held tight.

He switched the direction of his struggling and they both collapsed to the floor. For a heartbeat Olivia was prone, and he was back on his feet above her. A chair appeared above her as Sean smashed it down onto her head – she rolled and the chair splintered across her side instead, a stripe of hot pain searing her arm. For the first time in her life she felt an uneasy rustling in the pit of her stomach. Could she actually be in danger?

Sean tossed the broken chair aside and leapt at her, but she was up again and ready. She stepped aside as he flew past.

She had to concentrate. Had to think. He was fighting as though he meant to kill, and he was as fast as her, as strong as her. She felt a tingling in her arm as the wound pulled and softened, the edges joining and zipping together, the pain receding to a throb, then a warmness, then nothing. Sean paused before coming at her again, although his Red stamina meant he couldn't be tired. No, he was choosing to pause, to look at her with those wild blood-red slits. Maybe it was his lack of clothing, but he seemed more animal than human, in a simian crouch, his muscles bunching and writhing like coiled snakes, an earthy stink rolling off him. His chest rose and fell with long, ragged breaths, but it was not the breathing of exhaustion; it was the breathing of a creature no longer thinking with any semblance of reason, the breathing of insanity.

He came at her again.

* * *

The first time Terry heard a noise on his patrol he assumed it was a bird, or the wind rattling a window. Unexplained noises came with the job, and over the years he had spent too much time worrying about creaks and bangs, only to investigate and find a big load of nothing. These days he didn't bother worrying. Especially here – a dream job in a luxury mansion, a rich client and no danger. Easy money. Although when Terry neared the foot of the hall's central flight of stairs he heard another noise. Two unexplained noises – that was more unusual.

It couldn't be an intruder. The house was at the heart of a gated five-acre estate, enclosed by ten-foot-high walls topped with barbed wire. His colleagues at the main gates were the real security guards. Terry had the enviable position inside the extravagant mansion itself, as Olivia's "peace of mind" guard.

Maybe two noises deserved an investigation. He started climbing the red-carpeted stairs, peering at the paintings on the wall as he passed. What a place. As his foot came down on the fourth step he heard more noises and reassessed the situation. Two raised voices were echoing from somewhere beyond the top of the stairs, accompanied by sharp cracks and occasional crashes. One voice was female, screaming – Olivia. Another voice was male and growling. *An intruder.*

Terry raced to the top of the stairs, almost tripping over himself in haste, and stumbled into the corridor leading to Olivia's rooms. He pursued the noise to a bedroom door and had just put his hand on the handle when there was an awesome crash to his right. The wall exploded like a bomb had gone off and something flew out in a shower of rubble, spraying Terry with shattered plaster. When the thing hit the far wall of the corridor and slumped to the floor he realised it was Olivia. His stomach flipped. She wasn't moving.

He took an involuntary step back from the hole in the wall as another, larger figure hurtled through. It looked like a man but it was moving too fast for him to see it clearly. In a blur it swept across the corridor and descended on Olivia's small, crumpled body. A swirl of dust was flung into Terry's face from its passage and he spun away, eyes stinging. When he turned back a second later Olivia was impossibly back on her feet and unharmed, exchanging a lightning sequence of blows with the other figure.

Terry found himself rooted to the dusty carpet, unable to look away from the storm of violence before him. Seemingly unaware of his presence, Olivia battled the man – Terry could see it was a man now, a huge man – in a whirlwind of fists, her slight frame and lack of height causing her no difficulty in holding him off. Their movements were too fast for him to decipher if their blows were striking home, but he could hear her screaming and the man's inhuman bellowing.

The cacophony receded as Olivia pelted back down the corridor to raise the alarm. There was nothing he could do himself in this situation. Assistance of a special kind was needed.

* * *

"Arthan."

"Is that Mr Arthan?"

"No, just Arthan."

"Hello, Mr Arthan. This is Terry Davis. I'm a security guard at Oliviana."

"What do you want?"

"We've got a problem here. At Oliviana Park. I was given this number to call if anything, um, weird happened, and to ask for you. So I called it. I'm allowed to give you our location if—"

"Tell me what is happening."

"Someone is attacking Olivia. They're moving so fast, I couldn't even—"

"It's Sean. I'm on my way."

"Who's Sean? Hello?"

* * *

Olivia was panting as she staggered back to her feet. She had never been so tired. In fact, she couldn't remember ever being tired at all. Ever since she had been signed with the agency as a child, daily exercise had become as habitual as breathing and just as effortless, her Red power fuelling her training with an inexhaustible fire. Despite her body forever remaining that of a scrawny girl, she could lift weights all day without tiring, run for miles without breaking a sweat and get up the next morning feeling as fresh as the day before. But now, for the first time, her body was being punished beyond its capacity to rebound. Her legs were like string, her arms tenderised by a thousand bruises and cuts – all of which had healed but were now beginning to seep back through her skin, the building swell of injuries leaving their mark as an insistent burning.

She dodged a series of strikes to her face, spun out of Sean's attempted grab and battered a volley of punches back at him. She should be thankful, she told herself through clenched teeth, that she wasn't human. Those thousand blows she bore would have killed her several times over by now. She used her Red Control Ambiently, with no time to do anything but trust her sorcery to keep protecting her. If she could just pause for a moment to compose her thoughts there must be some other sorcery she could use against him, something to take him by surprise, but then she had never practised any other than Red anyway. Red Controls pushed her body and her opponent's beyond normal limits, hardened their muscles, readied their twitching nerves and fired their pumping blood, but it wasn't enough. Her reflexes remained sharp, but underneath she could feel her consciousness beginning to fray at the edges. The abilities she took for granted were slipping between her exhausted fingers as her opponent wore her down. She was healing herself more slowly; she had less energy in each dodge and each punch.

The screaming had stopped now. They were both too focused on the fight, hardened and sharpened on the stone of combat to steel spinning machines, to let themselves waste energy releasing emotion. The only sound was the squeaking of their feet on the floor and the occasional grunt of effort.

The fight had spilt down a flight of stairs at one point, and they now grappled in the long corridor of the east wing, watched sombrely by the paintings that lined the high walls. Sean's face bobbed in and out of darkness as they danced between the baths of light thrown by the tall lamps, but Olivia never took her eyes from him and the whirlwind of their fists never paused. They had both tried and discarded makeshift weapons invented from the ornaments and furniture around them, but had now hardened their skin such that no piece of wood or metal would be as effective as their fists.

Not that anything she did to him ever seemed to be effective. He was so strong, so *fast*. He was her Red brother, the same age as her, which was why they were evenly matched. She knew she didn't look his equal – he had at least a foot of height over her, and her arms felt barely as thick as his meaty fingers – but it was sorcery, not physical size, that mattered here. She leapt away from him to gain a split-second advantage then crashed her left fist into his side, but he slipped away at the last instant, turning the momentum into an attack of his own. As she blocked and whirled away she felt her limbs screaming. When would this end? Her muscles wailed at her to drop to her knees and give in, to let him fall on her and rip her apart, but she couldn't listen. All she could do was push every inch of her strength into each step, each strike and each moment that might be the opening she needed to prise his defences apart and destroy him.

She bent her focus back to the fight for the hundredth time, and continued fighting for her life. Underneath it all, under the layers of cold concentration and liquid-fire adrenaline, her mind still rang with confusion.

She had no idea why she was being attacked.

CHAPTER TWENTY-SIX

Burning eyes, searing pain, blackened flesh. A crunch as a stone fist ground muscle against bone, a hiss and a gasp as a sharp edge punctured skin and bubbled steaming blood. A roar and a whimper and a fat girl twisting and falling to smack like a thick steak on the hot, oily road.

Rupert's eyes snapped open and he tried to rise, then gasped as a torrent of chunky, bitter vomit rushed up his throat. He managed to reach his knees so he could spit the last stringy dribbles of sick to the carpet, but he didn't need to look down to know the rest was a foul-smelling stew ladled over his brand-new sweater. He closed his eyes again and tried to breathe.

It would be happening soon, or might be happening now. There was no time to gather his strength or worry about the bruises from his fall. He had to find his phone. He opened his eyes again and his bedroom started spinning like one of those fireworks. Agonising neon stripes and metal sparks, hurtling around with an occasional crunch as a stone fist hit bone, and an occasional wet smack as a fat girl's meat hit the road. He squinted and the lights seemed to fade. Maybe he could make out the door – no, his bed – shimmering in the scalding heat. The phone. Where was his phone?

He reached a trembling white hand out towards something before him, felt wood and flapped his fingers for a grip. *Pull yourself up, Rupert.* He thrust with his wasted legs and his hand slipped from the chair, his head cracked against the wood and he landed bodily on the carpet, the wet stink of vomit in his nose. Something beeped.

His phone was in his pocket. By lucky chance his shaking left hand was close enough to slide it out and take a feeble grip. With a grunt he rolled himself onto his back and felt the vomit on his sweater slide towards his face. His phone was still in his left hand, now close enough to his mouth. His fingers complained as he bent them to the touchscreen. Recent calls. Ian.

They hadn't spoken since Ian had been burned at the supermarket. This wasn't really the best time to clear the air, but he didn't know who else to call.

The phone rang, sounding more like an angry buzzing than the usual perky trilling. Two rings, three. Rupert closed his eyes.

"Yes?"

It didn't sound like Ian, but Rupert supposed it was him. He tried to talk but nothing came out but pain.

"What do you want, Rupert?"

Rupert. He was normally Rupe. "A vision."

Silence. Had he said it out loud? Rupert's entire body throbbed for a few seconds before Ian's voice sounded again in the blackness.

"What vision? What happened?"

He felt the vomit slide further, the warm soup dribbling down his neck. His right leg started spasming and he gritted his teeth.

"Naomi. Hurt. Come."

* * *

Arthan narrowed his eyes at the hefty entrance doors as he strode down the path. They were thick oak, square panelled, studded with brass and secured with a column of thick, gleaming locks. A tug with Orange Control and the locks obligingly slid open. He took the wide stone stairs two at a time and thrust open the doors, making a man in a black jacket whirl in surprise. The inside of the building was warm and musty, the

178

huge entrance hall reaching into shadows on all sides. Arthan felt the depth of the carpet beneath his feet, cast his eye around at the high walls groaning with ornaments and tapestries. A self-indulgent waste of money, just like the rest of this ridiculous place.

"Who are you?"

Arthan granted the man a brief look before resuming his march to the stairs. This was the human who had called him. "Arthan."

The man gaped, then scampered to Arthan's side as he mounted the main staircase.

"How did you—No one told me you were here!"

This didn't seem like it needed an answer, so Arthan didn't provide one. In any case, the man's nerves would probably not be settled by the news that it was child's play for any sorcerer to walk past those cretins guarding the main gate.

There were a few moments of blissful silence as they swept across the landing before the human started bleating again. "Shall I show you where they are?"

"I know."

They turned a corner and the trail of damage caused by Sean and Olivia became apparent. The carpet was ripped in ugly gaps and tears, windows were shattered with puddles of glass beneath, the oak cabinets that lined the corridor were mostly dented or caved in, sprawling drunkenly to the side. As they neared the far end of the corridor they had to leap over a missing section of floor where a splintered hole yawned into shadow beneath. Arthan didn't need his Green Control to know the two of them were close.

"I didn't think you'd be so young."

Arthan stopped mid-stride, whirled towards the human, and the man stumbled to an open-mouthed halt. Arthan forced his gritted teeth apart. He had a wild temptation to slap this simpleton halfway back down the long corridor. He drew a deep, slow breath. "Stay here and shut up."

Suffocated by the sorcery infusing Arthan's words, the human swayed as if bolted to the floor, his eyes turning glassy.

What an irritating creature. Belas could have the pleasure of dealing with him when he eventually arrived.

He had only taken a few steps further down the corridor when he heard a crash ahead. It was them. He broke into a faltering run, cursing his ungainly, childish body, and emerged into a huge, echoing hall. Feeling like he was running into a giant's mouth, he clattered on beneath the yawning ceiling into the depths of the hall, his eyes pinned on the two figures before him.

He summoned more power as he went, bringing a Yellow Control into shape behind his expanding well of sorcery. Ahead of him, Sean and Olivia were a blur. They were locked in a dense storm of combat in the centre of the hall, their movements flickering with coloured flashes of blood and tattered clothing as their limbs whirred with thrusts and parries, gunshot cracks echoing when they connected. One moment they were on their feet and the next they were on the floor, a bleak crunch sounding as a blow was landed, although it was impossible to tell who had been hit. Arthan closed to within a few metres. Where the hell was Belas?

He planted his feet and released power into his Control just as a dark shape crashed through a window pane in the right-hand corner of his vision, showering the floor with glass. Finally. He flashed a message to his fellow sorcerer's mind. *You took your time.*

He closed his eyes to concentrate on his Control, but he could hear Belas clambering to his feet beside him and brushing glass shards from his clothes.

"Sorry, old boy, bad visibility tonight. Had to take it steady. What's going on?"

Arthan snorted, eyes still closed. "I am sure you can figure that out." He felt his power sharpen to a point, and with a push he entered Sean's and Olivia's minds, then almost gasped at the sea of fire that engulfed him. They were overflowing with the violent, mindless heat of Red sorcery, pulsating, bloody vessels of fury. He doused his own emotions, knowing how easy it would be to be swept away by the tide, then grabbed both their minds in the vice of his power and clamped his will onto the roaring furnace inside them. He could tell Belas had already taken hold of their bodies with his own sorcery.

Once his connection was established, Arthan opened his eyes. The fighting hadn't stopped, but it had slowed. He flooded the fighters' minds with commands, shovelling ice onto the blaze, and felt the battle madness inside them begin to soften at the edges.

Without releasing pressure on the fighters' minds, Arthan glanced to the side. A trail of sweat had broken across Belas's brow as he strained to keep control of Sean's and Olivia's bodies. Arthan pumped more power into his hold on their emotions and felt the coolness of a small current of calm seeping through the murderous passion. Still resisting every step, the duelling pair were prised apart as if by invisible hands, Sean wailing as he was pulled away from his opponent, his flailing arms now meeting air. Olivia's lunges lost momentum as she also slid away across the marble floor. She stared blankly at Arthan and Belas as if only now aware of their presence.

With care Arthan let his Control rest. "She listens to reason." He looked to Belas. "But Sean cannot hear me – he has lost control."

Belas didn't reply. Sweat was running down his tanned face. Sean was a blur of movement, heaving against his invisible constraints, his screams echoing around the hall.

Arthan raised his eyebrows at the display. "His emotion feeds his power."

Belas managed a shaky nod. He glanced at Olivia, who was no longer struggling; then he must have released her from his Orange grip, because she sank to the floor. Arthan made his way over to where she lay in a ragged curl.

"What happened?" he asked.

She didn't move or respond, but he hadn't expected her to; she would be using all the energy she had left to heal herself. He couldn't hold back a grimace at the sight of her battered body, latticed with pink cuts and yet dark with cloudy bruises.

"Rupert texted me earlier." Belas's face was still drawn with effort. "He's gone with Ian to find Naomi. She's hurt."

"Hurt how?"

Belas made a noise that probably meant he didn't know.

Arthan frowned. "Find out. I will contact Marrin — we may need her help." He turned his focus inward and reached for power. The sea of thoughts opened before him, and he searched for the signature of Marrin's mind, but there was no sign of her.

Odd. Marrin must have closed herself to communication. What on earth was she doing?

* * *

"There she is."

Rupert peered through the windscreen in the direction Ian was pointing. The night's blackness painted smudges and swirls in empty spaces, creating figures everywhere, but among the mirages he could see a dark mound by the edge of the road. Ian applied the brakes and his car shuddered to a halt, its headlights sending stripes of bleached colour across Naomi's prone body. They clambered out, Rupert's legs still shaky from the prophecy, and Ian strode over to crouch beside her.

By the time Rupert had joined them Ian was already casting some kind of Control, presumably Purple. Rupert shivered and rubbed his arms, wishing he had brought a coat. Ian didn't seem to notice either the cold or that Rupert had joined them; he just kept frowning at Naomi and flexing his fingers like he was playing an invisible instrument. Rupert wondered what his friend could see before him. Maybe the network of her veins and muscles was strung before him like a neon web, the strings and knots ready to be tweaked and pulled. Ian hadn't previously been this focused; he was usually the one a few minutes behind Rupert in everything they did, chattering about something unrelated to the task in hand. That was before the fire. This new Ian didn't talk much, and looked at people in that odd way like they were problems to be solved, or information to be digested.

Rupert swallowed, the acrid stink of vomit still in his

throat, the shadows around him alive with blood and screams and the crunch of bone and tearing of flesh. When had life grown so dark? Ian was supposed to be the one Rupert could make jokes with and pretend nothing was wrong. Even though he was turned away from the headlights, Ian's scar could be seen carving its way across his nose and cheek, but if Rupert looked at him the right way he could imagine it was just a shadow reaching down his face and he was still the same old Ian.

Rupert jumped when Naomi groaned. She had been lifeless just minutes before. Ian pressed his hands against her arm and murmured something.

"Let go of me!" Naomi's eyes burst open.

Ian blinked, then withdrew further into the pooling shadows. Naomi looked around at Rupert and scrabbled on the pavement for purchase, but the effort seemed to tire her, and she subsided again.

"What did Sean do to you?" Now that Rupert's eyes were filling themselves with the darkness he could see that her black jeans were ripped.

Her round face turned to him, blotchy, red and quivering. The poor girl looked more ugly than ever. "I told him it was her!"

"What?" Rupert looked at Ian's blank face, then back at Naomi. "Who?"

"Kim's cat saw everything." Naomi seemed to focus on him for the first time. "Rosie. I tried to stop Sean going after her."

That was brave. Rupert had no idea who Rosie was, or what Naomi was talking about, but he knew it was dangerous to get in Sean's way when he was angry.

Ian resumed his work, kneading Naomi's back and muttering to himself. After a moment his hands stopped moving. "Naomi."

Naomi didn't answer, and Rupert wondered if she was entirely aware of her surroundings.

"You're—you're hurt badly," Ian said, his voice a shadow of its previous bitterness. "I may not be able to heal your legs."

183

Naomi looked at Ian for the first time, glaring into his scarred and twisted face. "My legs? Olivia killed Kim, now Sean is trying to kill Olivia! Who cares about my legs?"

Ian blinked. "You don't care? You might not be able to walk again."

"I am alive."

"Wait a minute!" Rupert grabbed her arm, a little too roughly, forgetting her injuries. She winced but turned her scowl towards him without speaking. "Olivia killed Kim? Not Sean?"

"Yes. And now she'll be killed, or she will kill Sean. Oh God, they might be both dead already – you have to call for help!"

"Yes, yes." Rupert rummaged for his mobile phone, unable to keep the grin from his face. "I'll call Arthan."

Ian was slumped on his knees; it seemed all his energy had leeched away into the night. He looked at Rupert, perhaps for the first time that evening. "What can you be happy about?"

"My prophecies don't work!" Rupert chuckled as the phone started ringing in his ear. "I don't know anything!"

Naomi glared at him and held her hand out for the phone. He passed it to her, filled with the realisation that Arthan could stop more murders, stem the flow of blood. Anything was possible – any call could change the future, any consequence could be avoided. Olivia had killed Kim, not Sean. Rupert's prophecies were useless – beautifully, pointlessly useless. He couldn't predict anything, no deaths could be foreseen, no stained hospital beds would bear their skeletal cargo on his account.

Nothing was his fault.

CHAPTER TWENTY-SEVEN

"Thank you, Naomi. I will call you if I need anything else." Arthan returned his mobile phone to his jacket pocket and frowned down at Sean's slumped body. So Naomi had been another casualty damaged in his wake. The violence that this boy had perpetrated was unwelcome, but Arthan couldn't help feeling a sense of respect for the brutal and unflinching manner in which Sean had set about his objective. He had caused destruction, but that was incidental to his purpose, not his goal in itself. Life requires great sacrifice of us all as the price of any small success.

It had taken Belas and Arthan nearly an hour to fully calm the boy. It would have been useful to have Marrin here to overpower him, but maybe even her skills wouldn't have been up to the occasion. Sean had now withdrawn into himself and seemed smaller, a pale young boy coiled on the floor where a beast had been snarling just minutes earlier. He had not made any movement to communicate, or even heal himself; he just lay there. Like Olivia, his wounds were multiple, obvious and appalling, his body a network of cuts and gouges, but Arthan knew there was no emergency. A Red sorcerer like Sean rarely had need of medical treatment; he could heal himself whenever he chose and return to perfect fitness. All the same, the sight of him was rather unpleasant.

Belas returned from the adjoining room, yawning.

Arthan frowned. "Where's Olivia?"

Belas shrugged in that infuriating way of his. "Wandered off somewhere. I've been having a kip – haven't seen her for a bit."

"Wandered off?" The extent of Belas's ineptitude never ceased to surprise him. "And you let her?"

Belas recoiled, raising his hands as if to protect himself. Arthan was still deciding on the best words to express his feelings at Belas's attitude when Olivia herself appeared in the doorway.

"Come and look at this!" She turned and marched from the room, seemingly back in full health. Belas moved to follow her, but Arthan stopped him with a silent command.

-Stay and watch Sean.

Without looking back, Arthan set off after her and trailed her presence to a nearby room, where he found her standing by a wall-mounted television screen. She stood with her arms folded, a defiant slant to her chin, her blue eyes glittering. Something about her prominent front teeth, or the way she wore her blond hair in a ponytail, made her look young, younger than her brothers and sisters. Maybe her body had already stopped ageing. He felt a surge of empathy at the possibility she was destined for his own fate of eternal adolescence. She pressed a button on the remote control she held and the black television screen burst into life.

A huge stadium appeared with rows of blue plastic seats rising up like a wave, hordes of wailing and hooting humans, waving banners and fluttering flags. A man's voice could be heard enthusing about history and achievement. A running track curved around the centre of the stadium, and Olivia's toothy grin was everywhere. Arthan recognised the posters. This was the day Olivia had run the marathon, one of Oliviana's orchestrated sporting events. Thousands of her fans had gone to cheer her on as she broke yet another world record. Arthan realised immediately why Olivia was showing the video. It proved she couldn't have killed Kim.

The commentator's voice droned on while Arthan considered his next steps. The field of suspects had just narrowed considerably. "… on this momentous day, the twenty-seventh of June, we will see another world record smashed by Olivia, the legend that…"

"Recognise the date?"

"I do," Arthan said.

"Recognise the stadium?" Her voice dripped with sarcasm. "It's in Cardiff, you know."

"I know."

On the screen, a gun fired and Olivia's small figure set off on the marathon. The event was shown live, and coverage had lasted all day. The cameras hadn't left Olivia for a minute. No one could have stood in for her, as no one could have completed the marathon as fast as she did. The event was a circus, the level of publicity surrounding it was sickening, and Arthan had never been able to find a way to accept that Olivia had spent her life endangering their code of secrecy for her own commercial gain, but there was no doubt the stunt had served Olivia well in at least one regard. It was a watertight alibi.

"So how exactly was I supposed to have murdered a girl in London?"

Arthan raised his hand for silence. "You have made your point. Switch it off."

She glared at him, but did as he asked, and the screen went mercifully black.

Arthan glared back at her. "Would you be happy for me to read your mind?"

* * *

-Are you there, Elizan?

As usual, the response from the great sorcerer's mind was immediate.

-Good evening, Arthan.

The mere sound of her mental voice reassured him. He closed his eyes to the watching faces of Belas, Sean and Olivia, and let himself focus on the inner conversation only he could hear.

-I must speak with you urgently, Elizan. We have need of your assistance.

-Please continue.

Although it was likely Elizan already knew what had happened, Arthan summarised the evening's events.

-I see. What did you learn from Olivia's mind?

-She is telling the truth. Olivia was at the Millennium Stadium all day – she couldn't have killed Kim. But I sense Naomi is telling the truth too. The cat saw Olivia kill Kim, and Naomi saw it in the cat's memory. There is no doubt over identification.

There was the briefest of pauses while Elizan considered this information. Or was she picking up on his underlying thoughts? Arthan tried to keep his mind clear.

-What do you believe happened?

What did he believe? Arthan felt the weight of this whole affair bear down on him, the pressure of Elizan's question pulling on the taut ropes of control that kept him level-headed while others panicked and looked to him for leadership. What did he believe? He believed in society, in people; he believed in justice and moral fortitude and the old way of the world, where people said what they stood for and actually stood for it. He believed in what people promised him and he expected them to deliver it. He did not believe any of the sorcerers he knew and trusted could have committed this crime, but the only thing he knew for certain was that he himself had not committed it. What did he believe happened? There were theories, thoughts that crossed his mind, but he couldn't bring himself to believe them. He cleared his mind of everything except one answer.

-It must have been Paros. Only Grey sorcerers can shape-shift. He must have disguised himself to look like Olivia and killed Kim whilst wearing her body. It is fortunate Paros chose Olivia as the one he would try to frame. Sean would have killed any of the other young sorcerers.

-Paros is not the only possibility. Why are you protecting Elliot?

Of course she had seen through him; he had been foolish to hope otherwise. Arthan began forming his thoughts to respond, but Elizan interrupted him.

-Do not pretend, Arthan. I know Elliot is a sorcerer. I know he has taken you into his confidence and you have been assisting him with his training, and I know you do not want to think he did this. But you must not be deceived by him.

Deceived by him? Arthan would have scoffed at this suggestion from anyone but Elizan. He wasn't deceived. People never deceived him; he could see through them like their faces were made of glass. Elizan always knew best, but in this, he couldn't help doubting her. The murderer couldn't be Elliot. On the surface it seemed an obvious conclusion: Elliot was a Grey sorcerer and had proven himself less than honest through his thievery, but he just didn't seem to fit. Elizan's advice was not to be dismissed lightly, but Arthan had spent time with the boy and could sense no sign in him of the darkness, the careless violence, that Kim's murder spoke of. The boy wore a mask of indifference that could be mistaken for callousness, but behind this, Arthan sensed something deeper.

-Elliot didn't do this. I have been inside his mind. He is not a killer.

-Be careful, Arthan. I am conducting an investigation of my own, into an evil presence I found watching my thoughts. I have encountered memories and emotions that lead to that boy. I fear he is involved. Do not let your judgement be clouded by loyalty.

-It isn't.

Arthan wondered what the evil presence was, but held back his question. It was not his place to ask questions of Elizan. Her voice continued.

-Or by an unwillingness to face your personal problems.

-What do you mean?

The mental voice in his head softened, the ice momentarily melting.

-Arthan. Be honest with yourself. You must know.

Arthan found himself biting back an angry retort, although he wasn't sure where it had come from. *You must know?* He let her words trickle through his mind like sand and observed their shifting patterns, waiting for them to settle. He decided not to wonder about what she meant. When Elizan spoke again the ice of her tone had returned.

-*I know one thing for a fact, Arthan. Paros is innocent. If nothing else, believe me in this.*

-How can you be sure?

-*Paros is innocent.*

Arthan was considering his next question when Elizan spoke again.

-*Arthan. Marrin has just contacted me. She has some information in connection with the murder. You should speak with her now.*

Arthan discarded his questions and shut off the mind link as she instructed. He had always followed Elizan's guidance without question. She must know best – she always knew best. Without opening his eyes, he reached out for Marrin's mind, realising with wonder that Elizan had somehow conducted mental conversations with both of them simultaneously.

-*Arthan.*

Marrin's mental voice was subdued, a whisper of its usual force.

-Marrin. Where are you? I tried to contact you earlier.

-*I hid my mind. I've been watching Elliot and Holly.*

That was odd. Elliot and Holly had been interviewing Paros today, but he had not expected Marrin to attend.

-Why?

-*I think Elliot is the murderer. Holly may be in danger.*

-You have been spying on them?

There was a long pause before Marrin replied.

-*We must be quick. Elliot may sense me. Can you get here?*

There was an undercurrent to her words, something she was keeping from him. Why were Elizan and Marrin so intent on accusing Elliot?

-I am needed here.

-*Elliot had a motive – Gordon told me. Can you come? Holly may be in danger.*

Despite Arthan's doubts over her claims, the way Marrin repeated this statement sent a chill through him. The idea of anything bad happening to Holly was unthinkable. He frowned.

She must be back home by now.

-Where are you?

-At Elliot's flat.

-Where is Holly?

Another long pause.

-She is with Elliot.

He felt her words like a cold slap in the face, but the meaning didn't take hold of him; he felt like he was listening to her talk to someone else.

-No, she isn't. She must be at our house.

Now he felt a sharpness creep into Marrin's mental voice.

-She is here. I will show you.

* * *

Marrin kept her mind linked to Arthan, opened her eyes and let him see through them. She could feel his presence there, a shadow behind her senses. She marched across the patchy lawn towards Elliot's front door, her Red Control giving her perfect vision in the darkness, and drew on Orange Control to twist the door handle on the inside. She didn't pause but barged through and continued down the narrow corridor to fling open the door at the end. Her hand snaked round to flick the light switch, and the room flooded with light. In front of her, Elliot and Holly lay under crumpled bedsheets.

Elliot sat bolt upright, blinking in the light, and his mouth formed a slow, silent circle. Miles away, linked through her mind, Marrin knew Arthan watched the scene that unfolded through her eyes.

-Arthan, Elliot is the killer. Come now.

The covers stirred beside Elliot, and Holly eased herself up beside him. Then her lidded eyes found Marrin in the doorway and she gasped and pulled the duvet over her naked chest.

Elliot seemed to be trying to speak, but failed. He looked at Holly, then joined her in staring at Marrin.

The scene remained frozen for a few seconds before Marrin stepped back out into the corridor, closing the door again. She shouldn't have confronted them yet. She knew it wasn't sensible, but she needed Arthan to come and she didn't know the right words to persuade him.

She felt for Arthan's presence in her mind, but it had already vanished.

CHAPTER TWENTY-EIGHT

Elliot pulled on his jeans, his thoughts careering in every direction.

"My clothes!" Holly had hauled the duvet up tight under her chin, her eyes locked on the door as if Marrin might reappear at any moment.

Elliot swept Holly's clothes up from the floor and flung them at her. He pushed on the door as if to shut it tighter, though there was no way he could secure the door that Marrin couldn't overcome. When he turned back, Holly's face was obscured by the shirt she was yanking down over her head.

"Why is she here?" Elliot grabbed his own shirt. "What is she doing here?"

Holly took an unsteady breath. She was now clothed, and rose from the bed. She combed her tangled hair with her fingers. "Don't panic. Marrin will keep our secret. We just need to talk to her, and explain."

Don't panic. Elliot's head pounded. He had woken into a living nightmare. "We don't know her! She's Arthan's friend!"

Holly took his hand. Her green eyes were still wide but her voice was flat and steady. "They're not close. Marrin is my great-grandmother – she'll listen to us."

She was right. Elliot took his own long breath, rested a hand on the wall and yanked on socks and shoes. His head was buzzing with questions yet still fogged with sleep. "OK. Let's talk to her."

He straightened his clothes and patted down his hair, as if that would help Marrin forget what she had seen. They opened the door together, to find her waiting with a scowl.

* * *

Sean watched Arthan's boyish face twitch and stir. He had been in silent mind communication for several minutes now; he must surely be about to open his eyes and reveal some information. When Sean had woken up, Briggs and Arthan had told him that Olivia had an alibi, and that despite what Naomi's cat had seen, she couldn't be the killer. Before Sean could even digest this, Arthan had gathered them all and announced he would contact Elizan for help. One of those useless guards had found them a room to occupy, and Sean, Briggs and Olivia were now sitting around a large oval oak table, waiting for Arthan to emerge from his world of thought.

Sean had caught Olivia looking at him twice, her eyes as sharp as glass, but she had said nothing to him. He didn't know whether to look back at her or just ignore her. The idea that he had attacked her and she was innocent was... annoying, but he couldn't do anything about that. Naomi had told him what the cat had seen and had left Sean with no doubt, and so he had acted on it. He shouldn't feel guilty. He kept his attention instead on Arthan. Briggs said Arthan had ended one mind conversation and started another, but Sean hadn't noticed any sign of this. Arthan just sat there in silence with his eyes shut tight, offering no other hint of activity than that infuriating twitching.

Arthan's eyes snapped open, and Sean half rose from his chair. "What did you find out?"

The Yellow sorcerer didn't reply. His doughy face had set like cement, his eyes hard and shining. Beside him, Sean could see Olivia shrinking back from the venom in that glare, but he met it, searching for answers.

Briggs put a hand on Arthan's shoulder. "What is it?"

Arthan's eyes finally focused on the others around the

table. "The murderer is Elliot."

Elliot? Sean's stomach twisted. It was Elliot.

Briggs's tanned brow wrinkled. "How do you know?"

"Elliot has sorcery. Somehow, he is a sorcerer." Arthan scowled, his face reddening. "I knew – I concealed his secret. I trusted him." His lip curled. "But now I see he has been deceiving me."

Sean felt a heat wash over him, searing, inflaming that rent in his heart which had driven him to Olivia's window. It was Elliot. His muscles tensed, as though slack chains had been jerked tight around him, choking off all else but the heat. He wanted to do something, to destroy something. He clenched his fists to stop himself moving.

"Are you certain?" Briggs said.

Arthan settled his gaze on Briggs but ignored the question. "I need you to get me to Elliot's flat. Now."

There was a steel edge to the command that seemed to trip up Briggs's protests. He spluttered a moment before finding his voice. "I need more time, Arthan. I'm exhausted from restraining Sean—"

"You're mostly recovered," Arthan countered, without dropping his glare. "Holly is in danger, and Marrin too."

Sean rounded the table to join Briggs and Arthan, shouldering past Olivia. He had to get there with them, although he had no idea how they would be travelling.

"You'll slow me down." Briggs was shaking his head. "I can go quicker alone."

"Take me now!" With this last barked command, Arthan rose to his feet as if the matter was decided.

Briggs wiped his brow and glanced at Sean and Olivia. "You should go home, Sean." He stepped away from them and placed his hand on Arthan's shoulder. "The two of you need rest."

"I don't!" Sean grabbed Briggs's arm, harder than he meant to. "And I'm coming!"

Briggs shook his head and waved a hand. "No, you must stay here."

At these words Sean felt his legs stiffen and his feet clamp to the floor. He grunted in effort, drawing on Red power as he strained at Briggs's Orange Control. Briggs stepped away from him and Arthan laid his own hand on Briggs's shoulder. Sean clawed at the air but couldn't reach them.

Briggs's free hand began moving fast, fingers fluttering. Sean pulled one foot from the floor and took a sluggish step forward, the air like treacle around him. He could feel the power building in Briggs, and out of the corner of his eye saw Olivia hastening out of the way. What was Briggs casting? At last he was released, and he leapt forward. He couldn't let them escape without him. But as he lunged for them, Briggs and Arthan lifted into the air as though they were held on wires, rising out of his reach. Sean wailed as they flew over his head towards the window, which opened to let them sail through.

The pair floated out of the window, then increased speed on reaching open air. The silhouette of their bodies shrank against the night's darkness as they moved away, joining the black, impossibly fast.

"Orange Control on his own body," Olivia said. "Of course."

Almost unaware of her, Sean screamed. Seeing Arthan and Briggs disappearing was like watching the last remains of his reason slipping into the night. His blood was rushing hot again, his sinews stretching and throbbing, his heart pounding with one name. Elliot.

A soft voice penetrated the red cloud. "Three things."

Sean looked blankly at Olivia. "What?"

Her arms were folded as she regarded him with a toothy grimace. Her eyes held a strange glint. "Get out of my house. Be a man and grieve for your sister." She ticked each instruction off with her fingers. Then, without warning, she flew from her chair at him, and Sean felt a sharp crack to his cheekbone as she struck him hard. Caught off guard and only partly healed, the blow spun him from his chair and onto the floor in a heap. He spat warm blood on the marble, a garish red shape splattered on cold white stone.

He heard her reedy voice again, this time above him. "But first, beg my forgiveness."

* * *

Elliot was taken aback by the scowl on Marrin's face, which seemed to be directed at him. She stood blocking the doorway to his bedroom as though she expected him and Holly to try and escape. He couldn't piece together what was happening. Why was she here?

Holly spoke first. "Marrin, I know this may be asking a lot, but we would not want Arthan to find out about this."

Marrin's face was a stone mask. "He is already on his way."

The blunt statement hit Elliot like a physical blow. *Already on his way.* He turned from Marrin to Holly. Her hand was over her mouth; she looked like she was about to be sick.

He tried to think of something to say, but all thoughts and words had vanished from his brain. Prickles of cool sweat tiptoed down the back of his neck.

"Why are you doing this, Marrin?" Holly sounded close to tears, her voice almost a squeak. "I know I should have spoken to Arthan – I know I should have – but not like this—"

"You know Kim was pregnant."

Holly faltered. "Yes – but why does that matter?"

"Gordon told me who the father was."

Elliot's mouth turned dry. Holly frowned, then shook her head as if to try and make sense of it. "Marrin, what is this all about?"

Her face still expressionless, Marrin replied immediately, as though she was unaware of the impact of her words. "Elliot is the murderer. Gordon saw Kim and Elliot go home together after the Christmas party. Elliot was the father of her child. He killed her to stop himself Fading when the child was born."

Elliot felt the bottom dropping out of his stomach. This couldn't be happening. Out of the corner of his eye he could see Holly's face turn towards him, but he couldn't meet her eyes yet. He couldn't think straight, he couldn't accept that he was here and that these heavy coils of shock were being looped

197

around him in a tightening knot. A few words escaped him. "Was it definitely mine?"

He heard Holly draw a sharp breath, and Marrin nodded. "I examined the body. The child was yours."

The child was his. A hand gripped Elliot's arm. "Elliot – what does she mean?"

Marrin interrupted before Elliot could think of a response. "Holly, I don't approve of you deceiving Arthan, but I'll give you the benefit of the doubt that this young man seduced you like he seduced Kim. Take my advice, go to Arthan and ask his forgiveness."

Elliot finally turned to Holly. "I didn't seduce Kim – that's not what happened."

Her face was a mess. A blotchy redness had crept up her cheeks, her mouth was twisted in an ugly grimace and tears were standing in her eyes. "I was going to leave him for you!" The fierceness of her shriek made Elliot step back. "I was going to leave my life for you!"

She shoved him hard. He stumbled and almost fell, Marrin making no move to support him. "When?" he heard himself say. "When were you going to? Next year? The year after?"

"You lied to me! I never lied to you!"

Elliot managed to stop himself shouting back, his heart beating in his ears. This situation was spinning out of control, his grip on the world spinning with it, wrenching him around, his head pounding. Holly stalked back to the bedside, her shoulders shaking. Elliot followed her, leaving Marrin in the doorway. He didn't cope well in emotional confrontations. What were the right things to say?

"I didn't lie to you." He couldn't keep an edge out of his voice.

"You did!" Holly was packing her bag, thrusting in her clothes with white fists. "You said there was no one else!"

"There isn't!" Elliot could hear his own voice rising. "There wasn't, there isn't! Kim was a mistake, a one-night mistake when I was drunk! She wasn't a someone else."

Holly barked a cold laugh. "Very funny."

"It wasn't supposed to be." Elliot slumped against the wall. Holly finished jamming her bag and pulled it onto her shoulder. She paused, her back to him, and for a brief moment Elliot hoped she was thinking about forgiving him.

"What did you mean, 'stop himself Fading'?" Holly's voice was barely a whisper, and she didn't turn round, but the question was directed at Marrin.

Instead a male voice answered.

"He is a sorcerer, Holly. Very capable. Very powerful. And very dangerous."

All hope of resolving the situation died as Elliot turned to see that two figures had joined Marrin in the doorway. Arthan and Briggs.

"We must talk, Holly, but not now. I have to deal with a murderer." Arthan turned to Elliot and his eyes hardened to stone. "Belas, hold him."

Briggs waved his right hand and Elliot felt the Control move over him like ice, a stiff blanket of sorcery spreading fast across his legs, his chest and his arms. He struggled but could no longer move. He was caught in an absurd position, leaning as if casually cemented in place against his bedroom wall.

"A sorcerer?" Holly turned from Arthan's cold stare to Elliot's frozen body. Her eyes begged Elliot to deny it. He heard her say something. He thought it was "Not more lies…"

Arthan stepped into the room and looked at the bed, the sheets still rumpled. "Your investigation is over, Holly. Elliot is the murderer. He deceived us all, as he deceived you about his affair with Kim."

Elliot realised his mouth was not held still. "That's not true, Holly! It's not true!" He wanted to make it right, to reverse this nightmare, but he knew that there was no longer any way to.

He could see tears sliding down her face, dripping from her chin with each thump of his aching head. "Who are you?" she murmured.

Arthan put a hand on Holly's arm to steer her away. "There is a car outside. Marrin will take you to her house." His voice held its usual monotony but his movements were stiff, his face dark.

Elliot felt like a pressure was building somewhere, in his brain, or in his power.

"Who are you!"

Now her voice was a scream. Elliot couldn't look away from her twisted face, but he could tell Arthan was closing his eyes to summon power. He felt the seep of Yellow Control into his mind, a thick, penetrating fog creeping over his senses. He was being sedated.

Deep inside him, an instinct rose, old and powerful. He was cornered, nearly captured. He had to escape. He had an indistinct vision, like a memory, of a thousand similar situations. *Do what you always do.* He summoned power fast, without thinking, and a flood of blistering energy seared through him. He had to get out. He focused his power.

Arthan and Briggs both flinched as his body strained at their hold. They kept their grip for only an instant, Briggs to his body and Arthan to his mind, before he overcame them. Elliot felt himself break the physical boundaries of his body, and with a rush, he dispersed. His blood, bone and flesh scattered and joined the air. He had vanished. His clothes drifted to the floor, empty. He was out. Hovering in the air – he *was* the air – he watched the room react from above. Holly darted forward to where he had disappeared. Arthan yelled something. Briggs threw his hands up and started searching the room. The air that was Elliot waited a moment longer, then he propelled himself over their heads and out of the bedroom. If they felt a breeze, they didn't show it. He flew out into the corridor and gusted down the dimly lit passageway to his front door. It was so easy to move like this, so natural, so instinctive. Invisible, a host of air, he banked through the doorway and up into the black sky.

Things seemed clearer now, as the night rushed to meet him and the world fell away. He felt the warm air caress him, enveloping him in its invisibility. He shot high into the nothingness, barrelling through the void, buildings rendered as pebbles in the dimly twinkling city beneath him, a sequinned black blanket of baubles and trifles.

He was in a difficult situation. Arthan knew about him and Holly, Holly knew about him and Kim. Everyone thought he was the murderer. But those problems were somewhere down below. He had escaped.

His flight of freedom carried him across London until he no longer knew where he was. The new world was a blur of grey cloud threads, streaks of stars and thick, buffeting winds. He slowed eventually and gazed all around as he flew. He was high above the clouds, but if he peered below and injected power into his sight, he saw a network of streets with pinprick lights dotting the grey landscape, toy cars rolling by and huddled humans traipsing along timeworn paths.

He could see all about him in a way that was impossible with physical eyes. He had no idea how it worked – he had no body, so how was he propelling himself through the air, how was he listening, how was he seeing? But however it worked, it was easy, and this formless shape he assumed felt more familiar to him than his own skin. He was himself in a different way, a better way. He felt like he did in his dreams, when he walked in Viros's shoes – free. Where should he go? It didn't matter. Nothing mattered. He propelled himself into the night air.

Time to disappear.

PART EIGHT
AWAKENING

A few days after Kim's death

CHAPTER TWENTY-NINE

A young boy paused with his football as Elliot strode past. The boy's gaze followed him. Soft light splashed over Elliot's footsteps as he rounded the corner and approached the girl's flat. The sun hid behind a cloud screen, poking occasional fingers through to stroke the mottled grey and tan houses and the leaning, whispering trees. There was a smell of dry leaves.

Would the boy remember him? It didn't matter.

He stopped in front of the door to the building. He could see the beads swaying on the other side of the glass on the upper door. The surface was murky but he could see his reflection. Olivia's toothy face shimmered in the marbled glass.

He felt the locks with his mind, and one by one they clicked and slid open at his will. He pushed the door forward and entered.

Another flight of stairs and he was at the door to 4e. Another set of locks – slower this time – and a quieter entry.

She lived here with her brother. A tidy place, with bare white walls and thick beige carpets: modern and boring.

Elliot padded across the floor in Olivia's white shoes. A cat was startled by his entry and raced away up the hall. I'm coming too. *He glanced at himself in a mirror he passed and saw a woman. It was him, and it was her. It was difficult to pin himself down sometimes; his body had stopped being his own a long time ago.*

He smothered a smirk as he crept along, thinking about the first time he had worn a woman's body, many years ago. He brought his mind back

205

to the present. There was a job to do here, a plan.

With each step a shape grew at his side. Drawing matter from inside his body, the shape stretched from his hand and sharpened, gleaming, into a sword. It swung by his side, a part of his arm. A foolish idea, perhaps — he could kill her with a breath — but the sword would feel more real. He had to make sure.

He came to a door with a floral scent — the girl's room. It opened at a touch, and he stepped in.

Predictably, the girl screamed. Even more predictably, she had been trained to use her power to defend herself. She tried to constrain him, to subdue him, to push him away. Most predictably of all, her attempts at self-defence were faint, so faint he barely felt them. He sent her to the ground with enough force to keep her there and stepped closer. She was panting squeaky, chugging breaths.

He raised the sword. She had clearly seen it, her eyes wide and white.

She was Blue. Her best attempt at disabling him was a bundled storm of sharp electricity that she summoned, centred in his stomach. Elliot supposed it would have hurt a weaker sorcerer and killed a human. He waved it aside.

She realised now that she was going to die; he saw it in her eyes. He remembered once before being poised over a sorcerer's life and facing a dilemma. Was it wrong to kill a sorcerer? He turned the thought around, let it wash away. He had a plan. He was following the plan.

She seemed about to speak, and Elliot waited. He didn't want to hear what she would say, but he didn't want to stop her.

"Why, Olivia? Why?" Kim stared up at Olivia's long-lashed eyes and into Elliot's.

Elliot looked away. He told himself he was Olivia, and looked back. He brought the sword down hard.

CHAPTER THIRTY

Elliot burst awake as if coming up for air. He sat bolt upright, cold sweat sticking his T-shirt to his back. He stared at a white sign. *A New You.*

He gripped the duvet like a lifeline. With each echoing heartbeat the outline of many beds thudded into dim focus, until eventually peace descended. Where was he?

A department store. It was dark. He remembered walking the streets last night, looking for somewhere to sleep. At least he had found a comfortable bed.

He tried to shake the dream out of his head. It was the worst one.

He clutched his legs. "I killed Kim." He said it aloud, his voice sounding odd in the emptiness.

It had been so real. Her white face, the heavy sword, the blood.

"I didn't kill Kim." But the dream had been so real.

Normal dreams weren't like this. Normal dreams were of the insubstantial, of people who told him strange things and then he found they had been someone else all along, and he was in another place that sprang from the mist when he turned his head. But he could touch these dreams of Viros. He could feel the solid earth beneath him – he had actually been there. They were just like memories. They weren't memories; he hadn't been there. But they were just like memories.

He lay awake until morning, until the locks creaked open and the strip lights flickered on, and then he vanished before the cleaners found him. Bleak thoughts wandered through him. He could smell the dreams, taste them, but he wasn't himself in them. In his dreams he looked at people and didn't feel anything. He didn't kill Kim. He wasn't there; he had been at work all day in the archives, reading. Did it all mean something, or was he just having nightmares? He didn't kill Kim, but someone did. As time passed, his dreams seemed more like reality and his waking life more like a dream. He was beginning to wonder which of the many shapes he wore was himself.

* * *

Elliot roamed the streets for days. He watched but did not touch the city. He drifted past London's curled iron railings, its barbed antennae, its black-stained brick walls and smells of cooked meat and household waste, past the creeping roll of traffic and the rising, many-windowed facades. He was just another ghost, like the glassy-eyed strangers who brushed past him with mobile phones stuck to their faces and their voices lost in the whirring, humming clatter. Sometimes he rode on buses, sometimes he took taxis, sometimes he slipped invisibly into the backs of cars and sat listening to the conversations of the occupants, sidling into their lives. Sometimes he flew, coasting unseen above the humans below. But mostly he walked, without thought or direction. He never got tired – his Red Control kept him strong. He stopped sleeping; there seemed no need, and it enabled him to escape his dreams. He ate out of boredom though he never felt hungry. He stole the food – he knew it was wrong, but he did it anyway.

He didn't take part in the world. He didn't feel the sun's heat. He didn't feel anything. He was never involved; no one could touch him. He wasn't there.

Kim had been pregnant. Everyone thought he was a murderer. He had to think, to be alone for a while to figure this out. What was he? What was he to do?

Maybe he should truly escape, and run away.

He thought of Holly. He could go to her, but after his betrayal with Kim he didn't know if she would even speak to him. He had been so drunk that night, and Holly had seemed so happy with Arthan, laughing and touching his arm, and Kim had been an unexpected comfort.

He tried to imagine the situation from Holly's perspective, but he had never understood why she stayed with Arthan. Was it such a betrayal for Elliot to sleep with Kim? Was it any worse?

Kim had been pregnant. She hadn't told him, or at least he didn't think she had. Had she told him and he had somehow forgotten, and suppressed the memories, and suppressed the white face and the cool, heavy sword he had brought down hard? He pushed it all aside.

He decided, for the hundredth time, not to run away yet.

* * *

He danced on a breeze, watching the city below him. A familiar snaking of the road caught his eye and he flew lower. He headed for the crowd of houses, the stretch of grass and the building that housed his flat, floating down through clumps of cloud fraying in the dewy sunlight, drifting as just another breeze.

When he rounded the building to approach his bedroom window he saw a figure standing at his open back door. Leaning limply against the frame, head dropped low. It was Holly. His heart leapt, then shrank, at the branded image of her twisted, blotchy face. He wanted to hurtle through the air and pull her into his arms, but he restrained himself. She must hate him, or at least she must want to hate him. He would have to respect the fact that he had hurt her, and it wouldn't help to appear out of thin air as a reminder of the sorcery he had kept secret.

He let himself glide closer on the wind. She looked up, but she must have been touched by the coolness of the air moving; she couldn't see him. He brushed past her shoulder and into the lounge, finding it as cluttered as the day he had left. It should have felt like coming home, but instead he felt like a stranger in someone else's house. Once out of sight of the doorway he made himself visible. He adopted a casual outfit of jeans and a sweatshirt. He worried over his hair, then walked out into view of the back door. Holly stood a few feet away, her back still turned.

"Hi."

When she turned round, Elliot looked for a sign she was glad to see him but saw nothing. Her eyes didn't widen, her mouth didn't twitch. "Hello, Elliot."

"How have you been?"

She shrugged. "Fine."

That shrug hit him hard. Hadn't she missed him? The idea flashed through his mind to read her thoughts, to understand her better, but he rejected it. He had to do this without sorcery. She stood in the door frame with the dull sky framing her in grey while Elliot shifted his feet, glaring at the tatty carpet then up again. She said nothing.

"What are you doing here?" His question sounded more confrontational than he had intended, but she didn't seem to notice.

"I was sent by Arthan." She gestured at the mess around them. "To tidy up, look around. To look for you."

"And if you found me? To contact him?"

"Yes." Now she looked at the carpet.

"Will you?"

She shook her head, still not looking up.

"Can he read it from your mind?"

She shook her head again. "I don't think he reads my mind."

"Thanks for not telling him."

She continued to stare at the floor. She looked so composed, her hair swept behind her perfect ears, clothed in iron-pressed professionalism, her world arranged in precise, ordered contrast to Elliot's chaos. "He said he would come over here later. You should go." She looked like she was building up to something. "You'll have to stay away for a while."

Elliot thought she was probably right, but he couldn't leave her yet. He ached to hug her, to make everything the way it was before she found out about Kim. "How are things at work?"

She gave no sign she had heard his question. "Elizan is trying to locate you. If you come near a sorcerer she can sense you better."

This revelation gave him a chill, and an instinctive urge to step further away. "Can she sense me now?"

"Perhaps. If she does I'll say I never saw you. I'll say you were invisible." Now she gave a small smile, but it held no humour. Had his concealment of his powers hurt her so much? More than his night with Kim?

"I'm sorry, Holly. About the secrets."

She looked up now and met his eyes. Hers were steely green, unwavering magnets with no trace of vulnerability. He had done this to her with his betrayal, hardened her, beaten her into emptiness.

"Which secrets?" Her gaze didn't waver. He wanted to look away, but he couldn't let himself off so lightly. She deserved him meeting her eye,

"The, er, the thing with me and Kim. And my sorcery."

She didn't respond.

Elliot watched her, trying to find the person he knew. He couldn't bear the silence for long. "What do you want me to say?"

"Are you sorry for killing Kim too?"

He stared. "You think I did it?"

"You did it."

"I didn't!" Of all the people to accuse him, he had never considered that Holly wouldn't believe him. "You know I was in work that day."

"That's what you told me."

"That's what happened!"

"That's what you think happened."

What was she talking about? He felt a tremor run through him, a flutter of nausea in his stomach. "Holly, you can't honestly believe I did this."

Holly dropped her gaze. "You told me about your dreams, Elliot. The murders from long ago, the murder of that young sorcerer, Tomar. Those are Viros's memories."

Elliot nodded. "I know." He no longer doubted this; he couldn't deny it.

"How do you think you became a sorcerer?" Holly lowered her voice, but there was an edge to her tone. "Sorcery only travels by blood, but your parents are human."

"I don't know how it happened!" Elliot felt his fists clenching at his sides, and with an effort he uncurled them. "Do you not think I've wondered about that?"

Holly's voice remained a horrible whisper. "Your parents are not your parents."

He felt a chill spreading up him, the nausea rising to his throat.

"Viros never died, Elliot. He faked his death. It was in your dream."

His insides turned to ice. "Stop."

"But it wasn't a dream. It was a memory."

Before Holly spoke again, something screamed denial inside him. "No." He knew what she was going to say next.

"You are Viros."

"No."

"You are him. You're a murderer. You faked your own death, vanished from the world and reappeared as Elliot. It's easy for a shape-shifter. I don't understand how you managed to make Paros your decoy – a new sorcerer shouldn't have been created as you didn't actually die – but somehow you arranged it, so that your death was believable."

Paros. The fake. That's why he was a fake. It made sense: Paros was a decoy, to support the illusion that Viros had died and his power had passed to another.

"That's not true." Elliot found his voice was hoarse, with none of the conviction he hoped for. "I'm not Viros – I'm Elliot. I'm me."

"I know you don't remember. You must have given yourself a new personality or something. But he's leaking back – in your dreams you remember yourself, and Viros is taking over. You talk like him, you joke like him. He's back, if he was ever gone, and he's you. It was you, Viros, who killed Kim. Perhaps

212

you've concealed it from yourself too and you think you really were in work, but you weren't. I don't know if you have two sides to you that are unaware of each other, or if deep down, you, Elliot, know what you did. But you did it. Your dreams tell you what really happened."

No. This couldn't be true. She couldn't be right. "Why are you doing this? You should be on my side." His voice cracked. "It's me, Elliot."

Her mouth twisted, and she made a sound that was too broken for a laugh. "On your side! You're lucky I was the one to find out. I never thought I would find the murderer, and now I've found him and I haven't told anyone. What a good job, Holly."

"Holly—"

"You need to go. Arthan might be here any second."

Elliot whirled as if he would find the other sorcerers behind him. The room was empty, but a hunted feeling gripped him. He saw in Holly's eyes what she thought of him. He was a murderer.

He could deny it again – he could keep denying it forever – but he couldn't escape the truth. He couldn't escape that presence deep inside his consciousness that weighed on him like an unseen anchor and pulled him with its greasy chain into the black-green depths. He couldn't escape that part of him that wanted to do things he shouldn't do, that wanted to gag his conscience and let his hands do the dark work they had always done, for hundreds and hundreds of years.

It was time to accept himself. He looked around the mess that was once his home but was now so unfamiliar. He had to go. He managed to walk as far as the lounge door before turning back.

"Holly."

"Go." She covered her mouth with a hand; her voice made a crack. "Go. Don't come back – stay away."

Elliot turned away. It was true. This wasn't a dream – this was real.

He was a murderer. Absently, he let his body dissolve into

the air. Time to disappear. He drifted through the flat as a ghost and out through the back door, feeling the wet tears on Holly's cheeks as he passed over them. He let himself be pulled up into the wind. Holly, his flat and his life got smaller behind him.

The clouds were darkening, and he blackened with them. The houses below shrank to tiny boxes and the sky widened to envelop him. As his heart sank with his spiralling thoughts, his body floated up to join the nothingness.

Elliot no longer existed. There was no reason to stay, nothing to do but drift away.

*   *   *

He watched the train pull into the station. The red carriages were painted in blood. He felt sick again, and his head pounded. The doors opened and the passengers poured out in a noise-less, murky stream. What had happened to him? He had been a normal person with a normal life, then he had been overtaken by a darkness that drowned everything that was once real.

He stepped onto the train and found a seat with no one nearby. He was in his own shape, his old jeans, his rumpled hair, his easy slouch. But was it his own shape or an unwitting disguise? Could he be Viros? How could he know who he was?

The train began to pull away from his old life. He placed a hand on the window as if to hold on to it, then gazed at his familiar skin, knuckles and fingers for what felt like the first time. After watching the houses pass by for some minutes, he looked at the dark, wet spots on his lap and realised he had been crying.

As Holly's words fully took hold of him something snapped in his mind, and he felt a Control break that he hadn't even known he had ever cast. But now he remembered. It was a Control he had cast nineteen years ago, a Control that had wiped his mind clean. A Control that had held years of memo-ries locked away from his consciousness, memories that now tumbled out into his unprepared mind.

He remembered everything in vivid detail.

PART NINE
MEMORY

1715

CHAPTER THIRTY-ONE

Charles Ward shouldered his way through the inn. After the sharpness of the evening air the stench of beer was rather a shock, but he tried not to let it show, as if he was a frequent visitor to these places. A meandering fog of smoke made it difficult to discern either the faces of the drinkers or the tables that butted him in the gloom as he came. The flickering sconces mounted occasionally on the walls cast the faces he did see into ghoulish caricature, confusing his vision further. He didn't even know which face he was looking for; all he could look for was a red coat and hat. Very strange. Fashions had become very bold in certain circles, but Charles had never heard of anyone wearing a red hat before.

Once he saw the man it was evidently the person he sought. The red was so vivid it was provoking glances from the surrounding tables. Murmurs drifted to Charles's ears as he made his way over to sit down opposite the red-garbed gentleman. He caught one or two words – *odd, foreign* – as he sat down and tucked his coat tails under him. He removed his hat, flattened his wig and tried not to look nervous. He wore his plain grey coat and white waistcoat, which he hoped made him look normal and reassured any onlooker that he wasn't a partner to his companion's eccentricity. He held out his hand. "Charles Ward."

"A pleasure," the gentleman replied, accepting the hand but

neglecting to offer his own name.

"You appear to have attracted quite some attention."

The red-coated gentleman nodded, a twitch of a smile touching his lips. He certainly looked foreign. He wore no wig, and his oily black hair was slicked across his head. His nose was long and sharp, his eyes darting and his skin an unusual olive tone. He cut a striking figure. He had the look of a crow, Charles decided – a smart, red-coated crow. His waxed moustache danced whenever his mouth twitched, which was often – the man had an energy about him. But he was also silent, so Charles prompted him.

"I received your note," Charles said in a low voice. "It perplexed me."

The moustache twitched. "Indeed?" The gentleman's voice was deep and mellow.

Charles nodded, but the man made no further comment. Charles tried again. "I have never seen such a thing before."

The gentleman gave another of his twitching smiles.

After a pause in which nothing further came, Charles made another attempt. "I cannot imagine how you made it. It is a delightful trick."

"Indeed."

Charles prepared to prompt him again, wondering if the other man's conversation would consist entirely of nods and fragments of sentences, but he was interrupted by the red-coated gentleman, who now launched into a speech.

"Many years ago I was servant to a Mr Whitelock. My master, God save him, died, but before doing so he bade me fulfil him a number of final tasks. Our meeting today is one of these tasks. My own name is of no importance."

Charles had been about to ask the gentleman's name again, and this last sentence cut the words off in his throat, exactly as if the red-coated man had known what he was thinking. But of course, that was impossible.

The gentleman continued, moustache dancing all the while. "My task today is to place three items into your care and to deliver to you a message from my master. He interested himself in you greatly, though you were but a baby when he died. On his deathbed he trusted to me the letter you found on your doorstep yesterday morning. The one that perplexed you."

"But that's quite impossible!"

And it was. The note had indeed been left on the doorstep of Charles's shop in Watling Street. He had arrived for work as normal early yesterday morning and found it placed there – a small white envelope. Picking it up, he had seen it was addressed to him, in a cursive and foreign-looking hand – the hand, he now supposed, of the red-coated gentleman. But on tearing open the envelope, Charles had found a folded note penned in another hand, and it was this note that had been so perplexing.

The note set out a concise and accurate summary of Charles's life. His date of birth, his name, his job, his address – all correct to the letter. It was strange to find this information presented to him in such an unexpected fashion, but it was nothing compared to what came next. The note proceeded to detail private and personal elements of his life. The place he had first spent the night with a woman, her name, the words she had whispered in his ear. The amount of money he had stolen from his father's room as a child. The gift he had bought his wife and not yet given her. Secrets, both those cherished and those darkly concealed. The note even described his dream from the previous night – and in every surreal detail. The next sentence ran, *You read this note at precisely nineteen minutes past seven.* Charles had checked the shop clock – the note was correct. The final tantalising sentence instructed him to *Go to the George Inn in Southwark at half past eight tomorrow night. Look for a man in a red coat and hat. He will explain.*

And yet the red-coated gentleman now claimed that the writer that knew so many things about him was his late master. It was impossible. According to the gentleman, his master had died when Charles was small, and none of the events in the note would have happened by that point.

"It is not impossible."

"What?" Charles jerked himself out of thought.

"It is not impossible," the gentleman repeated. "It is merely beyond the capabilities of most men."

There was a silence. Was this all he was going to say? Where was the explanation promised in the note?

The red-coated gentleman smiled, as if he had heard something amusing. "The note, in hand with the envelope that enclosed it, is an Enchantment. An Enchantment is an object that has been invested with sorcery, and a method for releasing that sorcery. In the case of this Enchantment, the method is the opening of the envelope. Thus, when you opened the envelope, the sorcery was released. What is most interesting to me, although perhaps not to you at this moment, is the appearance of it. Even should one know the note is produced by sorcery, it must have seemed my master had a vision of the future. But he didn't. And by the way, I assure you that what I tell you is the truth. My master did entrust me with the envelope before he died, when you were a tiny child, and I did not open it before delivering it to your shop." The red-coated gentleman took a sip of his ale. "So, as I say, the contents of the note are not produced by use of Premonition. Divining such little accidents so much of a way in the future would be impossible even for my master, who was greatly powerful. It is done a different way. Your breaking of the envelope's seal releases the sorcery, and it does what it has been set there for. It looks into the mind of the nearest person – in this instance, you. It searches out in your memory the answers to its questions: who was your first love, what did you dream of the night just past, and so forth. When this is done, a sorcery of a different kind releases itself, and this second sorcery causes the answers to be recorded in ink on the paper inside the envelope, in my master's hand. A difficult Enchantment, requiring two effects that need be precisely arranged, but it was no trouble for my master. All of this sorcery comes about before there is time to draw a breath, and when you open the envelope, it is already complete. And so it appears that it was written there the whole time. Most ingenious. I personally find this method just as impressive as if my master had divined these secrets of yours from his deathbed.

But my master had a liking for the theatrical – I imagine the impression of prophecy appealed to him."

Charles gaped at the gentleman, overwhelmed by this barrage of quite bizarre conversation. "Sorcery?" he said finally.

"Yes." The gentleman nodded. "My master was a sorcerer."

How should one respond to such a thing? Charles sipped his own drink, wondering if he should make his excuses and leave. *The man is mad*, he thought.

"I assure you I'm not mad," the gentleman said.

Charles stared at him again. Was he reading his mind?

"Yes, I am," the gentleman said, with a playful dance of his moustache. He held up one elegant hand. A large ring with a yellow stone adorned his middle finger. "This ring is another Enchantment, one of a small number of generous gifts my master left in my care when he passed." The moustache tipped to one side. "He named it the Reading Ring. Wearing of the ring activates its sorcery, which is similar to that of the envelope, in that it goes forth to read the thoughts of the person closest to the ring-wearer. However, rather than asking of the person's mind certain questions, the Reading Ring takes all of the thoughts it reads and channels them into the ring-wearer's mind. Thus, whilst I wear this ring, I can hear your thoughts."

This was altogether too much to take seriously. Charles snorted. "That's not possible."

The gentleman smiled his twitchy smile. He removed the ring and placed it on the table between them. "If you wish to, try it for yourself."

Charles looked at the ring, then back at the gentleman. It appeared to be an ordinary ring, if a little showy. Why not? He reached out to take it.

The gentleman held up a hand. "One moment, please," he said. "I would prefer you not to read my own thoughts. I am ashamed to admit I am most jealous of my privacy." As he said this last word he tapped his temple with one of his long fingers. "I will leave you for a short time. Please try the ring, and please ensure it is found back on the table upon my return, so that I may keep my own secrets. You are kind to indulge me."

221

He tapped his temple again, rose from the table and swept away into the crowds of drinkers.

* * *

Several minutes later, the red-coated gentleman reappeared. Charles marvelled at him as he came – who was this fascinating creature? The ring was back on the table and Charles sat where he had before, drinkers' elbows still jostling at his head, but his hands were now trembling. "It is incredible!" he said as the gentleman seated himself.

After the gentleman had left the table, Charles had slipped the ring on his finger and a voice had burst alive in his head. He had realised it was a consciousness, a flow of thoughts he could understand as if it were his own. But it had not been his own; it had been the flow of thoughts of the burly gentleman leaning against the wall behind his right shoulder. Charles had listened to the man's ale-addled wonderings, then shifted forward in his seat. Doing so meant that he had been closer to a well-dressed man to his right than the burly man behind, and the stream of thought he heard snapped into another. The well-dressed man was more lucid, and Charles became aware that he was soon to leave and visit a friend who had fallen ill. The device was incredible.

Charles could not help gabbling to the red-coated gentleman about his experience, although he knew he must be well acquainted with the wonders of wearing the ring. The gentleman listened with a politely inclined head, the moustache twitching occasionally. Finally Charles ran out of words, and a pause arrived in his outpouring of wonder.

The gentleman took advantage and broke in. "I have now demonstrated the truth of my claims for the Reading Ring. I would ask the favour of you now to trust the remainder of my tale." He paused as though expecting something, so Charles nodded, suddenly exhausted. "I am forever indebted to my master for his leaving me wonderful gifts. This ring and other such items are endlessly useful to me and permit me to profit from the skills my master had, in a small way. But he has given you a far more powerful gift. You are not like me, or the other men in this inn." He leant forward at this point, to peer at Charles as he breathed his soft words. "You can do all the things my master did. With no Enchantments."

The gentleman's examination of him was very searching, and Charles made a little chuckle to try and dispel the intensity of it. He motioned towards the ring on the table. "I cannot do such things as this!"

The gentleman's gaze did not waver. "Yes, you can. You have it running in your blood. Most of sorcery's parts you will need to learn. These you cannot command now, as you have not practised, although with practice you will truly learn them." The moustache danced, and the gentleman winked. "But there is one part of sorcery you already have. You have had the way of performing this sorcery from the day you were born."

"What sorcery?"

"The sorcery to disguise yourself. To change your shape."

Charles froze. His heart stopped beating. How could this man know? He had tried to forget it all, to convince himself it had stopped, that those days were merely nightmares he had once had. The incidents in his youth. The times when people had run screaming and he had not known why until he saw his changing, shifting face in a puddle's reflection. The times he had wished to be someone else and found himself changed in a heartbeat, in a widening circle of twisted, fearful faces. They had accused him of witchcraft. He had never tried or wanted to understand it, had decided it was an illness, a strange and evil one. No one knew, not his family, not his wife, not a single soul; he had left every memory of it far behind him long ago. He had suppressed it so well that he had nearly forgotten himself, until now. Now the nightmare was seeping back, the drinkers around him shifting and stretching like his reflection, the pale faces staring at him once more. What could his horrible condition have to do with this gentleman?

The man opposite him was waiting, watching, and no doubt listening to Charles think. The gentleman nodded, although Charles couldn't imagine why, and reached below the table. When his hands returned to the table they bore two large books.

"These books were written by my master." The gentleman held up each one in turn. "This book gives some of how my master came to his powers himself. And this book tells not only of why he has passed to you such powers but gives also some lessons on using what is within you."

Charles took the offered books with numb hands.

"My master relates these things in these books far better than such a one as I could ever explain them." The gentleman held a hand up with a single finger extended. "I have but one thing more to tell before I leave."

"You are leaving?" It could not be. Charles had so many questions for this strange gentleman.

"The books will answer your questions. Yes, I must go. But before I do, listen well. You will learn in these books that there are others, others like you. They meet Wednesday next, at noon, at Fetter Lane, opposite Dean Street. You should go and see them. Together you might do great things."

With that the gentleman rose. Charles rose too, not knowing what to do but certain that he couldn't let him leave. This was the only man who knew what he was, the only man he could talk to about his terrible illness.

"Please." The gentleman put a hand lightly on Charles's shoulder. "I must go, and please do not follow me. Take yourself to Fetter Lane, at noon on Wednesday. You will find there many people of like mind with whom you may appease your concerns."

Charles protested, and followed the gentleman while he did. He needed to talk this over more, to consider these impossible ideas further. He tailed the bright red coat as it weaved through the inn. A wreath of smoke obscured Charles's vision and the coat disappeared for a second. He pushed forward to find it, and was relieved a second later to see the gentleman framed by the inn's doorway, the red cloth glowing in the candlelight against the dimness of the street beyond. Charles stepped towards him then froze in horror as a figure pounced from the shadows of the doorway. The next moment the gentleman was on the floor, wrestling with the figure. The shapes of their bodies were dark, tumbling around in the half-light. The figure that attacked was animal-like, a jerky shadow with misshapen hands and back. For a second the light revealed its face. Pale skin, a swollen jaw and hungry eyes. Charles made a half-step forward, thinking he should help but finding his feet unwilling to do so, and then it was over. The figure rolled off and lay still. So did the gentleman.

Charles rushed forward, and realised a large, dark-haired man was at his side, rushing with him. They bent over the gentleman sprawled across the doorway, and Charles gasped to see the red of his coat was mingled with a deeper shade. He pulled the coat aside to find the gentleman's waistcoat soaked with blood, a jagged rip in the cloth right by his heart, and beneath it an open, leering wound.

"He's dead."

It was the voice of the dark-haired man next to him. Charles looked up and met the man's honest, sad eyes. He looked over at the attacker and saw a knife lying beside the prone body, stained with the gentleman's blood.

The dark-haired man didn't seem to be trembling or panting like Charles was. He looked an unsavoury type, with a long scar running down beneath his left eye. Charles opened his mouth to say something, and the red-coated gentleman moved.

His hands twitched, then came alive. His eyes opened, and he glanced at the two of them leaning over him. Before Charles's eyes the knife wound in the gentleman's chest lightened, tightened and smoothed out. The skin closed over, and the wound was gone.

The gentleman ignored their stares and pushed himself to his feet, showing no sign of injury. Charles and the man with the scar stepped back as the gentleman crossed to the other body and knelt by it. Charles could make out dark stains on the other body, which remained still. The gentleman's elegant fingers felt the attacker's face and neck, and he let out a sigh.

"Thank you both for your concern." The gentleman

addressed both Charles and the man with the scar, without acknowledging that he knew Charles. "I am unharmed. The other party, I am afraid, is dead, but that is not my problem or yours. I propose we leave the area in our own various directions. It would be best if we are not found here together." The gentleman tipped his red hat at them, and addressed one last sentence at Charles's open-mouthed stare before leaving. "Do not be distressed. This happens to me often. I am well prepared for it."

With these last words, the gentleman patted his red coat and winked. He then spun on his heel and vanished into the dark.

The silence was broken by the man with the scar, who had crouched to examine the body. "I don't think they are men."

Charles looked down at him. "I beg your pardon?"

The man grinned. "Pardon granted. I said, I don't think they're men. These things. They are something else." He rose to his feet and shook his head at the body, before extending a hairy hand towards Charles. "I'm Victor. Pleasure to meet you, Charles."

"How do you know me?" Charles frowned, but accepted the offered hand all the same.

Victor grinned again. "I must confess I've been watching you."

Then his face wobbled. The wrinkles softened and broke, the scar shrank and his skin swam. Charles gasped as before his eyes the man shrank into a shorter, fairer man, with a lively and sharp face. It looked like another grin could break across his face at any moment.

"That red-coated fellow met with me a few days past," Victor said, now standing in over-large clothes and shoes. "I am just like you, Charles. Victor Heath. Shape-changer."

"You are like me?" Charles's question came out sounding a little stupid, but Victor gave another broad smile as though Charles had paid him a compliment.

"Yes I am, Charles, yes I am. I apologise for lying to you – I knew very well Red wasn't dead. But I had to keep my guise of the passing stranger. I'm sure you understand."

Charles realised he was still holding Victor's hand, which had shrunk in his grip. He felt a smile creep across his face. Another sorcerer. An ally. A friend. He shook Victor's hand again. "A pleasure to make your acquaintance, Victor."

* * *

"What was that thing that attacked the gentleman?"

Victor pursed his lips, as though this was a theoretical question rather than an uneasy reflection on the violent and harrowing experience just recently visited on them. "I'm not certain. But I have seen Red attacked by creatures like that before. Perhaps they would steal his Enchantments. He has plenty."

Victor had offered to join Charles on his walk home, and now they ghosted together through the night, the houses drifting by like black ships, their breath misting in front and floating off behind.

"What of the others?" Charles asked as they drew closer to his home. "How did they seem?"

"Oh, a mixture of folk." Victor had told Charles that he had met the red-coated gentleman – or Red, as he referred to him – six days ago, and had since returned to the George every evening, each time disguised in a different shape, to watch Red meet other sorcerers. "Men, women, some of quality, some not. All of the same age." He sniffed, wrinkling his nose. "Some dull, some irritating. All have different sorceries they perform best in. But none can do as we can."

"Oh?"

Victor patted the books that Charles clutched to his chest. "You should read these. Everything is explained. We are Grey sorcerers, we two, the only ones. We can achieve all the sorcery that the others can; all that is required of us is practice. But." Victor paused at this point, presumably to create a dramatic moment. "None of them can alter their shape, no matter how they practise. It is all explained in the books."

Charles hugged the books a little closer, quickened his stride to keep up with his animated companion and nodded for

Victor to continue. His head was spinning so fast with all this information that he decided it was best to let Victor talk and spend his own silence attempting to accept what was happening. Though it was difficult to keep his mind on any one notion long enough to consider it before Victor assailed him with yet another unexpected issue. The man was like gunpowder.

It seemed that while Charles had spent his life suppressing his abilities, Victor had spent his life embracing them. Victor said he changed shape most frequently, adopting an endless myriad of disguises and rarely using his real body. He assured Charles the spry body he currently "wore" was his true one, although Charles realised he had no way of knowing for certain. But then, perhaps it wasn't important what Victor truly looked like. He had the luxury to choose his face to suit his mood, and Victor saw no reason not to take advantage of this, rather than trying to display every side of his nature with the single cast of features he had chanced to have been born with. A man who wore his lounging clothes to an evening dinner would be considered ill-mannered, so why would it be anything less than polite to wear not only the right outfit for the occasion but also the right body?

However, to Charles, the most beguiling part of Victor's powers was the least ostentatious. Victor had learnt that his shape-shifting could be used to make himself invisible. He said he spent days at a time in this insubstantial form, unseen by the world, just wandering, listening and watching. His words lit a spark in Charles's mind; Charles often wished he could vanish and leave all life's troubles behind, and now he could. Who would not yearn for such freedom, such anonymity, such unaccountability?

It was all so strange and marvellous, and yet, despite the incredible stories Victor told and the wonders he described, Charles felt a quiet discomfort.

"I won't meet with the others," he said, interrupting one of Victor's stories.

They were turning into Charles's street, but his words yanked Victor to an abrupt halt at the corner. He turned a frowning face to Charles, as though his companion had set him some fiendish riddle. "Why?"

It was hard to explain. Charles pressed on down the grey, puddled street, and he could hear Victor's boots splashing in his wake, seeming to demand an answer. Mere yards ahead, Charles could already see the ebbing light of his window, his warm, dusty home waiting for him where sorcery did not fit. This new world of impossible powers was so unfamiliar, so wild and untamed. "I can't."

Victor chuckled as he caught him up, as though Charles had made a joke. "You can do anything you choose now. You are a sorcerer."

"But I don't want to be." Now Charles himself stopped, while they were still in shadow. He didn't want to get too close to his house in Victor's company; if they were seen he would have to introduce him. The icy wind snaked about them where they stood huddled on the cobbles. In the dimness Charles almost felt invisible already. Just another coat in the night, that was all he wanted to be. "I am glad to have met you, Victor, but I fear the path of sorcery is not one I can follow."

Charles expected another chuckle at this, but his companion just sighed, and when Victor spoke again he sounded sincere, although he had turned his head away from the light ahead and so his features were lost in the black-and-grey fabric of the shadows. "I sometimes think such things also. Whilst I first imagined meeting the other sorcerers would be entertaining, I have not seen a single one of them I would greatly want to spend time with. In truth you are the only sorcerer I wanted to meet, Charles. We are the same, you and I."

Charles couldn't help smiling, his lips smarting in the sharp night air. Victor was right – they were the same. He had always been different to everyone else, but here was a man just like him. A man of a thousand faces.

But what of the other sorcerers? Victor said there were fourteen in total, which meant twelve others with unnatural powers, twelve others who would want Charles to join them in their new and strange world. Charles shivered, and tried to sink further into his warm coat. "I shouldn't like to miss any important news…"

"But you would rather not go to the meeting."

Charles nodded. Reading the books was one thing; accepting that he too may have unnatural powers was one thing, in private with no one else to know. But to meet with other sorcerers was an almost public admission of his own strangeness. He had to retain a guise of normality to his life, at least for a while longer. He had a wife and two children.

"So don't go." Victor shrugged. "I shall attend, watch the proceedings and report back to you."

How Charles admired him. Victor seemed not to have a care in the world; every incident was a trifle to him. With relief Charles decided immediately to accept Victor's offer. "Perhaps I could ask of you to pass a message of some difficulty I had in attending, and then once I am more accustomed to… all this, I could meet some of them, perhaps."

Victor shrugged again, rubbing his hands together to warm them. "You could. But why give any such message? You could simply not come, and I could advise them I am the only Grey sorcerer, and that Red advised me as such."

"Oh, you mustn't deceive them so wildly." Charles saw no reason to lie. He might decide to meet these people in the future. "Please just tell that I cannot attend."

"Very good, Charles." Victor winked, his bright eyes gleaming in the gloom. "I shall make a good show of it, don't fret, and you shall live your life as normal. How does that please you?"

Charles considered this, and smiled. "That pleases me very much."

They shook hands, said their farewells, and Victor vanished into the shadows. Charles breathed easily as he turned the handle to his door. There was no need to worry – everything would stay exactly as it was.

Even so, as he stepped across the threshold back into his life, the two books Red had given him weighed heavily in his arms.

CHAPTER THIRTY-TWO

Charles edged around the wall to watch Victor stride out of the door onto Fetter Lane, chuckling to himself. Victor trotted down the steps, turned a jaunty right in Charles's direction and made his way down the street with a grin on his face and his hands in his pockets. He peered in the windows of the houses he passed, slowing occasionally to examine some object of interest. He was in the rather bizarre shape of a tall, gangly man, with an oversized double-peaked powdered wig and a long, flapping coat. Charles could hear his shoes clacking on the cobblestones as he wandered closer.

Victor didn't so much as glance towards Charles as he approached, and it seemed he was going to sail past, but he took a sudden, smart turn down the side alley where Charles waited. Absurdly, Charles's first thought was to run, but he scolded himself for this foolishness and stood his ground while Victor entered the alley and perched on a low wall a few feet away.

The tall figure gazed around, beaming. "Well, dear Charles! Did that amuse you as much as it did me?"

Charles looked down at himself to check he was still invisible, and he was; there was nothing but air where his body should be. But it seemed Victor had found him anyway. He watched the air shimmer around himself as he reappeared, felt the usual burn in his throat as his sorcery flowed, and commanded his body to solidify into his familiar bones and flesh housed in his usual grey coat. "How could you tell I was here?"

Victor grinned and finally made eye contact with him. "I heard you cough."

"Ah, well." A polite enquiry after Victor's health nearly escaped Charles's lips, but he stopped himself, deciding he was well within his rights to omit pleasantries and turn straight to the point that was rankling him. "Why did you tell them you are the only Grey sorcerer?"

Charles wondered if Victor had realised he had been in the meeting invisibly the whole time, but no surprise registered on that long, thin face.

"I thought it best." It was accompanied by the usual shrug, which seemed to follow Victor to whichever body he wore.

Was that all Victor had to say on the matter? "That was not as we agreed!"

Another shrug. "You could have appeared to them and demonstrated me a liar, if you wished to."

Charles sighed, and felt the heat of irritation already fading. It was very difficult to be angry with Victor; he was so relaxed it was infectious.

When Victor told the other sorcerers that he was the only Grey sorcerer, Charles had been certain they would find it odd – after all, there were two sorcerers of every other colour – but no one had questioned it. And Victor was right: Charles had felt no desire to prove them wrong. He had watched the meeting silently and unseen from Victor's shoulder, just as he used to hide under a blanket when he was a child, in a safe haven where no one could see him and he couldn't be touched by the world's troubles.

Now that Charles had discovered the ability to vanish, the thought of disappearing was a constant allure. He had found himself waking in the night this last week and sneaking out of the house, invisible, to roam the streets. It was an addiction. He had never felt so free as when he drifted through the city unseen, the wandering beggars and thieves of the night staring straight through him. He stopped being Charles on those

232

nights, and became nobody. A watching emptiness.

"What opinion did you have on the names?"

Stirred from his thoughts, it took Charles a moment to recall what Victor was talking about. A woman called Elizabeth Carter had proposed at the meeting that each sorcerer should adopt a sorcerer's name, as a method of keeping their identities secret from anyone spying on them. "The idea had some worth."

Victor snorted a laugh. "You don't need to act for me! It was ridiculous. That woman was ridiculous."

He had snorted like that in the meeting when the idea was suggested, loudly enough that everyone could hear him. He had attracted some frowning looks from the other sorcerers, and went on to attract several more during the course of the meeting. He had laughed and joked throughout, his brash voice echoing around the hall while the rest of the sorcerers had spoken in hushed whispers.

"Elizan! Do you think she paid the most care to the name endings for Yellow sorcerers to be certain her own sorcerer name was to her liking?" Victor's eyes were live with humour.

A chuckle escaped Charles. He never found himself so amused as he did in Victor's company. "It seems likely."

Victor stretched his long legs out and yawned. "They are a pack of fools."

"You must admit your own sorcerer name sounds rather grand."

"Viros." Victor made a face, his skin wrinkling up. "It is ridiculous."

Charles smiled. The names were a little childish. But despite Victor's groans and scoffs, the other sorcerers had agreed to adopt them, and from then on had practised using the new names. The intention was never to mention their real names again. Victor had made several dry comments about the hordes of dangerous villains who must be seeking to discover their identities, and told everyone in tones of grave concern that he had seen an eavesdropper lurking in the doorway masquerading as a ginger cat. Charles had stifled a laugh at this warning, but the other sorcerers had not looked so amused. One red-faced man told Victor rather snappily that it was vital to preserve the secrecy of their talents, and that Victor would do well to cooperate or leave. Victor had grinned at him until the man broke eye contact.

The larger part of the discussions had been about the aims of the group. The others all seemed to feel as though they should put their skills to some noble purpose. For his part Charles felt tense about the idea of using his sorcery for anything apart from his secret night walks, and Victor just didn't seem to care.

The other sorcerers had eventually decided the best initial course was to each hone their own skills and think further on how they could be used. They would reconvene in a month. Victor had declared at this point that he would not be attending. The red-faced man had pronounced this to be "no great loss" rather loudly, at which Victor sent him another grin, this one somehow intimidating.

The proceedings were not quite concluded when Victor had sprung up and left, and Charles had slipped out through a window himself.

"They talk in circles." Victor twirled his finger to emphasise the point. "One moment they wish to be shrouded in secrecy, and the next they wish to change the world. They cannot do both!"

"I suppose not."

Victor clambered to his feet. "We should meet again."

"Of course," Charles replied automatically. "It has been good to see you, Victor."

The long face winked, eyes sparkling. "Do not worry, Charles, I can recognise a rejection. A 'good to see you', with no proposed date for a future meeting. I understand. You have a family." He slapped his hands on his coat and beamed, before extending his bony hand. "Farewell, then. I shall perhaps see you here and about in any case."

Charles didn't know what to say, so he just shook. Victor was right – Charles had enjoyed their time together, but the thought of arranging another meeting with Victor made him pause. The man was just so unpredictable. Perhaps it was best to part ways.

"Goodbye, Charles."

"Goodbye, Victor."

Charles watched him saunter back out onto the street, reminding himself again that this tall scarecrow was the same short, wiry man he had met before. Although it was impossible to tell for sure which, if any, of the disguises were Victor's own original body, Charles now had a strong feeling it was that nimble, lively fellow who had strolled home with him through the night. That body had suited Victor; he had seemed comfortable in it.

He wondered if he would recognise Victor if he ever saw him again.

CHAPTER THIRTY-THREE

1760

Charles drifted along London's damp, undulating streets. It was late, dark and wonderful. This was how he loved to be. The night was a mist he joined and wove between; the people around him emerged from the swirl like echoes of the ghost he had become. He was safe. He was not a person to be approached, accosted or avoided; he wasn't there. He was the shadowed bricks, he was the oily gutters, he was the lowering fog, he was a secret that couldn't be found, a person that couldn't be named. As he paused by a doorway, he glanced down and saw the glow from a lamp shining through his body to shimmer in the puddle beneath his feet. Invisibly, he smiled.

He looked up at the sign on the wall, wondering why he had come here. It was the address he sought, a row of looming, bleached townhouses lined with tall, staring panelled windows. Very grand indeed. He floated past the darkened doors and down some steps with spear-headed black iron railings to a peeling, grime-stained doorway beneath the street level. Perhaps not so grand.

When he stood in the gloom next to the door he paused again. It was ajar, and he heard voices. He put an invisible finger to the gap and let the end of it drift inside like a wisp of smoke, then let his whole body stretch and uncoil to follow his finger in a thin, silky trail, threading himself through the gap without disturbing the door, and promptly found himself reinstated on the inside.

A table, two chairs, a wooden cabinet and a fireplace were all squeezed into a cramped, damp-smelling room. It looked like a storeroom that had been hastily converted to a dining room, with the dust and cobwebs yet to be cleared. Over the table two men were arguing. They were complete opposites: one was stooped and elderly, with worn clothing and wild, raw eyes, while the other was young and clean-pressed, dressed in a frilled shirt and a long blue coat with gleaming buttons.

Charles sidled into the room as quietly as possible, glancing down more than once to check he was still invisible, although the men seemed so engrossed in their debate that even if he had burst in fully visible and dancing a jig they might not have noticed.

"I must find this Mr Lewis!"

"Yes, so you said." The younger man scowled at the other. "It is not my concern. I do not know Mr Lewis."

"But he was here!" The old man jabbed a finger on the table. "With my own eyes I saw him here – he lived here!"

The younger man narrowed his eyes. Charles wished he hadn't come inside. He kept as still as possible and held his breath until the young man spoke. "You are certain?"

"Of course I am certain – beyond all doubt I am certain!" The old man's voice rose to a screech. "He stood where you stand now! A man as tall and thin as a scarecrow. He has my daughter!" He fixed the younger man with a venomous look. "I am not leaving. Someone in this wretched place must know where to find Mr Lewis."

"Well." The young man smiled, in a way that Charles found a little sinister. "We shall have to bring an end to this."

A tall scarecrow. The description found a partner in Charles's memory. Victor.

The old man had fallen silent, his eyes turned glazed and

vacant. The young man took a step back towards the fireplace, and his hand closed around the poker. Charles gasped before he could stop himself, but the other men didn't react. Charles melted himself back into a wispy trail and slipped back through the gap in the door. He had to interrupt this argument quickly. He materialised outside the door and administered a few firm raps. There was the sound of hasty movement, and through the crack Charles saw the young man return the poker to the fireplace and dash to the door. When he opened it and saw Charles, a broad grin broke across his face.

"Charles! Wonderful to see you!"

"Victor?"

The young man winked. "Didn't you recognise me?"

Another disguise. Like the others, it was unnerving.

Victor ushered Charles into the room. The old man was still frozen to the spot, his eyes fixed on the fireplace where Victor had stood a moment before.

"Is he taken ill?" Charles asked.

"Oh, he's fine." Victor waved a hand, and the old man jerked out of his stupor. He stared about him until his eyes settled on Victor.

"There you are! We haven't finished!"

"Come with me." The mellow voice of this young guise of Victor's was as smooth as a cat's purr. He took the old man by the hand and hustled him out of the door, and Charles found himself alone. He remained where he stood, marvelling at the clutter and disarray, wondering when Victor would come back. He noticed a hat on the chair and had just taken it up when Victor returned.

"Sorry, Charles, merely a friend of mine who was passing by. Now you have my full attention!"

Victor beamed at him, then his brow furrowed as his gaze fell to the hat in Charles's hand.

"Your friend's hat, I think." Charles held it up. "You can still catch him, perhaps?"

"Oh no, I shan't bother." Victor nestled into a shabby chair and held a hand out for the hat, which Charles passed to him.

"He walks too fast."

"It is frightfully cold." Charles thought the old man had looked rather too frail to be out walking in this weather. "He shall come back for it, no doubt."

"I shouldn't think so." Victor threw the hat into the corner of the room to join a pile of dusty, indiscernible objects. "Enough about him. How are you, Charles?"

"Oh, very well, thank you. I have your address from your letters, so I thought to pay you a visit. I hope you have not fallen on bad times."

Victor grinned and turned in his chair to look round the poky room, as if for the first time. "This is Mr Lewis's lodging. It suits his status. This fellow" – Victor tapped his chest – "lives somewhere much grander, I assure you."

Charles gazed at the brass buttons gleaming on Victor's coat. What strange multiple lives Victor must lead. "So tell me, who was that gentleman who just left?"

"No one of consequence."

"Why were you arguing so?"

The other sorcerer arched an elegant eyebrow. "We were arguing?"

Charles felt his cheeks flush. "Yes, um, I did not really intend to, but I entered once already. Before I knocked. I saw the two of you in some kind of quarrel."

"Ah." A smirk. "It seems one never knows if you are about, Charles. Well, the story is as dreary as it is long, but if you insist I shall impart the short form of it. That cantankerous old man, like many a cantankerous old man, has a well-shaped and sweet-lipped daughter, and like many a pig-headed father is rather protective of her, and rather suspicious towards her suitors." He waggled his eyebrows in a wild manner. "Of course, you have guessed I am one such suitor." Charles had not guessed, but he supposed that was the meaning of Victor's eyebrow movements. "The old rogue is forever tormenting the poor girl. She begged me on hands and knees to send him away. As you no doubt surmised from our conversation, I have been wearing my Mr Lewis disguise to court her, scarecrow that he is, and so

I chose this one to get rid of him."

Charles knew it would be polite to turn the discussion to a different topic, but he found this one far too curious to abandon yet. "You used Yellow Control on the gentleman, I think?" Charles hadn't realised it at the time, but that must have been why the old man froze. "To… restrain him, I suppose?"

"Yes, of course." Victor made his way over to a wooden cabinet and opened the door. "Yellow is a useful one in a tight spot, or even in a looser spot, come to that! I read everybody's thoughts. Knowing the minds of others can be of great help."

"That seems somewhat wrong." Charles never used his powers on another person. To invade another man's mind, his private thoughts – if nothing else, it must be rude.

"It isn't wrong," Victor said, rummaging in the cabinet for something. "It is merely using our powers to their fullest. You should try it. Why learn these skills if you will never use them?"

"I wish to understand them," Charles said. "Why did you take up the poker?"

Victor cast him a pained look over his shoulder. "You embarrass me, Charles. I know I should not fear the old fellow – he was far too feeble to trouble me – but my nerves are as fragile as any man's. The old devil was growing agitated and I thought he might become violent. Of course I didn't need both Yellow Control and the poker to defend myself, but… well, Charles, I was scared."

Victor had never seemed one to scare easily, but Charles did not voice this opinion. As intriguing as he found Victor's dalliance with this girl, good manners required him to let the subject drop. "I am sorry for all the questions. I was merely curious."

"Let us forget the matter." Victor returned from the cabinet with an odd-looking wine bottle in hand. "Come and sit down, I have something to show you. Are you still studying like a lunatic?"

Certainly he didn't consider himself a lunatic, but Charles did find himself writing notes on sorcery and experiment-ing with Controls most hours of the day, and often the night too. There was so much to learn. Charles occupied one of the wooden chairs and Victor filled the other. "I have been researching rather a great deal, yes."

Victor cackled as if Charles had made a joke, throwing his handsome young face back and displaying a fine set of white teeth. Victor's disguises unsettled Charles. It was like talking to a complete stranger who knew all about him. "Ah, dear Charles," Victor sighed. "I read all your letters, you know. You must have invented as many Controls as there are in Whitelock's book."

"No, you flatter me. Not nearly that many."

"Have you tried splitting yourself up much further?"

The way Victor described it made it sound gruesome.

"I have, um, experimented with multiple Grey manifestations. But I am no longer pursuing that line of enquiry."

"Oh?"

Charles said nothing. The truth was he had no desire to revisit those experiments to divide himself into two separate bodies. He had made a clone of himself with relative ease, and had found he could see and hear and think in both bodies, which was astounding, if somewhat confusing. But he had found that if he remained split in two for a few days, the clone began to act a little unexpectedly. He would catch the clone looking at him out of the corner of his eye, or notice it pausing before enacting Charles's intentions. It almost seemed as if the clone was starting to think independently, and was becoming someone else. The thought had made cold sweat form on Charles's neck. He had merged the clone back into himself and resolved never to try it again.

"Well, you shall be interested in this in any case." Victor tapped the odd bottle that he had placed on the table beside two plain stemmed glasses. "I have finally succeeded in obtaining it. It was made by Whitelock himself, an astonishing thing."

Charles leant forward in his seat to examine the bottle. It was a green wine bottle. The label had peeled off years before but had left a faint impression on the thick glass. It looked ordinary, if very old, except for a strange-looking cap. In place of a cork, a wooden stopper sat in its neck with a thin stick rising from it. At the top of the stick was a cog, mounted so that it would spin freely. The cog was not connected to anything and appeared entirely useless. "It is quite odd. Where did you find it?"

Victor shook his head, as if that didn't matter. "Turn the cog."

Charles did as he was told, and as he turned the cog something shimmered at the bottom of the bottle. A puddle of red, glossy liquid had appeared. The bottle had certainly been empty a moment before.

He glanced at Victor, who motioned for him to continue. Charles spun the cog, and the level of red liquid crept upwards. He spun it some more, and some more, and the bottle filled and filled. After he had whirled the cog for a minute or so, the bottle was full.

"It is wine?"

Victor nodded. "It is."

"An Enchantment?"

"Indeed."

"Fascinating!" Charles examined the cog mechanism with renewed energy. The only Enchantment he had ever seen was the Reading Ring that Red had showed him all those years ago. He had been so overwhelmed that day he had barely taken anything in. Now he had the opportunity to examine this device with the benefit of all he had learnt about sorcery over the years. "So how does it work?"

"I have no idea."

"It must be invested with a Blue Control to create wine." Charles picked the device up and was surprised that the glass was cool to the touch. "And so the classic Blue obstacle of power consumption is overcome. Each spin casts hundreds of Blue Controls and the user expends no effort – it is extraordinary! One can only suppose other Controls could be applied similarly, perhaps even in combination." He looked up at Victor again. "But how is the Control put inside the device?"

"Who knows?" Victor laughed, throwing open his hands with apparent joy at his own lack of knowledge. "I knew it would interest you. All I know is it works. And it never fails, it never wears out."

"Whereas a Control may only be cast so often before the sorcerer tires and must stop."

"Exactly."

"Very interesting."

"And it is an interesting vintage too." Victor waved his hand and the wooden stopper rose from the bottle. The bottle then rose into the air and poured itself into Charles's empty glass.

Charles's attention was caught by this demonstration of Victor's Orange Control. "Why do you wave your hand when you use your power?"

"It seems right," Victor said.

"My studies have shown that such movements have no effect on using Control. Summoning power is a physical process that can be aided by such movements, but certainly the casting itself is an endeavour entirely of the mind."

Victor leant back in his chair, stretched out like a cat and swilled his wine at arm's length. "A clever theory, Charles, but the hand movements seem right to me. What do you think of the wine?"

Charles took a sip and felt the warm kiss of plums and black pepper in his throat. "It is very good." He peered again at the Enchanted bottle. "Very good indeed."

"It is likely this bottle was Whitelock's personal wine cellar. An inexpensive way of staying fully stocked of one's favourite wine."

Even though they had barely touched their glasses, Victor twisted the cog to fill the bottle again. Charles smiled at Victor's delight with his Enchantment, and wondered how he had got hold of it. Victor was a man who seemed to get whatever he wanted.

"The strength of a Control could be multiplied many times using Enchantments," Charles thought aloud. "And any person could use them, not just sorcerers."

"I know," said Victor, his smile vanishing. "It is a worry. You know that woman Elizan has banned the making of any more? For once she is talking some sense."

"Why?" It seemed impossible that Victor would ever worry about anything.

"Think about it, Charles – we must be careful! Imagine if a human found one of these. It would be a threat to our invincibility."

Charles could not help laughing. "We are not invincible!"

"We are!" Victor leant forward in his chair, his eyes suddenly bright and intense. "In all the parts of life we are! We are a different race, a higher race – other men cannot do what we do. Once we have mastery of our skills no one may stop us. You have read the books, more closely than I. You know well what we can do, what we will be able to do. We may strengthen our bodies, harden them against any physical attacks. We can read thoughts, see the future – we cannot be surprised or deceived. And we do not age. Have you noticed? Nearly fifty years have passed since we met Red in the inn! My hair stays black, my limbs stay strong! Our lives might last forever!"

A familiar emptiness stabbed at Charles's heart. "But the lives of our families and our friends will not. They wither and die around us." He stared at his own hand resting on the chair, the skin milky pale and smooth. "Why should one wish to live forever?"

"Oh. Yes. I was most sorry to hear about your wife."

Without looking up, Charles gave the now habitual brave smile and spoke the mechanical words. "She had a long life, and a happy one. And she died peacefully."

"How are your boys?"

"Fully grown. One has two children of his own."

"You are a grandfather! Wonderful news!"

While he appreciated Victor's attempt to lift the mood, Charles couldn't raise a smile. "I do not see them any more. I have stopped ageing while my family continue; I am frozen in time while they move on. I do not fit."

"You could age yourself," Victor said. "A grey hair here, a wrinkle there."

Charles shook his head. "It does not work like that. Our

245

shape-shifting only mirrors the subject of our Control, and it is only skin-deep. If we could change ourselves inside as well, change our bones and blood and muscle to another's, perhaps we would age in the body we assumed." He sighed. "But it matters not. I do not belong in my family any longer. I am different."

Victor nodded, his lively eyes turned still. "Yes, you are. We are both different from the rest."

And very different to each other, Charles thought as he sipped the wine.

* * *

"Where is your young lady then?" Charles asked.

He had stayed for dinner at Victor's insistence. He had kept meaning to leave, but as the cog kept spinning and the wine kept flowing, he found himself staying hour after hour. Now they slumped in the same two chairs surrounded by dirty plates and empty glasses, and Charles's head was full of a rosy fog and his stomach hosted a warm glow.

"Lady? Oh, the girl. She is not joining us tonight. We have the evening reserved for men. Unless you are inviting a woman?"

Charles stiffened. "My wife is barely a year in her grave."

Victor held his hands up. "Apologies, apologies. I meant no offence."

His tension evaporating, Charles slumped into the chair once more. "I know you didn't, do not worry." He sighed. "You are right in any case – I should think of seeking companionship. After all, I am perhaps destined to live forever."

"True." His brows rising, a smile tugged Victor's lips. "You'll need a patient one. A woman who will enjoy a relationship with your study door."

Charles chuckled. "I suppose my secrecy might be difficult to live with." An entertaining thought struck him. "In fact, why do I not marry a sorcerer! Then I would not need to hide anything."

Victor's face tightened. "I would not, Charles. They are an

ill-humoured lot."

"But it would work beautifully!" Charles pursued his idea, wondering why Victor was not finding it amusing. "She would not age – she would be at my side for centuries. It is a fine notion!"

The other man scowled. "They are all sour baggages. If there was a charming girl among them I would agree, Charles, I assure you I would, but there is no such one."

Charles laughed at Victor's expression. "I said it in jest, I didn't—" He paused with a sudden insight. "You don't want me near them."

"What?"

"You don't want me to meet the other sorcerers." Charles thought back to their previous meetings, and it started falling into place. "That was your true aim in persuading me not to attend their gathering."

"Come now, Charles, I have no hidden motive." Victor waved a hand as if to brush the suggestion aside. "Their gatherings are dull – you heard the first one yourself. Go to another and bore yourself if you wish."

"I don't wish to! But I don't wish to be tricked either. I see now why you didn't want me to meet them." Charles felt himself shiver. It was suddenly so clear, everything Victor had said, everything he had done.

"And why is that?" Victor's tone held nothing but polite enquiry, but his gaze was fixed on Charles.

"You told me yourself. You are almost invincible, but not quite. The only danger, our only weakness, is a Grey sorcerer baby. But there is only one other apart from you who can parent a Grey sorcerer, and that is me." Charles half wished he could stop talking, as he had a feeling he was bringing himself trouble, but he felt drunk and bold and the words kept marching from his lips. "You cannot deny the idea troubles you! If I father a child with a sorcerer, the child will be Grey – it says so in Whitelock's book. And then one of us will die."

"You could be the one to die," Victor said.

"True, but it is a great risk for you. That is why you keep

me from the others, to keep yourself safe. Is that not so?"

Charles was breathing heavily. Victor looked at him for a few moments. His eyes flickered, and Charles wasn't sure if he was going to yell or weep. In the end he just sat back in his chair.

"You caught me." He closed his eyes and shook his head. "I am sorry, Charles. It was wrong of me to deceive you. I am a coward – I worry about things. The dangers, as you put it. When you weren't keen to meet the others, I thought it for the best to suggest that you stay away, best for both of us. You must see I was protecting you too; I know I can withstand a woman's charms, but can you? What if you fell in love with a female sorcerer? Love is blind, as they say. You might end up Fading yourself, and would thus give your life in payment for a night of foolish passion."

Charles did not say anything. He stared at the charcoal ribbons of wood grain in the table top. Each wave in the wood was a year of life, he had heard. He waited to see what else Victor would say.

"No, I should not make such excuses." Victor cleared his throat. "I was not trying to protect you, I was protecting myself. I was selfish to hide you away, Charles, and to be truthful, yes, that was why I first sought you out. But… it's changed now."

Charles looked up at the sound of a slight waver in Victor's voice. Incredibly, he thought he saw a shimmer in the other man's eyes. Just a moment earlier he would have sworn Victor would never reveal such weakness. A certainty gripped him: in all the times they had spent together, through all the faces Victor had worn, this was the closest he had ever come to seeing the person within. The many costumes, the voices, the grins and the jokes, they all distracted and shielded, but they were not real. Charles felt his own walls rising as if in reaction, his spirit coiling, his body tingling with the urge to vanish and escape any risk of being similarly exposed.

"I am not a man with friends, Charles," Victor said. "I gather acquaintances, but never friends."

Charles looked away, leaving the quiet statement to stretch

out between them. It was almost unbelievable. Victor was relaxed, witty, charming, everything Charles wasn't – how could he not have friends? But the person who made acquaintances so readily was not Victor, the grinning rogue who charmed ladies was not Victor, and it was not Victor who enjoyed the companionship of those around him. The empty laughing belonged to his disguises, the cast of puppets he lurked behind. Their doll-like joy did not warm Victor; it only reflected its glossy light on him like a stage onto its audience, dwindling to dusty shadows when the show was over.

Situations like this made Charles uncomfortable. There was too much emotion in the air. He coughed to shatter the silence, then spoke as steadily as he could to Victor's bowed head. "You have at least one friend."

Victor looked up, his young face wide-eyed. "We are still friends?"

"We should not have drunk so much wine. It has made us melancholy."

Looking somewhat lost and entirely without his usual self-assurance, Victor wiped his wet eyes. "Thank you."

"I am not myself." Charles produced a weak smile. "I am sorry for getting so animated."

The other man shook his head. "I'm sorry for misleading you." The serious, true face held for a few moments longer before a familiar smirk tweaked the corner of Victor's lips. "But I swear to you I spoke the truth on at least one count. They are all sour baggages."

Charles couldn't contain a snort of laughter, and Victor beamed. They both returned to their reclining positions in their chairs as if the creases of their argument were already being smoothed flat.

Victor raised his glass. Feeling that he knew what the other man was toasting, although he couldn't quite put it into words, Charles half raised his in return.

Despite all their differences, watching Victor felt somehow like looking in a mirror.

CHAPTER THIRTY-FOUR

1995

Charles heard the front door slam. *The maid.* He was review-ing some thought-provoking experiments he had been conducting on body-temperature Control, but they would have to wait. She would be in here in moments with her inquisi-tive eyes and that damned noisy vacuum cleaner. He swept the papers into a pile and shoved them in a drawer. He cast an eye around the study for any other incriminating evidence, but thankfully the small room was, for once, tidy.

He looked up from his desk as the study door swung open to reveal not the maid but himself standing in the doorway. Or at least someone who looked exactly like him.

"Victor?"

The man who looked like him nodded.

"Very good." Charles chuckled, easing back into his chair. "You made me jump. How did you get in?"

Victor wore an odd expression. He stepped into the room but did not look Charles in the eye. "There's something we have to… something I have to do."

Charles felt a chill tiptoe down his spine. Something was wrong.

The man who looked like him but wasn't approached the desk, and Charles felt as though it wasn't real, as if he was watching a film of himself. But while the rumpled shirt and coat, the thin shoulders and deep-set gaze held a lifetime of familiarity, the gait, expression and darting eyes were entirely unlike his own. Victor unwrapped a bundle Charles hadn't noticed he was carrying. A small pink arm emerged, then another, then a tiny, wrinkled face. Charles gasped. The baby had its ankle circled with a white plastic tag, its saucer eyes now blinking open to gawk at its surroundings. Victor laid it down on Charles's desk, nestled in blankets. Charles stared, speechless, as Victor proceeded to unwrap a worn silver pocket mirror, wipe its grimy face with an end of the blanket and prop it against a book on the desk so that it was facing Charles.

Charles found his voice. "What's going on, Victor? Where did that baby come from?"

Victor stepped away from the desk, and Charles could see he was every inch a replica of himself: his frame, his clothes, his hands, his face. The grey coat that Victor wore was an exact copy of the coat that still hung in his wardrobe upstairs, although the real version was now rather more threadbare after all this time. The copy that Victor wore looked newer, a fresh relic from over two hundred years ago. "Do you see this mirror, Charles?"

Charles glanced at the mirror, seeing his own wide eyes reflected in its thick glass. "Yes?"

Then, as if drawn by a magnet, he found his gaze tugged back to that circle of glass to see it shining brightly enough to blind him, as though it reflected a beam of sunlight that had found its way into the dark room. He tried to turn his head but felt strapped in place, his chin pulled forward and eyelids peeled back for him to stare at the dazzling circle. His mouth felt salty; he thirsted for something. The circle seemed to grow, or perhaps it was shining even more fiercely. He thought he heard Victor speak.

"It's working. I want you to do exactly as I say."

"An Enchantment." The circle continued expanding, the

dusty books and patterned carpet fading to shadows beside its brilliance.

"Yes, it is. Look at me."

"I—I can't." Charles could do nothing but stare at the blazing white circle that was filling his vision. The thirst intensified. Victor's voice was faint, and the room receded until Charles felt like he was floating in the bath of light.

A whisper came from far away. "Not ready yet."

The circle was now all Charles could perceive. It enveloped him; there was nothing but the light – he drank it in, it filled his mind.

"Look at me," a voice murmured. Charles felt an urge to look but couldn't stop gorging himself on the burning light, luxuriating in it spreading through his body, quenching his thirst and warming his limbs. It coursed through him, into his eyes and out to the tips of his fingers and toes.

"Look at me."

The words struck like a hammer blow, the light disappeared in a blink and Charles's head snapped involuntarily towards Victor. He was back in the dusty study in his scratchy armchair, the baby wailing on the desk and Victor standing before him in Charles's own shape with an unreadable expression on his face. Charles knew very simply that he could not look away until Victor allowed it.

Victor nodded. "It worked."

"What is going on, Victor?" Charles heard the tremble in his own voice.

Victor remained impassive. How many thousands of times had Charles looked at that face, his face, in a mirror, and known what he was thinking? Now he knew nothing of what was happening within.

"I want you to do exactly as I say," Victor repeated.

"I don't understand. What did that Enchantment do?"

"Charles, I... Please be quiet."

Charles felt his jaw fall limp. He could no longer talk but his thoughts raced. Why was Victor here? What was he going to do to that baby? He must have lost his mind.

"I have not lost my mind!" Victor spun away and began examining the bookcase.

Charles had a desperate thought to slip from his chair, snatch the baby and run for the door while Victor's back was turned, but it seemed that Victor would know before he had risen from his seat. A grunt sounded from Victor's direction to confirm this.

"Stay there, Charles. Do not escape."

The invisible ropes tightened around Charles so that it was painful even to try to move. He was held fast by a power far greater than he could resist. Victor's Enchantment must be reading his mind and controlling his body.

When the other sorcerer turned back around, Charles noticed that Victor's eyes – Charles's eyes – were reddened. "No, Charles. The Enchantment lets me command you, but the mind-reading is a trick I came up with myself. A new Grey Control. You would be impressed."

If Charles could talk he would have laughed.

Victor blinked, and his forehead wrinkled. "What can be funny about this?"

Charles found his jaw was freed. "Why don't you tell me what you want? You have used this Enchantment to restrain me – it must be important."

Victor slumped into the chair opposite the desk and looked at his hands. The baby's cries had died down to faint gurgles, otherwise Charles would not have heard Victor's next words. "It is important."

"Well then, tell me." Charles was amazed at the sound of his own measured words. He wasn't experienced in managing crises; he was experienced only in spending day after day sitting in this room with his books and his thoughts. Who knew he could cope with such a shocking intrusion? Perhaps the Enchantment was keeping him subdued.

"You've always been calm. You're a good influence on me." Victor turned to look at Charles, a smile on his lips, his cheeks blotchy, his eyes glinting, shining and wet. "I've been living with you for such a long time now."

Charles didn't know what Victor meant, but he felt the power of his words like a weight pushing into his chest, driving the breath from him. He forced a breath in and sighed. "We are friends, Victor. Why are you treating me like this?"

"I have to."

"Have to do what?"

Victor rose and paced the carpet. Charles still could not move his head, so Victor's body passed out of his field of vision each time he stepped too far from the desk, as though Charles was watching a play and Victor was continually exiting and entering the stage. "The idea for the Grey Control came from one of your letters, Charles. You said if we shrank a part of ourselves small enough, we could become nothing more than a tiny splinter in someone else's body. A part of the person, unnoticed, untraceable, but always there. A useful ally."

While the talk of this strange Grey Control was distracting, Charles realised Victor was avoiding his question. Why would Victor want him to do something but not tell him what it was?

"I'll tell you." Victor shook his head, stopped pacing, and when he looked at Charles again his face was blank, his gaze vacant. "I am going to ask you to transform yourself into the shape of this child and erase your own memory."

For a moment the world seemed to slow down. A second dragged by, Charles's thoughts moving like thick mud, Victor's words making no sense in his ears. "I don't understand."

"I don't need you to understand." Victor broke eye contact. "I just need you to do it."

Charles could hear the baby gurgling from its blankets on the desk. "You want me to change into the baby?"

"Yes, completely change. In your letters you say you have found a way to change yourself with Grey Control so that the inside changes too. So that the new body will grow like a real body, as we spoke of before."

"Yes, but I've never—"

"I want you to change into the baby like that," Victor said. "So that you will grow. And then I want you to remove your own memory."

Victor's instructions ran in confused tangles, fragments of their conversation returning again and again to whisper in Charles's ear. *Change into the baby. There's something I have to do. Remove your own memory. It's important.* Charles's insides roiled while his body was tied in place to sit and stare across the desk. "You are going to kill me."

The other sorcerer shook his head. "Your power would transfer to the nearest available Host, who could be much more difficult to cope with."

"You want to control me. Is that it? Am I some threat to you?"

Victor looked at him as though Charles was the one who was being irrational. "You are the only threat to me. You have always been the only threat."

"This is about Fading again? I am not going to take a sorcerer wife, Victor. You must know that – you are reading my mind!"

Victor banged the desk with his fist, just missing the wriggling child. "It has just happened! Verrin and Haris have produced seven children. Seven sorcerers have died."

"What? When did this happen?"

Victor looked at him with raw eyes. "No one suspected they would do this – they are sensible people, like you, Charles – but the desire to have children is an urge they could not resist. They hid the children so that the babies lived and the other sorcerers died. I am safe for today – only a Grey child can kill me – but what happens when you meet a woman sorcerer and feel urges you cannot resist?"

"When is that ever likely to happen?" Somewhere inside, Charles felt the shock at the news of the seven Fadings, but the spiralling bleakness of his situation rendered all other concerns distant and hollow. "You seem to be listening to my mind anyway – you would know before I ever produced a child."

Victor slumped into the chair opposite the desk, and his body slipped back into the shape of the small, wiry man Charles had first met so many years before. "But how will I stop you? You are too strong a sorcerer now." He gestured at the mirror on the table between them. "Only Enchantments can control you. I must use the power I have while I still have the opportunity."

With his heartbeat pounding in his ears, Charles strained against the grip of the Enchantment holding him but could not move a muscle. He tried to summon power to vanish, to move himself by Orange force, to move Victor, to break the mirror, but nothing happened. He could feel the command *Do not escape* sunk deep in his mind, branded on his thoughts by the Enchantment, and any notion he had to disobey was clamped in cold iron before he could even begin.

Was this really how it ended? Charles had thought he had centuries left, to research, to study, to explore the world. "I am your only friend, Victor. You are killing me, whether you think of it that way or not. The person I am will be gone."

Victor was gazing at nothing. He shook his head. "We were never friends. I pretended to be your friend so that I could keep an eye on you. You are just a threat."

"No, that's not true. I know you, Victor."

"You don't."

I do, Charles thought. And he knew Victor must have heard the thought too, through that strange Grey Control he talked about – a piece of Victor hidden within him? He shivered, and stopped struggling against the Enchantment. It was too strong; there was no point.

He knew he might only have a few seconds left, but he couldn't focus on any one thing. His mind wandering, he found himself recalling tiny moments from his long life, cast up before him for a final examination. Flaky red paint on a wooden fence, bitter coffee in a foggy railside café, sharp frost crystals on his fingers plunged in snow, a head on his shoulder, a warm hand through his hair. It was a while before he realised nothing had happened.

"You know, I always liked to hide." Charles closed his eyes and thought of disappearing, becoming a ghost again, a nothingness. "When I was with you I felt visible, and it scared me."

Victor whispered something. Charles thought it was "It

scared me too."

"I am your friend, Victor." A cracked and hollow voice, so unlike his. Was he losing himself already? "You don't have to do this."

Victor looked up. For the first time Charles noticed the large scar that ran from Victor's forehead through his right eye and down his cheek. Had that been there when they first met all those years ago?

"They happen," said Victor. He rose to his feet, his eyes dead. "It all continues. And these things happen." His voice dropped to a whisper. "Do it now, Charles. Change, and then wipe your memory."

Charles bent every fibre of his being to resist, but it was a command; he could not refuse. His mind rent in two, he found some part of himself coolly preparing for the Control to become the baby while another part screamed at him to stop. He would need to condense himself to a smaller size and shape-shift in a deeper way, a biological transformation, so that his new shape would grow from the inside. He wasn't going to adopt a new disguise; he was going to truly change. His body strained at the invisible ropes that held him. His conscious mind reared in futile mutiny and crumbled.

Pulled by unyielding forces, he summoned his power and cast a true changing of himself. He felt his body melt, dissolve, contract and recompose. A full recomposition, his cells transposed, old for new. He had changed shape a thousand times before but it had only ever been skin-deep. This was different – he could feel it was different – every part of him was changed, he was becoming someone else. As his body melted into a new arrangement of blood and lungs and heart, he felt an ache at the loss of himself that was in no way physical. When it was over he was the baby and no trace of Charles remained other than in his mind. The whole process took only a second.

He looked up from the seat of his chair at Victor, through the eyes of a baby. He felt his fragile limbs flailing as he began toppling over, but Victor caught him up in his arms. Charles's sight was blurred and he could not move his head to look at

258

himself but knew he was an exact copy of the child that lay on the desk, a wide-eyed infant in the arms of the one who had brought his end. He couldn't stop himself summoning power to follow Victor's command for the next and final step, but he found some corner of his mind was still free and reached out with Yellow Control to the other sorcerer.

-Victor!

-*What?*

-This will not help you. I will have no memory, but I still might grow up and father a Grey child.

-*You will be easier to control.*

-Where will the new version of me live? Who will look after me? You are making a problem for yourself.

-*Many babies are abandoned – you'll be adopted.*

Charles knew the inevitable was coming, and he felt the pressure build as he was forced to prepare the final Control, but still he groped for an escape.

-What about the real baby? Where will he go?

-*Far away.*

Charles strained to Resist with every inch of his body and power.

-*Goodbye, Charles. I'll be keeping a close eye on you.*

Charles's last struggle collapsed. He released his power for the last time as Charles Ward and erased his own memory. Some part of him realised that although he was going to finally be hidden, and hidden even from himself inside this child, actually that hadn't been what he'd really wanted. He wanted to be with people, to live and talk and laugh. Who would want to be invisible? His thoughts became vague, then vanished into smoke as he tried to chase them. His memories disappeared and his life drained away as he wondered what would happen to him next. He wondered who he would be next. He would have a new life. He would be a new person. This was the last time he would ever truly be himself.

PART TEN
IDENTITY

A few days after Kim's death

CHAPTER THIRTY-FIVE

The train jerked to a halt. It took Elliot a moment to realise where he was, and a few moments more to remember who he was. He was Charles.

Lines of passengers were filing off the train and marching past the window. The white sign on the platform read *Oxford*. Had he been asleep? He stared at his pale, shaking hands. He had been asleep his whole life.

He wasn't Viros; Victor was Viros. He rose from his seat as the train doors slid shut. Why had he dreamt Viros's memories? It didn't matter; he knew now that they weren't his. He was Charles. As if a wall in his mind had collapsed, he was now conscious of the hundreds of years of his life that floated there, that he had never known were locked away inside him. The world looked different through these altered eyes. He had the same body, he was the same person, and yet he wasn't. It was as if he had stepped off the stage after playing a part for so long that he had forgotten he was acting. Millions of moments from his life as Charles weighed on him and shaped his perspective. He felt different, but couldn't tell if it was just his memory changing or his own self. Maybe they were one and the same. As the seconds passed it became harder to remember how he had felt just a few moments before when he was just Elliot; now he was Charles too.

No matter who he was, he was innocent – he wasn't a

murderer. It must have been Viros. Paros was a decoy, and Viros was still alive. He, Charles, had been friends with the notorious killer, the Grey sorcerer who everyone had feared. He felt sick. Only Viros would have been prepared to kill to stop Kim and Elliot's Grey child being born. The train's engine whirred. Elliot decided to go back; he didn't need to disappear any more.

The train pulled away from the station as he was gathering his possessions. The screen of his mobile phone caught his eye before he put it in his pocket. He had a missed call and a text message, both from Holly.

We need to talk. Jay said you've changed your number but I couldn't help trying anyway. Hope that you get this message. I don't want to leave things the way we did the day you disappeared.

He read the message again. *I don't want to leave things the way we did the day you disappeared.*

The day he disappeared? But he had seen her earlier today in his flat. He collapsed back into his seat, staring at the tiny, significant words, questions swirling in his head, answers clicking into place. In his flat earlier Holly had been so different, Elliot had looked for the girl he knew. She had been so cold; she had been changed. An answer clicked. It hadn't been Holly at his flat today – it had been someone disguised as Holly. It had been Viros.

Why had Viros disguised himself as Holly? What did the start of Holly's message mean – why had Jay said that Elliot had changed his mobile number when he hadn't? Why would Jay lie?

His phone dropped out of his hand and he heard it crack as it hit the floor. Memories of Jay flashed past his eyes. A good friend, the best friend, always loyal, always there. Same school, same class, always close. Other friends drifted away to different places and different jobs, but Jay stayed near. Elliot had liked him from the start. That easy grin. That casual manner. That infectious laugh.

A slow and dreadful acceptance uncoiled in Elliot's stomach. Jay was always interested in his jobs, his hobbies, what he was doing, but especially in the girls Elliot dated, and he always wanted details, descriptions, names. Elliot heard Victor's last words to him, to Charles. *I'll be keeping a close eye on you.* He heard Victor's laughter echoing from many mouths. Laughter from a tall, scarecrow-looking man, a young man in an expensive coat, a wiry man with a long scar through his right eye, from all of Victor's disguises. Laughter from Olivia's mouth as Victor raised the sword over Kim. Laughter from Jay's mouth as he and Elliot talked and joked together, year after year after year, echoing, infectious laughter.

The final answer clicked. Elliot vanished, leaving his clothes to flutter to the floor, and flew out of the train through an open window. He had to go back and find Holly – he had to tell someone. Jay was Viros.

* * *

"Did he say where he was going?" Holly asked.

"He said he needed to get away."

Holly toyed with her coffee cup. "I suppose he does."

Across the table Jay smiled in response. His company reminded her of Elliot, and made it seem a little like Elliot was there too. She couldn't help looking around yet again at the customers milling in the café, hoping each half-hidden face would be revealed as Elliot. Ever since that night when he had vanished she had been expecting to find him around every corner, waiting for her with his unkempt hair and lazy smile.

The café chatter washed over them and pooled in their silence. She stared at the varnished-wood table top, tracing its dark lines to where they disappeared beneath her pale hands. She had never had a proper conversation with Jay before; she probably should have made more effort with Elliot's best friend. Perhaps now it was too late.

She had always thought of Jay as an influence Elliot needed to break away from, but she could see now that behind the childish laughter there was a more careful presence, something older, that watched her with an experience and understanding. She trusted him, but she found herself wishing she hadn't met with him. To have confirmation that Elliot had left London and wasn't returning had left her feeling empty, as if all her warmth had leaked away with him.

"Did he say anything about me?"

Jay didn't respond immediately, and Holly wondered if he had heard her over the clamour of conversation, but at last he shook his head. "No, sorry."

She told herself it didn't matter and didn't mean anything. The buzzing of talk increased and pressed in on her. She ignored it, and ignored any suggestion from her trembling fingers that her poise might be crumbling. As it often did at such times, her hand moved to her belly, but she covered the gesture by straightening her top and Jay didn't seem to notice. Perhaps she should tell him. No one knew she was pregnant – it would be such a relief to say it out loud.

For the hundredth time she mentally ran through her options, the logical conclusions unchanged and uncomfortable. She couldn't tell Arthan about the baby; he would know as well as her that it was Elliot's and not his. She had to keep it from the other sorcerers because sorcerer babies were forbidden, despite the fact that Elliot's child would be Grey and so the only person to Fade would be Elliot himself. The thought made her feel sick. How she wished she could talk to him. If he knew about the baby maybe he would come back and they could work out what to do. She glanced across the table at Jay, who was quiet, watching her. Maybe she could trust Elliot's best friend to keep a secret.

"What's up?"

Holly shook her head. "Nothing."

Jay drained his coffee. "You need cheering up." He grinned. "Why don't we go and find a drink of something stronger? I've got a bottle of champagne gathering dust back at mine."

Holly managed a smile. "What are we celebrating?"

"We'll think of something."

Strangely, Holly found herself tempted, but she shook away the feeling. "I can't. Another coffee instead?"

"Right you are." Jay didn't seem offended by her refusal. He set off towards the counter before she could insist that she would pay for the drinks. She sighed and rose from her chair to follow; she couldn't let him pay for everything.

By the time she had squeezed through the throng of tables and pushchairs and the crossing streams of people, Jay was already ordering their drinks. As she approached she saw him reach into his pocket. If she hadn't been so determined to get to him before he opened his wallet she wouldn't have been watching him so closely, and wouldn't have noticed what happened when he drew his hand out. In the split second before his arm was raised she saw a slice of skin peel away from his empty palm and crinkle into the shape of a tattered bank note. Jay passed the bank note to the woman behind the counter, who held it up to the light, opened the till drawer and gave Jay back his change.

When Jay turned round with the tray of drinks Holly hadn't moved. She stood, staring. "Hi! Did you get bored without my witty company?"

"Yes!" Holly forced herself to laugh, praying it sounded natural. "I have to go now though. Sorry." She knew it would look odd to leave after suggesting another drink, but she couldn't think of an excuse and now she couldn't bear to stay a minute longer.

"Oh. OK." Jay glanced down at the drinks with a wrinkled brow, then recovered his smile. "No problem. I'll see you around soon?"

"Of course," Holly said. She tried to smile and failed. "Bye."

She felt the heat rising in her cheeks as he found a space to rest the tray, beamed at her and then hugged her goodbye. She almost ran from the café, feeling even more exposed as she plunged out into the biting air. She didn't look back, but trotted along the street as fast as she dared. She needed space to think.

Jay was a sorcerer. A Grey sorcerer – he had shape-shifted his hand to create money. How could that be? Who was he? She froze mid-step as it all fell into place.

She started moving again, and broke into a run. Belas's offices were closer than Arthan's, so she headed in that direction.

Overhead, she heard a peal of thunder rumble in the clear sky.

CHAPTER THIRTY-SIX

The mists of memory swam around Elizan, hollow voices echoing in her wake as she walked in his body, taking his steps through his life. The outside world glared at her where she nested inside his head, shrank from her in the face of his laughter. Through centuries she lounged and grinned, tasting every breath he drew like it was her own. She flexed his fingers, she shrugged his shoulders, she summoned his power. She was Viros.

-*Why are you still here?*

The interruption shook her concentration and she found herself ejected from Viros's kaleidoscope memories into the shifting blackness of mental space. She sighed, and ignored the question.

-*You said this wouldn't take long, and we're still bloody here. You know all you need to know: Elliot is Viros. Now get out of my head and go after him.*

This woman was relentless. Elizan steered away from the insistent voice and reasserted herself on Viros's memories. It was a challenge to keep one's head clear during such a complex mind interaction; Viros's and Danielle's thoughts intruded on her own like radio static. However, it was vital that she persevered – there was something important she had to find.

-*What? What is this oh-so-important thing you keep going on about?*

-Danielle, please. Let me concentrate.

-I didn't sign up for any of this, you know. Some stupid sorcerer dies and lumbers me with her power, that's bad enough. Using my head as a magnifying glass to look at that spy in your head is worse. I'm not your servant. What are you trying to find, anyway? If you want to help your sorcerer friends, why don't you go and actually help them instead of lazing around here, poking about in my head? I know you're strong enough to stop Elliot – I've seen inside your mind.

-You have learnt so much, Danielle. But please, trust me. I cannot tell what it is, but something is not right. I need to keep looking.

-And if you find it?

Drifting in the world of thought, Elizan watched the years of Viros's memories falling before her like leaves, some green with freshness, some tattered with age, millions of moments cascading over time. There was something in there, somewhere.

-If you find it will you go after him?

-Yes.

At last Danielle's mental voice fell silent, allowing Elizan to give her full attention to the memories. Examining this spy inside her own mind, through the window of Danielle's mind, required a level of mental focus that tested Elizan's Yellow ability to its strained limits. The abundance of Viros's memories that she could access through this captive creature inside her own mind was exhilarating, an uninhibited intrusion into the mind of the enemy who had haunted her for so long. But it was almost too much to contend with. There seemed no way of controlling the tide – the memories spilt into her in a blaring, thrashing torrent, enslaving her senses, spinning her head into his. She felt she must have pawed her way through every inch of his miserable life, and yet so much more remained.

He was different to what she had expected. Or at least what she thought she had expected. It was hard to recall exactly how she had felt when she had lived out there in her own mind, when she had composed herself in that small, peaceful room in her beautiful home and explained carefully to Danielle the method by which they must link their minds. She was spending too long in here – she knew that. It was affecting her.

He wasn't exactly evil. It seemed wrong to allow him this concession even in her own mind, but she had to admit that he wasn't hateful; that emotion did not drive him. It was more an absence of something, a missing part of his psychology that didn't stop him at the boundary of acceptable behaviour and stay his hand when he reached for what he wanted.

It was while she dwelt on him, rifling through the years of his wanderings, that she felt her mind brush past another presence in his memory, a familiar and strong beat in Viros's heart, another person who was instantly recognisable.

That was it!

-What? You found something?

Elizan homed in on the memory like a moth to a flame, unravelling the flickering weeks and days in the twine of Viros's life, to where the branches of thought joined and met at the moment she sought. There! There was a separation, and a merging. Elizan dove into the past and found herself inside Viros's memories once more, looking out through his eyes at a cramped and cluttered cellar room. She sat in his body at a table with another man, a slight man with his hands in his lap and his eyes on Viros, a half-empty bottle of wine between them. The shape of the slight man's mind was clear, his thoughts a pure signature. It was Elliot.

-Him? Not Viros?

There was no doubt: the man was Elliot, and Elliot was not Viros.

The sense of Elliot ran through Viros's memories like veins through living rock, and Elizan was unable to deny the boy's presence was there. His identity was linked to Viros, he was in Viros – he was Viros. But something had never felt right; some part of the rhythm had always seemed off-kilter, muted and distorted, and now she saw why. They were not the same person – they were just linked.

She watched through Viros's eyes as he implanted a tiny Grey hook of himself in his companion across the wooden table and lodged a spy in the man's unsuspecting mind. The man was certainly Elliot, although it seemed he was called Charles at this time. Unknown to Elliot, the spy burrowed deep and settled in his mind just as another of Viros's spies had settled in Elizan's own mind, an invisible thread of power keeping it leashed to its owner.

Elizan shivered with the emotions Viros had felt when the connection was made, was shaken by his disorientation over the spy's awareness and his silent exultation over his success. How many other spies had he implanted in unknowing hosts? She sensed there had been many. She sensed too what Viros himself hadn't realised in his clumsy application of Grey power: the spy he left in Elliot's mind was placed differently to the one he had placed in Elizan's. Viros had never been a good sorcerer, and this Grey trick of his was not thoroughly designed. Both the spy in her head and the one in Elliot's were inserted deep into the consciousness – this was Viros's deceit, his way of slipping unseen behind the mind's defences – but the spy in Elliot's mind made a stronger link, a deeper connection that left a lasting imprint on both him and Viros. They were forever joined from that moment, and in all Viros's memories afterwards, Elizan sensed Elliot's presence coursing through each thought.

They were separate, and yet their minds breathed as one.

-What the hell's going on? You're thinking too fast.

-I am sorry, Danielle. I should not rush the investigation like this. I need to examine this memory carefully, but it seems I have found what I was looking for.

-Elliot is not Viros?

-That is correct. We were mistaken.

-But you said you knew it was him.

-Their minds have been linked, using one of Viros's spies… It is hard to explain.

-Well, don't bother. If you say you've figured it out then I believe you. Now you'd better go.

-Go where?

-Go to get Viros.

-No, I must examine these memories further. Besides, we know now Viros is not Elliot.

-So what? You still need to stop him. How long do you think I'm going to sit here and listen to your prattling thoughts?

-We must carry on. I can find Viros best from afar.

Elizan felt a powerful jolt. She blinked open her heavy eyes to find herself back on the wooden chair in the small white room. Danielle scowled at her from where she lay on the bed.

"Let me back in," Elizan said. "I need to carry on."

"No way." Danielle's lips screwed up. "Time to go."

"Please. Let me back in."

"No!" Danielle flung a pillow to one side and wiped her eyes with a sleeve. "Do you know what you have done to me? I have seen it all through your messing around inside my head! You have poured it all into me! I can feel them dying, all those people."

Elizan leant closer and put an arm on the other woman's heaving shoulder. "I am sorry, Danielle. The mind-linking is intense, especially when one's mind is untrained for it. I should not have put you through this, but the circumstances have become so desperate—"

"I'm going with you."

"I beg your pardon?"

"You heard." Danielle narrowed her eyes. "You need someone with you who's got some guts. I want to find that bastard too. You know what might happen if we don't – I've seen it in your thoughts!"

"Prophecy is an uncertain art. What you saw may not come to pass."

Danielle scoffed. "Don't make excuses. Why don't you tell me the real reason why you don't want to go?"

The real reason. Elizan strangled her own panic with an iron fist of Yellow Control. She spoke in a whisper to the floor. "What reason?"

"Because of that deal you made with Viros."

Elizan looked up, her heart beating. The words to deny it rose to her lips, but she realised it was no use and let her excuses melt away unvoiced. She heaved a sigh. "You know about that?"

Danielle rolled her eyes. "Of course, it kept running through your mind. You found him inside that farmer's mind, the Host, after you thought he had died. And you let him live."

"I—Yes. He said he would never kill again."

"As long as you kept it secret that he was still alive."

Her mouth dry, Elizan dropped her gaze to her own hands folded in her lap. So many years and so many worries, but the same smooth, pale fingers never changed. "I have not told a soul."

"Yeah, I know."

Elizan heard her own voice crack. "I told the Blue girl that Viros lived, when she interviewed me, then I erased her memory of it." She breathed out. "I have ached to share this burden for a very long time."

"Well it's a good job you didn't, because he was watching you all the time through the spy, so he would have known."

Elizan sought for control of herself, but felt mutinous, hot tears in her eyes. "You think it was right, what I did?"

"Sure, why not?" Danielle shrugged. "No more murders for as long as he gets away with it. It was a decent trade. It worked for a long time. But who cares, it's done now. He's killing again, and you need to go and stop him instead of sitting around feeling guilty."

With a broken sigh Elizan sank into her chair, feeling the tears now rolling freely down her cheeks. "That's not it." What was left of her control was crumbling, the mortar cracking, bricks shifting in the walls.

"What?"

"Of course I feel guilty that I helped him hide. I made everyone believe Paros was really the Host, that he was really a sorcerer and that Viros was dead. But I live with my choice." She wiped her eyes. "That's not why I can't leave here."

Danielle frowned. "Then why?"

Elizan rose unsteadily to her feet. "I don't think I can explain. I cannot leave."

"Why not?"

"I cannot."

Elizan made her way to the door, but she heard Danielle rise from the bed to follow her.

"But why not?"

Elizan flushed. "Because I cannot!" She heard herself make a sound somewhere between a cough and a whimper and stumbled out of the door.

She only managed five paces before collapsing into a ball. Danielle's grating voice harangued her, Viros's misty, violent memories surrounded her, the air pressed in on her and she shut her eyes tight. No matter what she saw, no matter how her feelings ripped her apart, no matter what anyone thought, she had to stay here inside her stone walls, where she was safe.

CHAPTER THIRTY-SEVEN

Elliot shot into the grand entrance hall through the cracks around the front door and paused, hovering invisibly. He could tell that Holly wasn't in the house; even with his senses enhanced by Red Control he could hear no movement other than the rhythmic humming of the refrigerator and the murmuring pipes of the central heating system, but something made him decide to check more thoroughly.

He spread his Green awareness through the house, the edges of his senses expanding in a widening net. Elliot hated being there. It had been Arthan's home for decades, a sprawling Georgian mansion crammed with antiques that perhaps reminded him of his youth. Signs of Arthan's relationship with Holly were obvious to Elliot's enhanced awareness: her clothes, her bag, her books, her toothbrush, her lingering, stirring scent.

Charles's awoken mind skirted over the scattered possessions and was drawn to the thick walls that had stood here as long as he had lived, the bricks that had been laid in his youth. He ignored his turbulent feelings; Charles knew how insignificant his lust for Holly became when measured against the vast, evolving surge of history.

He pressed his awareness into every corner of every room, to be rewarded with a deluge of sensations, sounds and aromas. Cracked paint, thick glass, scratchy carpet, stained mug, dusty books, feather pillow, damp glass. He felt pressed up against

277

every part of the house at once, seeping into the solid walls, Holly's and Arthan's memories forced into his senses. Elliot's mind ached, and Charles felt numb, but there was no time to dwell on himself. He had to find Holly and warn her that Jay was Viros before that dry, bleeding feeling in his gut became reality. Violence was coming.

There was no one in the house. The thought of going near the other sorcerers, particularly Arthan, turned his stomach, but he had to find Holly. If she wasn't here she was most likely to be at the office.

Elliot couldn't help lingering for a second longer. He didn't want to look through this window into Holly and Arthan's life, didn't want to know that they had lived here for so long, so happily, but while his Green Control held he was intensely aware of every inch of the house and couldn't drag himself away yet. The evidence of every moment they had shared was a stab in his heart, but he couldn't put down the knife.

Something caught his attention. Under the mattress in the bedroom, an item was hidden. Without needing to be in the room, he could see it as clearly as if he held it in front of his face. A pack of pregnancy tests. Half empty.

-Elliot.

The voice in his head collided with his thoughts. He blinked, and his senses shrank back towards him.

-It is Elizan. I must speak with you.

His physical body coalesced in the entrance hall and Charles gathered himself to try and think straight. Elizan was the only remaining original sorcerer apart from him and Viros. What did she want with him? He had never had a mind conversation but he had studied it years before; it was a simple application of Yellow Control. He formed his response and pulsed it back at Elizan's mind, uncertain of how to address her.

-I hear you, Elizan.

-Please listen carefully. I have located a presence in my mind, a being that was spying on me. I discovered that the spy was a part of Viros, split from him using Grey Control yet linked to his mind by a communicating thread. I have trapped the spy in my mind, blinded it using Yellow Control

278

and examined its memories through the connection with Viros's mind. I know everything, Elliot. I know you are Charles, I know you are not Kim's murderer, I know it was Viros, I know Viros is Jay.

Elliot breathed out. An ally.

-You have to help me, Elizan. All of the other—

-There is more. Viros planted more spies than just the one in my mind. You have one too.

A spy inside him? He couldn't sense anything, but the idea seemed plausible. Charles suddenly remembered that Victor had read his mind using a new Grey Control.

-He is still reading my mind?

-The spy has been within you for many years – it was implanted long before you became Elliot. Viros knows everything you know. I will show you. Please do not resist.

There was a building pressure on Elliot's temples as he felt Elizan extend her power towards him. He tried to relax and let her take control. With a lurch he felt his focus turn inward, and suddenly he was surrounded by murky blackness, examining his own mind using Yellow Control, guided by Elizan's mental hand.

-You cannot see this without help from another sorcerer. It is like a blemish on your face – I must hold the mirror. Do you see it?

Charles could see it, sitting there among the mists of thought. It was like a lump of coal in a pile of apples. Something alien was nestled inside his own mind and yet he had been unaware. It was an odd thing. It almost had the mental presence of a person, a glimmer of the same sentience he felt from Elizan's mind touching his own. Yet he could see it wasn't a person; it was a reduced form of life, a tiny, simple creature lurking inside his brain and absorbing the information it found. A spy.

-You can isolate it so that it sees and hears nothing. It responds to Yellow Control as though it is part of you.

He could see the thread of power she had spoken about. Through the eyes of his sorcery it seemed to glow, a tendril of thought that wound from the spy out of his mind into the distance and connected the creature to its master. Viros.

Charles probed inside his mind with Yellow Control, with Elizan guiding him. When he gripped the tiny spy inside him it felt strangely as though he was seizing a part of his own mind, but a part that thought on its own. He closed his mental hand around the spy and shut down its senses. It remained lodged in him like a cancer but would not overhear anything further from his mind.

-Good. We can talk freely now – Viros is no longer listening.

With a start Elliot remembered what he had been doing when Elizan contacted him. Holly was in danger. He dropped his mental focus and found himself back in the grand hallway. He ran for the door, forgetting for a moment to travel using Grey Control.

-Elliot. What is wrong?

Elliot heaved open the door. There was no time to think. He had to get to Holly before Viros did.

-Elizan, you must come to help. I think Holly is pregnant. With my baby.

-When did you find out? Does Viros know?

Elliot took a step outside the house and just had time to notice a thin figure standing on the other side of the street before he heard a rushing of air and felt a sharp pain in his chest. He looked down to see the wooden handle of a kitchen knife jutting out of his shirt. He lifted his hands to the handle just as his legs weakened and he dropped to his knees.

He squinted at the scrawny figure across the road, metal glinting in its bony hands. The scene seemed too bright, the sunlight burning on every white wall and every car bonnet. Even the pitted and cracked road surface stood out in glossy contrast, the white-painted lines underlining the indistinct shape of his assailant. The way the figure stood with hunched shoulders touched a memory. "Gordon?"

Gordon's hands opened and the two other knives arced through the air towards Elliot. With a hard smack he felt one sink deep into his chest, then another. He coughed and felt thick blood spill from his mouth.

A reedy voice screamed somewhere, but when Elliot lifted

his head again the bright world had blurred into red and grey smears. "I loved her! I don't care if you know!"

Voiceless, Elliot opened his mouth and felt himself keeling over. His body was growing numb. The street was getting dark.

"I stabbed you in the front. I'm not afraid."

The world swirled upside down, Elliot's and Charles's thoughts evaporated, he slumped to the ground and his face hit the pavement with a crack.

* * *

Holly stared at her own deathly pale face in the mirrored lift doors while they creaked, groaned, then finally slid open. She slipped through the widening gap, sped past the vacant reception desk and through the glass double doors to emerge onto the open floor of Briggs and Co.

A thin face appeared from behind a nearby desk. She almost didn't recognise him; he wore the same pressed pinstripe shirt and his usual perfectly sculpted hairstyle, but his lively eyes were now pale, sunken stones. "Holly?"

"Hello, Rupert." Holly realised she was breathless and her legs were aching. Discovering Jay's identity had lent her temporary energy that was now draining away into the thin blue carpet tiles. "Is anyone else here?"

Rupert hurried round the desk to join her, adjusting his glasses as he came. He glanced to the side in the direction of a closed office door, then produced an unconvincing smile. "Er, yeah. I think they're busy."

There was no time for games. Holly gave Rupert only one further appraising look before marching towards the closed door.

"Sorry, Holly, you can't go in there—"

She heard his steps falter as she reached the door. *I can go in there.* She wrenched the door open and surveyed the scene inside.

Perched side by side on metal stools against the wall, staring at her open-mouthed, were Olivia Gale and Sean. What was Olivia doing here? She wore the same red-and-white-streaked tracksuit Holly had seen her wear on the television, as if she didn't own any other clothes, the huge letters *G A L E* marching down her side. Sean wore a tracksuit too, although his was faded and unbranded. In the middle of the small, bare room was a colourful circular rug, and upon it sat Briggs, his legs crossed, his eyes squeezed shut, his hands outstretched over the rug. The scene held still for a second before his eyes flashed open.

"Blast it! You broke my concentration!" He glared up at Holly, then faltered when their eyes met. "Are you OK?"

"What are you doing?"

Briggs's tanned face flushed a deeper shade. She noticed his suit was in disarray and his tie hung half knotted and forgotten around his neck. She had never seen him with even a hair out of place before. From the rug before him he picked up a small object, which looked to be a plain wristwatch, and held it to his ear, but didn't answer.

"He's trying to make an Enchantment," said a voice from the doorway.

"What?" Holly whirled to face Rupert, who winced.

"I know." Rupert rubbed the back of his neck and averted his eyes. "We shouldn't have done it."

Behind her in the room, Holly heard the creak of a metal stool, and then felt a touch on her shoulder.

"Briggs, Rupert and Ian have been researching Enchantments for months." Sean's voice was measured and careful. "We have to use every weapon we have. If they can really make one then we can use it to catch Elliot."

"Oh?" Holly let the syllable hang between them, then turned to face him. Her hairline was barely level with his stony jaw, but she held his eye without flinching. However righteous he would make himself seem now, he was the same red-eyed thug who had broken her legs in his blind rage. She didn't expect an apology from him – he wasn't the type; he would always be convinced of his choices – but she wasn't about to let him forget what he'd done. She looked then to Olivia, who returned her gaze equally, her young face grim.

"I am helping too." Olivia glanced at Sean. "My family need me."

A change of heart, Holly thought, remembering how her phone message to Olivia had been ignored. She cast her gaze around the group, who were all watching her. "Enchantments are dangerous – that's why Elizan banned them."

"I can't even get it to work," said Briggs, still sitting on the floor.

"You've been doing this for months? Why were you researching Enchantments in the first place?"

Briggs didn't look up.

"To sell them," Sean said.

"You idiot!" Holly bit back the rest of the torrent of recrimination on her tongue. She had to stay focused on why she was here, despite the enormity of Briggs's actions. She couldn't believe he would contemplate selling Enchantments to the public. "Does Arthan know about this?"

Briggs nodded. "He said that—"

"Where is he? I need to speak to him."

"At his office. He—"

Holly interrupted him again, this time by walking out of the room past Rupert's lost stare to the nearest desk, where she snatched up the phone. She watched the others talking as she dialled. Had they always been so vacant, so purposeless?

"This is Arthan."

"It's me."

"Holly." There was a brief silence at the other end of the phone. They had barely spoken since the night Elliot had disappeared. "Something's wrong."

"Yes. You're chasing the wrong person. Elliot is not the murderer."

"Yes, he is." As always Arthan's young voice held no doubt, he that spoke with pure certainty. Had that been what she'd found attractive in him? He provided answers in an uncertain world. "Where are you? I can feel something... Danger."

"At Briggs's."

"I'm coming. I'll make Yellow contact. Holly – are you

OK?"

Why was everyone asking her that? She opened her mouth to tell him she didn't need anyone's help then realised that wasn't why he was asking. He was asking because he sensed that something in her had changed; the tightening cords of threat were forming a knot of cold steel inside her, an unexpected inner hardness. "I'm fine."

The line went dead. Holly opened her mind to receive Arthan's contact, replaced the receiver and returned to the office room where Briggs, Rupert, Olivia and Sean were milling around. Arthan's voice sounded again, but this time inside her head.

-I'm on my way now. Has Elliot contacted you?

-No, but Jay has, Elliot's friend. He is Viros.

-Elizan killed Viros years ago. This murder is not Viros's doing, it is Elliot's – wait, Elizan is contacting me.

Holly watched Rupert loiter in the corner, picking his nails. He had always been so composed, but it seemed this crisis had pulled him apart. Which personality was a front and which was a temporary aberration? Perhaps you only meet your true self when your defences are pulled down. Arthan's voice returned.

-Viros is alive. Elizan has just told me.

-So you didn't believe me, but you believe Elizan?

-I don't believe all she says. She thinks, as you do, that Elliot is innocent. He has fooled both of you. But it is true that Viros lives – I can feel the truth of that.

-He hasn't fooled us—

-Holly. Viros is coming for you.

He was coming. The news sank into her skin and bypassed her usual thought processes to condense somewhere in her stomach, a focused, emotionless resolve. "Viros is coming."

Rupert's mouth fell open, while the others just stared.

-Stay out of sight and stay with the others. I'll be there as fast as I can.

Olivia and Sean got up, looking around. Holly stepped into the centre of the room while Briggs and Rupert shrank into themselves. She felt a rising within her, her power summoning in readiness, her fingers flexing. It was time to be ready. He was coming. She picked up the wristwatch from the floor and examined its white face, while in her mind she sent a message back to Arthan.

-I saw Jay use Grey sorcery, Arthan. He is a Grey sorcerer like Elliot. Jay killed Kim to stop himself Fading when her baby was born. He is Viros.

Holly knew Viros would try and kill her if he knew she was pregnant. She guessed he must know already – that was why he was coming. But she wouldn't tell Arthan, not yet.

-*Think logically. You want to believe that Jay is Viros and Elliot is innocent. Do you have proof?*

-I don't need proof – nothing else makes sense. I am right.

Holly turned her attention to Rupert again, who flinched under her glare. "Where is Naomi?"

"Downstairs," he said. "Shall I get her?"

"Yes. We need her help."

Briggs chuckled and shook his head. "I don't think Naomi will be much help."

Rupert disappeared out of the doorway and Holly spun to face Briggs. "What the hell were you thinking?"

Briggs spluttered, his usually slicked-back hair falling into his eyes. "What? What's that?"

Holly grimaced at the sight of him. She had heard rumours in the past that creating Enchantments could have side effects. "The Enchantments. You tried to make Enchantments to sell to humans. How could you?"

Briggs was saved by the sound of the door opening behind Holly, and she turned to see Marrin thrusting her way into the room with Ian hovering behind her, his pale face visible over her squat frame.

"What's going on?"

"Marrin! How terrific to see you!" Briggs leapt to his feet, his eyes bulging. "Viros is coming! We need your help."

Marrin took in the room with a sweep of her tiny, piercing eyes. "Where is Arthan?"

"On his way," said Holly.

"Gordon?"

"I don't know."

Marrin turned and marched back out of the door.

"Marrin!" Briggs said. "Where are you going?"

"I'm going to find Gordon," Marrin said over her broad shoulder, and then she was gone.

"Marrin!" Briggs's face was reddening. "Stay here with us!"

Holly turned from him. He was no use to her in his present state. Inside her head, Arthan's voice whispered at her.

-Elliot has poisoned your mind. You twist the facts to suit his lies. He has such a hold over you. If Jay is a Grey sorcerer it does not mean Elliot is innocent. There is a far simpler explanation. Elliot is Jay, and Jay is Viros. They are all the same person. He can change his shape, he can split himself in two, or in any way he wishes.

Holly turned the dial on the wristwatch and watched the hands revolve. Briggs had been trying to implant Orange Control in this innocuous piece of metal. If he had succeeded, any amount of power he wished could have been loaded into the dial, enough to overcome any sorcerer's Resistance. Could the creation of such a weapon be justified?

-Elliot has proven that you cannot trust him. He is not what he seems. Elliot is the murderer – you must accept it. He seduced Kim and then killed her to save his own skin. He is dangerous and he must be stopped.

Holly turned to Briggs, who was looking at the floor, his eyes glazed. "What sort of Enchantment have you been trying to make? Briggs!"

He blinked and seemed to wake up. "Orange." He cleared his throat while she waited for more. "When you stop the watch it should stop the targeted person from moving. But the Control won't stick."

"I want you to stop making it."

"Look, I know it's illegal. I just thought—"

"Teach me the method instead."

Briggs's mouth hung open. "Teach you?"

-Elliot has deceived you – I know it is not your fault. He made you betray me. You cannot see him clearly. But your relationship with him is not real – you must not stay with him, you must come back to me. Listen to me.

She sought inside herself for the strength to tell Arthan

what she had always avoided. *I don't love you any more. I'm sorry. I was weak to go to Elliot, weak not to tell you, and you shouldn't forgive me. I owe you the truth. I don't want to be with him, and I don't want to be with you.*

Even in this inner mind conversation, where she didn't have to sound the words aloud, she couldn't quite manage to say it. But she felt like he had realised anyway.

She nodded to Briggs. "Teach me. I will make a Blue Enchantment, one that will do more than stop Viros from moving."

There was silence in the room, and silence from Arthan in her mind. For once, there was silence inside her too. No voice of doubt, no inner talk, no questions. She knew what she had to do.

-I'm sorry, Arthan.

CHAPTER THIRTY-EIGHT

Sean could feel his power coursing through him, his hackles rising and his muscles bunching. Arthan had sent him and Olivia a mind communication, filling in the missing information Holly hadn't had time to provide. Viros was behind it all, he was still alive, and he was the one who had murdered Kim. Worst of all, he had walked among them disguised as a friend, calling himself Elliot. Sean's blood throbbed with red heat. Finally, he would avenge his sister.

He glanced across to the other side of the entrance, where Olivia lounged against the brick wall. Stationed in the grey-slabbed street outside Briggs & Co's glass doors, they were the only barrier between those within and the approaching danger. He knew his sister's lidded eyes concealed a watching readiness, an instinctive ability to react fuelled by her Red power. People must assume her scrawny, girlish limbs meant she was weak; they would have no idea what she was capable of. He respected her strength. Although she hadn't said so, he knew she respected him too; he had tried to kill her because Naomi had told him she was the enemy, and in his position she would have done the same. It was the Red way, the way of action. Seek your objectives and accomplish them, seek your enemies and destroy them. It must have been his determination to avenge Kim that inspired Olivia to join him.

When he'd fought his Red sister he had found her a close

match for his strength, but now he had the right target it would not be anything like an even contest. He and Olivia were an unstoppable force. They would grind Elliot's bones with their fists.

He watched empty-eyed pedestrians hustle along the pavement before him, heads ducked, coats wrapped tight, mouths hanging loose. They were sheep intent on their mundane agendas. They had no idea they were passing within touching distance of real power. Sean cast his gaze across them as they trailed by, the fading light no hindrance to his Red eyesight, and watched for any sign of *him*.

A wry voice sounded behind him. "And how exactly would you see me?"

Sean and Olivia spun to see Elliot standing behind them in the office reception area, just a few feet away. He was smiling, as though he was still a trusted work colleague and not a known murderer. Sean tensed to pounce but noticed Olivia make a slight motion with her hand. *OK, we bide our time.*

Elliot laughed, a childish, grating sound. "Red sorcerers are always so confident. An unstoppable force!"

Sean growled. "You crept past invisibly, like a coward."

"I did." Elliot grinned. "But actually, I need to ask you something." He coughed, and looked at the floor, then back at them. "Where is Holly?"

Sean gasped as something took hold of him and an unseen force moved his lips against his will. "She's on the second floor, in Room 4."

Elliot nodded. "Thank you."

"Now!" Olivia leapt towards Elliot.

Sean surged across the space between him and his target, his Red power flooding his limbs. He swept his colossal arm forward with enough strength to crush Elliot's face.

Split seconds before contact Sean heard a crack and a scream and felt the rush of air as Olivia was hurled aside with immense force. Impossibly fast, Elliot's hands were on Sean's neck and he found himself held to the floor on his knees. Elliot's fingers dug into his shoulder and Sean heard the sharp snap of a bone. Pain was spreading through him somewhere, but it was numb and distant. What had happened? Pinned on his side, he battered Elliot uselessly, his blows seeming to fall on solid rock rather than flesh, while his opponent murmured to himself.

"I have stopped an unstoppable force."

"Viros!"

Sean was unable to look away from the floor, but he recognised Holly's voice.

"A stapler?" Elliot chuckled. "What are you going to do with that?"

There was a crunching sound, and something exploded.

* * *

Holly watched the man who looked like Elliot topple backwards, his head a tangled red mess of flesh, Sean sliding from his hands. She crunched the stapler again. Elliot's leg erupted in a cloud of blood. Holly crunched the stapler again. His shoulder exploded.

"I'm going to kill you," she answered in a whisper.

She reached the foot of the stairs and kept walking towards him. As soon as she had heard the sound of his voice at the entrance she had come for him, and as soon as she had descended within eyeshot of the entrance he had seen her, but he hadn't thought her a threat. She used the stapler again. And again. And again. She gazed at the body in front of her as it melted and exploded. She had thought she wouldn't be ready to do it, that she would hesitate, but she didn't falter and continued crunching the stapler. She wasn't scared; she wasn't a meek Blue sorcerer. She wasn't another of Viros's victims; she wouldn't leave a Host in her wake. She thought of her father, unsuspecting of his future until power was thrust into him. She thought of him Fading, when his body had curled up in her arms. Viros hadn't killed her parents but he had killed many other parents, and their children had felt what she felt. The emptiness. She crunched the stapler.

She watched the violent results as the sorcery in the stapler

291

unleashed, over and over, the Blue Control to create matter. The same Blue Control everyone thought was so harmless, so useless, in its usual small dose. Once Briggs had explained the method of creating an Enchantment she found she had an instinct for the process that Briggs lacked, and she had realised how Blue sorcery would lend itself to creating what she needed: a weapon. With an Enchantment, the Resistance of any victim could be overcome no matter how powerful they were, and the size of the dose was limitless. It was all too easy to prime the stapler to create a large quantity of explosive material inside the body of whoever it was pointed at. Adding a burst of fire inside and throughout the material produced a concentrated and ferocious explosion.

The body before her was no longer a body – it was a soup of guts, bone and blood. Sean scuttled out of the way of the spreading mess, and Holly noticed Olivia had regained her feet and was watching with her hand over her mouth. A rank, wet, meaty smell rose from the slick floor, and when Holly looked down she saw her trousers were drenched brown and red, but she kept crunching the stapler as she marched on, each explosion spraying her with more of his blood.

Was he dead?

The stapler reached the last of its staples and she stopped, breathing hard. The Enchantment clicked emptily in her hand, but no more explosions came.

She watched the murky pool swill around her feet. Ripples from the last explosion ran across its dark surface and stilled.

"What happened?"

It was Arthan. He pushed his way through the glass doors into the entrance hall, his face white as he took in the bloody carpet covering the marble floor.

No one answered him. Sean and Olivia stood staring at Holly. They both looked unsteady on their feet, and most likely had some broken bones, judging by the sounds Holly had heard during the fight.

"Holly." Arthan stood before her. He looked at the stapler for a long moment. "An Enchantment."

"Yes."

He glanced again at the scattered remains. "That was Viros?"

"Yes." She let no doubt creep into her tone; it had to be him. Viros had worn Elliot's body, but Elliot wouldn't have hurt Sean and Olivia like he had. She could question herself, she could assume that he was acting in self-defence, as it was true they had attacked him and not the other way round. But it had to be him. She refused to listen to the voice that insisted she didn't know who she had just killed.

Arthan lowered his voice. "Are we over?"

She nodded.

"We need to talk about it." His eyes were wide and shining. He looked more than ever like an adolescent.

Holly looked at the pool of blood again. It was dark, dark red. "Let's go back upstairs."

* * *

"They cannot stop him."

At the sound of Elizan's voice, Danielle looked up from her suitcase with a start. It was the first time the woman had spoken in about an hour; she had been sitting there in that golden gown with her head hanging as if she'd passed out. Danielle had almost forgotten she was there. She tossed a pile of crumpled clothes into the case. "Could you stop him?"

"If I was there, perhaps. I don't know."

"Then why don't you go to help?"

Elizan didn't reply. Danielle scoffed, and scooped up another bundle of clothes. She couldn't wait to escape this room; it had been her prison for the last few weeks. She'd seen enough white walls and heard enough soft music to last her a lifetime. What she needed was a battered old sofa, a television and a fag. After such a long time away from home, she might even be able to spend an hour in Scott's company without slapping his stupid, smug face. But the best part of all would be to get away from this ridiculous drip of a woman.

"I'm scared to leave."

Danielle stopped packing and stared at Elizan's bowed head. "What?"

"I'm scared to leave this house."

She was sitting in the same chair she had perched on beside the bed ever since Danielle had known her, wearing the same regal outfit, the same perfect, rippling hair, but she looked a lot smaller now. Just a normal person.

Danielle dumped herself on the bed and cracked her knuckles while she turned things over in her head. "Why?"

The slim shoulders gave a small shrug. "I don't know. After so many years in this place... time has changed me. I only exist in here. All my Yellow sorcery, and I cannot even overcome the fear in my own mind. I am so helpless, I just can't—"

"You just need to get out there." Danielle blew a gum bubble that swelled until it burst. "You're stuck in a rut."

For some reason Elizan smiled, finally looking up from the floor. "You are uniquely perceptive."

"Am I?" Danielle wondered what the hell that meant.

"You are." Her smile vanished again. "But I cannot leave here. I wish I could. Viros must be stopped."

Danielle grunted in agreement. "He's better off dead, that one."

"They all think I am so strong." Elizan croaked a laugh while tears rolled down her white marble cheeks. A small whimper came out.

"This is pathetic." Danielle stood up. "I've had enough of your whingeing."

Elizan sniffed. "I know you want to leave. I won't stop you."

"You're coming with me." Danielle grabbed Elizan's slender wrist and yanked her out of the chair. The woman stumbled and almost tripped over her gown, but Danielle grabbed the other arm and pulled her to her feet.

"Danielle! Stop!"

"No. We're going, now." Danielle marched to the door, dragging Elizan behind her, her fingers dug tight into Elizan's wrist. The woman flailed and whimpered but didn't break away.

Why wasn't she using her sorcery to fight back? Danielle knew she couldn't force Elizan to do anything, but she dragged her anyway. "It's time to do something. You know what you need to do and you're going to do it now. You're going to leave this house and you're going to stop Viros."

CHAPTER THIRTY-NINE

"I don't think he's dead," Rupert whispered.

Ian turned his face towards Rupert, the puckered scar winding into view. "Why?"

"A bad feeling."

They were sitting side by side on the floor on the edge of the open office space of Briggs & Co. Rupert watched the blue carpet swirl in time with his stomach and heard a sound like a mixture of a ringing telephone and a cackling laugh. He leant back against the wall to stop himself pitching forwards. He tasted vomit. He felt like he always did when the Premonitions took hold of him, although this time there were no visions, just an emotional foreshadowing of what he knew was to come. It didn't feel good.

"They know he's not dead. Look at them." Rupert gazed at Holly and Arthan, who were still pacing up and down, occasionally leaning close and muttering a few words.

How long had it been since Holly and Arthan had burst up the stairs to announce that Viros had never died, he had come to kill Holly and he was now downstairs reduced to a puddle of bloody remains? Five minutes ago? It felt like it had been hours, each idle minute stretching further and further. There was nothing to do but scuttle about like rats awaiting the impending flood.

Arthan had sent Sean and Olivia away to recover from

their injuries, although Rupert had sensed their unsteadiness was less about broken bones than broken minds. The fearless Red sorcerers.

They weren't the only ones willing to escape. After teaching Holly how to make the Enchantment, Briggs had shut himself in an office and hadn't emerged. Naomi was wrapped in a world of her own, slunk against the wall with her head bowed, while Rupert and Ian had stopped resisting and sunk to the floor in exhaustion. They were all finding their own way to shut out the bitter taste that swam in the air, the sense of what could be coming. Viros's body had been destroyed, but no one was convinced it was over. He was either dead or he couldn't be stopped; they were waiting to find out which.

Rupert reminded himself again that Viros was looking for Holly, not him. The sensible course of action was for him to get up and walk out. He had nothing to offer Holly as protection; sacrificing himself was completely without reason. *Get up, Rupert.* His legs didn't obey. *Get up.* Some idiotic sense of conformity kept him here with the rest of them. It couldn't be bravery; he didn't feel brave. He felt like his heart was chasing his stomach and his muscles had turned to water.

"He might be dead." Ian was looking at him. He smiled, making his scar twist. "We've already established your predictions are useless."

"I know."

"I was joking."

Rupert nodded. "I know."

Was this the first time in his life he couldn't bring himself to see the funny side? Maybe he had been deceiving himself all along. Laughter was a shield against the truth: life was horribly serious. "I'm sorry about your face, Ian. I shouldn't have laughed when it happened."

"I'm glad it happened." Ian traced a finger down his face, following the gnarled contours of his wound. "It tore a hole in my mask. Now I see the real scars. Everything we see is an illusion – you cannot see someone by looking at them. No one is who you think they are."

298

Rupert hugged his knees. He knew he should say something; he sensed that his friend was spiralling deeper into some dark place and it wouldn't be long until he was out of reach. But all he could think of was death. His predictions were useless – he knew this with a calm and logical conviction. The accurate predictions were indistinguishable from the false ones. But he also knew, with a contradicting certainty that came from somewhere else inside him, that what he was feeling shuddering through his bones was going to happen. What use was knowing anything when his own fallible mind gave him falsities as knowledge? All he could rely on was his instinct for the truth. "We're going to die."

"Elizan will save us."

There was no trace of concern in Ian's voice. *Is he trying to reassure me or does he really believe it?*

Rupert stared at his pale, thin, shaking hands. "I hope so." He knew she wouldn't.

* * *

Arthan paced up and down the office floor. He was surrounded by incompetence. Naomi, Rupert and Ian were slumped on the floor in useless heaps and seemed resigned to accept whatever fate Viros chose to deliver to them. Briggs had not only surpassed his usual idiocy by breaking the ban on Enchantments in an attempt to wring himself some additional profit, but when the opportunity had arisen for him to put his dishonourable project toward a worthwhile end he had failed to produce anything! Now he was hiding in an office with his brain unhinged from his dabbling in Enchantments, of no use to anyone. Marrin had abandoned them all to go and find Gordon for some incomprehensible reason, and Sean and Olivia had been sent running with their tails between their legs. It was only Holly who had impeded Viros with any material effect. She didn't let it show, but she had always been strong. Arthan knew her outburst about wanting to be on her own was just a symptom of the strain she was under. He would give her time.

The sense of danger surrounded him like a palpable smell.

Despite how convincingly Holly had destroyed Viros's body, every instinct warned him it was too early to assume they were safe. Ever since Kim's murder, Arthan had sensed a dark presence in every shadow, and the discovery that Elliot had been the murderer had given a name to the enemy. But now that Elizan had revealed that Viros lived, it changed everything. Viros was mindless. It had been so long since the days when Viros had roamed the country that Arthan had put it all out of his mind long ago, but he could never forget the sheer callousness shown in those crimes. Viros had no respect for anything, or for anyone; he had killed people merely because they got in his way. He would not be easily stopped. Arthan had sent mental messages to Elizan requesting she come to their aid, but had so far been unable to connect with her. They needed someone with her experience and power. A First Caster to stop a First Caster.

There was a gasp, and Arthan whirled around. Like some hideous, stricken moon, Naomi's pale face rose from her lap. "The blood's gone!"

"What do you mean?" Holly said.

"The insects in the entrance hall – they've been watching. They just told me the blood on the floor is all gone!"

He is coming. Arthan took in the silent faces around him with a final glance. He knew that despite their knowledge of the man within, they couldn't stop seeing him as the boy standing before them. His immature body had always held him back, but he succeeded in spite of it. He was still the one they looked to for direction. "I'll stall him. You three – go with Holly, take the back stairs."

"You can't stop him, Arthan," Holly said, her green eyes unwavering. "We may as well stay together."

Arthan addressed Rupert. "Remember Holly is his target. Don't split up – stay with her."

"OK." Rupert stood up, slowly, his eyes like saucers.

"Go!" Arthan said.

Holly gave him a hard look, then turned on her heel and walked towards the door that led to the back stairs. Ian, Rupert and Naomi scuttled after her. Arthan grimaced. He knew they wouldn't provide her with any meaningful protection. It was down to him.

He wiped his clammy hands on his suit and looked around, but could see no one. He reached out with Yellow Control but sensed nothing. He wondered if Viros was standing inches from his face. He swallowed and began moving through the tables.

The blue carpet tiles crunched as he crept over them. The desks were still piled with papers for a normal day's work and the computers and printers still hummed. A phone rang, the insistent rings punctuating the silence.

When he was halfway across the room the double doors slid open. With his hands in his pockets, smiling as though he hadn't a care in the world, Elliot stepped into the room and raised his eyebrows at Arthan. "Are you looking for me?"

Arthan didn't reply. His power roared alive inside him at the sight of that smug face, the memory of discovering Elliot was the killer springing fresh and livid into his mind: the rumpled bedsheets, Holly's flushed face, Elliot's hand on her arm. He twisted the searing fire inside him into sharp Red Control – toughened his skin, sharpened his senses – and then summoned more power to try and predict Elliot's next move.

He was about to cast a Control to invade his enemy's mind when a man materialised next to Elliot. Arthan paused. It was another Elliot, identical to the first. The same shabby clothes, the same ruffled hair, the same lean face, but a different expression. The new Elliot's eyes twitched back and forth; the first Elliot smirked.

The second Elliot was the one who spoke next. "This man isn't me, Arthan. He is Viros."

A ploy. Arthan forced Yellow Control into the first Elliot's mind. He passed inside and found the information he sought, then glared at the second Elliot. "I have just read your friend's mind – I know the truth. He is Viros, and so are you. You are both a part of him."

"You're wrong," the second Elliot said. "Why do you think

301

you can read his mind? Viros is a First Caster — you can't read him. He is making false thoughts for you to read."

Arthan scoffed. "Yellow Control cannot be used to make false thoughts. And I can read any sorcerer other than Elizan, First Caster or not."

The first Elliot was still grinning.

"He is using Grey Control, not Yellow," the second Elliot said. "Try to read me instead."

Arthan saw no reason not to. All this conversation just bought Holly more time to escape. He extended his power towards the second Elliot... but met nothing. The well of silence around him sent Arthan's thoughts spiralling. Why couldn't he read him? If he couldn't read the first Elliot either and he really had been shown false thoughts, what was the purpose of the deception?

"I am stopping you with Resistance." The second Elliot glanced at the first. "I am a First Caster, like Viros. I didn't know who I was until now. My name is Charles Ward — that's my real name."

Arthan ignored his churning inner questions. He could not waver now. "You try to hide behind other names, but you cannot escape who you are and what you have done. You are Viros." He glared at them both. "You are both Viros, one person in two bodies. And your disguise is not even very convincing — only one of you is talking."

"He is Viros! He killed Kim, not me!" The second Elliot trailed off and looked at his companion, who continued to grin. "It's a decoy," he said. Then he vanished.

A moment later the first Elliot vanished too, and Arthan was alone. He felt himself growing hot, and clenched his fists. Viros had been within touching distance and had slipped through his fingers. He swore and kicked a nearby desk.

He sent his power around the office floor but already knew he wouldn't sense anyone there. Viros would be on his way after Holly. Elizan said she didn't know why Holly was Viros's target, but she did know, and Arthan knew too. Despite the risk to herself and others, despite any love she still felt for Arthan,

Holly must be pregnant with Elliot's baby. Now that Arthan admitted this to himself, he didn't feel the expected storm of emotion, only a cold, dead fear of the consequences. Viros would do anything to stop a Grey sorcerer being born. His heart pounding, Arthan turned and ran for the back stairs.

He sent power into his own mind, pouring ice on his own feelings with Yellow Control, but his thoughts remained in disarray. The words of the second Elliot swam in his head. *I didn't know who I was until now.*

If each of them really had been a separate person, then they couldn't both be Viros. If Viros was the one in disguise, then who was the other? Elliot? Charles Ward?

Could he have been so wrong?

* * *

Elliot hurtled invisibly towards the group ahead. At his desperate speed everyone seemed to be moving in slow motion, other than the invisible presence he followed, which pelted through the air as fast as he did. The four ahead had barely made their way out of the back office door – Naomi cringed behind the corner of a nearby wall, Ian and Rupert were fleeing in the direction of the main street, and Holly was slowing to a halt. They were not in eyeshot yet, but Elliot could see them with his power as though he stood at their side. Rupert flung a wild-eyed look over his shoulder to scream at Holly to keep running, but she ignored him and turned to face her pursuer. Elliot didn't know if she could sense his approach. The presence ahead of him reached her and materialised as a familiar figure. A wiry build, jeans and a polo shirt, a shaved head and a wry grin. Jay.

While Elliot sped towards them a thin metal spike grew from Jay's arm and lengthened and sharpened into the shape of a sword. The hilt detached from his body and dropped into his hand, and he hefted the weapon in the air.

Holly was standing unmoving and unarmed. Elliot could see she had no Enchantment, no defence, but she was holding her chin high, looking at Jay.

Elliot asserted his physical body behind them, just as the sword came down upon Holly. "Jay!"

The sword stopped. Jay turned to look at him, smiled and lowered the weapon. "Hi, El."

Elliot felt himself sway where he stood. He had done it; he had got here in time. Although he had no plan for what he would do now he was here.

Hi, El. Should it have been "Hi, Charles"? Elliot and Charles swirled in the same body and thought with the same brain. He was a mess, a tangled web of screaming memories and echoing fears. He hadn't recovered from Gordon's attack, either in body or mind. How had Gordon found such capacity to hate him? He had died, bleeding on that hot pavement, and now he stood here. His heart raced, his blood pounded. His voice came out thin and shadowy. "Put the sword away, Jay."

Jay smiled. His old, familiar Jay smile. "No problem, mate. No problem."

The sword shrank back into Jay's body, the metal glinting as it disappeared into his arm. Holly staggered backwards although she hadn't been touched, as if she had been held in place by invisible hands.

The three of them stood there for a moment. Rupert, Ian and Naomi were nowhere to be seen. There was no one else in the narrow alley, no sound but the muted hum of traffic in the street beyond. Elliot tried to comprehend that this was the same friend who he trusted above all others, who had been about to kill Holly. He couldn't think of anything appropriate to say. "Why do you use a sword?"

Jay shrugged. "Habit."

That shrug made Elliot's jaw clench. He told himself to stay calm but couldn't help spitting his words out like they were poison. "So you are Viros."

Jay pulled a face. "I always hated those stupid names. I'm Victor, not Viros."

"I remember everything now." Elliot found he was shaking, his words coming with difficulty. "You've been lying to me my whole life – both my life as Charles and my life as Elliot."

Elliot sent a silent message to Holly to run, but she either ignored him or didn't hear. She stood rooted to the spot, her eyes gleaming as she stared at Jay.

Jay sighed. "What can I say, El? It wasn't personal."

"It was personal!" Elliot knew he should keep his concentration; Jay only needed a second, sword or no sword, to kill Holly. But he couldn't stop his voice rising to a shriek. "How long did you have that mirror Enchantment? How many decades were you planning on betraying me?"

Jay made a small chuckle. It sounded hollow, empty. "As if I plan. You know me. I collected Enchantments because they were useful. I only decided to take your memory away when all those other sorcerers Faded. It put me on edge."

"Put you on edge?" Holly's face had gone red. "My family died that day!"

Jay looked back and forth at them. He ran a hand through his hair. "I wanted to keep you under control." He jerked up his head and laughed, a loud bark, harsh and incongruent in the quiet alley. "Despite my best efforts, you found the other sorcerers! Took a job with them, and managed to get two of them pregnant!" Elliot noticed Holly's hand move to her stomach while Jay grinned, wrinkling his eyes. "Never would have picked you out as a ladies' man."

Charles had never been a ladies' man. He had never been a man for people at all; he was more comfortable alone. Elliot shook his head, another memory coming back to him. "Those messages at work, that dead bird – you sent them."

Jay blinked, and the grin evaporated. "You're my biggest problem." He sighed. "If only I still had that mirror Enchantment. I could control you now and avoid this debate."

"A debate? This isn't a debate."

Jay's eyes flickered as he stared at Elliot. "You're right." Even as he spoke, he lunged forward at Elliot.

Elliot's power ignited without thought. He swerved aside to avoid Jay's swinging arm. His body had reacted before his mind and it took him that second to realise that Jay had been trying to hit him. Something turned in his stomach. He swung

305

a fist back at Jay's face. For those first few moments it was just like every time they had brawled in the past, when a discussion had got overheated or they had both had too much to drink. But in each of those times they had fought as humans, and now they fought as sorcerers. Jay ducked the fist and swung his own towards Elliot in a blur. Elliot blocked with an arm hardened to stone while his other arm whirred back to counter. He heard a crunch as his fist met Jay's bones, but the injury didn't slow Jay down; he cut at Elliot's throat with a scything hand. Elliot felt something crumple in his windpipe and staggered backwards, choking, then leapt at Jay again. With a wild shriek Holly hurled herself at him too, but Jay dodged them both and danced away.

Holly was screaming something, her face flushed and raw.

Elliot ran after him, his head pounding, tasting blood in his mouth. He managed to entangle his leg in Jay's and sent him to the floor in a heap. He closed upon him, but Jay writhed away and regained his feet. As he grappled for a hold on Jay's body, Elliot heard his voice in his mind.

-You're going to kill me to save Holly. I'm going to kill Holly to save myself. We're the same.

Something in these words made Elliot truly lose control. He didn't know or care why he was fighting any more. He just wanted to fight. He ducked inside Jay's defences and pelted him with blows that were glanced aside, sending him off balance. Elliot fought with savage instinct, the speed of his own movements becoming too fast for his eyes to follow. He felt himself hurtling around the alley, heard windows breaking, brick walls cracking. He heard someone screaming and thought it was his own voice. He smelt fire. He saw clouds of ragged smoke rising and showers of jagged stone, and felt the pavement crack beneath his feet. He battered Jay blindly, senselessly, knowing it made no difference. The memory of Gordon's knife in his chest was still lurid in his memory, and while the searing pain and seeping blood had been real, it had not lasted. Elliot's and Jay's injuries from this fight would not last either. Even if Jay's body was physically destroyed he could use Grey Control to reconstruct himself again. Elliot could not harm Jay and Jay could not harm him, but he fought anyway.

-*It's going to happen. I have to protect myself.*

Elliot clenched his teeth and pushed his strained muscles to work harder. Their fight had taken them a distance along the alley away from Holly, but if Elliot let Jay slip past he would be upon her in a second. There was no physical force that could impede them but each other.

Without warning Jay vanished, and without a thought Elliot vanished too. He could still sense Jay with his power, he could still fight him, but the ferocity of their battle was no longer limited by their physical environment. Air resistance had been limiting their speed and the raw matter of the physical world had been limiting the hardness of their bodies. Now they were insubstantial, pure power in the air. They were no longer of the physical world; they occupied the same space but moved through it like ghosts. Elliot saw the scene of destruction they had caused in the alley as though he looked through a glass screen: a grey veil had fallen over the world – the rubble and splintered glass and twisted metal didn't look like they could be real.

Unhinged from the world, their strikes and parries were thrusts of pure force, limitless in their power and intensity. For an instant Jay broke from Elliot's grip and swept towards Holly. Elliot surged after him and managed to slow his progress, and then contain him again. For a moment Holly was just a few feet away, still screaming at the air, then Elliot landed a violent blow on Jay that sent him cannoning away from the alley into a bustling street. Vacant-eyed commuters traipsed along the pavement, unaware of the sorcerers that rocketed through the same space they occupied. Elliot and Jay veered and dived and collided, unyielding. Elliot held him, felt him straining at his control, attempting to slip away again, but he clung on. His invisible self burned.

Inside Elliot's disembodied mind, Jay's voice continued.

-*I had that Splinter in your head for years – I've heard every thought you ever had. Until today, when you shut it off. I've lived your life – I know you better than anyone.*

-I know you too.

-There's a link between us. Do you feel it? That Splinter in your brain did more than just listen to your thoughts. It has leaked me into you. We are far more alike than Charles and I ever were.

-I *am* Charles. And I am nothing like you.

That was all he had to hold on to: his identity. Charles or Elliot, it made no difference. A name didn't change who he was.

Elliot crashed his power against Jay's again and again, like waves against the rocks. They flew through London's streets, through its walls and buildings. Glass, brick, stone and steel were no barrier; the two of them were of another world that had no substance, only thought and power. They flew through chanting mouths and staring eyes, past the washed-out glass towers, patched roads and blinking lights that surrounded them but meant nothing. The world was not important. There was nothing else but to fight and to stop Jay killing Holly.

Elliot still felt the look of pure venom in Arthan's eyes when he saw Holly in his bedroom that night, still felt the shock on Holly's white face when she found out he was a sorcerer, still felt the sick feeling in his stomach that had started when she found out he had fathered Kim's child. He knew he hadn't done everything right. His life had been spent idling, coasting through fog with no direction. But now he could do something. He had to save her.

For a split second Elliot lost concentration, and Jay broke out of his grip again and shot towards Holly. Elliot screamed without noise as he bent all his strength to catching him. With the eyes of his power he saw Jay lunge for Holly, rejoining physical space. Elliot crashed into him with the full force of his sorcery and tore him away from her with inches to spare. They spun into the side of a building, and Elliot felt the stone walls shatter around them as they barraged back into the real world. Dissolving his body again, Elliot ensnared Jay in his power and redoubled his attacks. He couldn't let him escape again.

While the building tumbled to the ground, screams of terror floated from the mouths of pale humans, and as their struggle reached blistering intensity, Elliot looked within

308

himself. He could feel the presence of Viros's spy inside him, the Splinter as Viros called it. The spy was the key – it was the bond that linked them, that combined their personalities. They were one and they were two and they were three. Viros's spy was part of him and a part of Viros and yet was also independent. It was like an unborn child.

It was like a child. The idea collided with his spinning thoughts. Charles remembered when he had cloned himself many years before and had caught his clone looking at him differently, thinking for itself. When did a separated part of a Grey sorcerer start to become somebody else?

It was like a child. If the spy truly behaved like an unborn child, then if it was separated from him and from Jay it would be a new sorcerer. A sorcerer birth.

It was a way out. It was a chance.

Jay's voice pierced Elliot's thoughts, while their bodiless presences continued to grapple and thrash among the sliding rubble and panicked crowds.

-We are the same. The same things happen. Remember the old man who saw you break into Arthan Associates. You thought about killing him, just like I would, and let him go like I used to let people go. We walk the same path.

-I didn't hurt the old man.

But I hurt others. I hurt Holly. I hurt Arthan – I betrayed him after he had supported me, just to satisfy my desire. Elliot searched for the reasons. What made him different to Viros?

-I haven't been myself.

Elliot felt his defences weakening and flooded his efforts with more power. He felt the life of the spy flickering inside him. It wasn't Viros, and it wasn't him, but it wasn't separate from them. There was no way of knowing what would happen if it was cut loose.

-You should accept responsibility. I accept responsibility for all I have done. Do you deny responsibility for your personality because it is inherited from me? Should I blame my father for all my actions?

As their fight continued Elliot found the outside world growing dimmer, the buildings, faces and sirens fading to transparency and Holly's figure disappearing beneath the fog. He didn't need to focus on what was out there any more. He let go of his senses and entered a world of pure darkness. He was just a sentient force, unseeing, unhearing, unfeeling.

There was nothing now but him and his enemy. He fought in the void. He could tell Jay was there, he could hold him and hurt him, but he couldn't see him or know where he was. He could barely identify himself. With all the world taken away, did he really even know why he fought?

-We must decide where our responsibility starts and ends. That is where our identity starts and ends.

-*When you have lived as long as I, you realise identity means nothing. None of it matters. We label ourselves with anything we want, but the same things happen.*

The words echoed through Elliot in the blackness. What was going to happen? Jay was going to kill Holly to stop a Grey child being born. Elliot was strong enough to stop him, but not strong enough to kill him. They were at an impasse. They were nothing, the pair of them; they were unstoppable and invincible.

He had a choice. He could stop fighting and Holly would die. Or he could separate the spy from himself and Jay.

In a world of emptiness, what else was there but choices? Elliot searched for himself, trying to find that place within that told him who he was.

-No, Jay. We are who we are. We make our choices. You know me. I'm your friend, your only friend.

The void consumed them. The memory of life faded with every passing second. Their conscious minds coalesced as they spun together in glinting fragments forming a rising tornado of thought. He was losing his grip on himself. Was Jay fighting him or becoming him, or was he becoming Jay?

-*We are still friends?*

Elliot reached inside himself with Grey Control towards the tiny spy that rested there. He tried not to think about what he was doing. He held the spy in the grip of his power, his life balanced on the future of this fragile creature. It would

310

only take a second to cut the connection between the spy and himself and Jay.

It was strange how now, at the most important moment of his life, he didn't even know why he did what he did. Was that where his true self resided? In the gap between reason and decision?

Elliot had made his choice. He cut the connection.

He felt the spy release from them, an independent identity now, a child newly born – a Grey sorcerer child. He felt the surge as power flooded in a torrent to the spy, a transfer of sorcery that would leave either him or Jay with no power and with nothing left to do but Fade.

Here he was.

Without thought, without feeling, he drifted in the void and waited to see if he would live or die.

PART ELEVEN
THE SORCERER WITHIN

Three months after Kim's death

CHAPTER FORTY

Arthan rifled through his papers. *Where are those invoices?* It was at times like this when he needed Holly – she always knew where everything was. He picked up a faded folder and the bottom came loose in his hands, spilling a small avalanche of paper onto the floor. He growled, and bent to pick the sheets up.

When the door to his office opened Arthan felt a weight rise from his chest. It was around this time that Holly arrived at work; this would be her now.

It wasn't Holly but Elliot who stood in the doorway. Arthan stiffened.

"Is now a good time?"

Arthan continued retrieving his papers and didn't reply. *It will never be a good time.* He hadn't seen Elliot since the day Viros had attacked the office; he hadn't wanted to see him. He had returned to his normal routine as fast as possible.

Elliot entered the office and sat down in the chair opposite the desk as though Arthan had signalled to him that he could come in. He looked as scruffy as always – he wasn't wearing a tie, his shirt was creased, his hair was uncombed. Arthan picked up his cigar from its holder and clamped it between his lips. Looking at Elliot's expression made him want to kick something, but he sat down instead and held his gaze. He would not be the one to break eye contact first.

"I came to apologise," Elliot said with an incongruous smile.

"Oh?"

"To apologise for everything." Elliot spread his hands wide. "I know what I did. You deserve to hate me."

"I don't," Arthan said, and was surprised to find that he meant it. He sighed and exhaled cigar smoke. The silence wandered for a few moments before Arthan spoke again. "Your colleagues are all sorry for believing you were the murderer. Myself included." He frowned. "We thought what we were doing was right."

"I know."

Arthan cleared his throat and straightened in his chair. "Whatever else you've done, it is thanks to you that Holly is still alive. You saved her when no one else could, even Elizan."

It hurt to thank this boy, but Arthan felt better after doing it. Credit should be given where it was due. The thought that Elizan had failed still troubled him. He had sent numerous messages asking her what had happened that day, but she hadn't responded. He refused to entertain the rumours that she had somehow lost her power, but the fact remained that she hadn't come to their aid when they needed her.

Elliot met his gaze. "I was lucky, that's all."

Yes, you were. Arthan watched the rings of smoke waft up into the air, circling and stretching to frayed threads and then dissolving into nothing. He was never lucky. It always seemed to be his shoulders that problems were stood on, his desk that work was piled on, his relationships that failed. He glared at the ceiling. At least he didn't have to watch Holly and Elliot continue their foolish dalliance. He was proud of her for finally rejecting Elliot's advances. Perhaps it was better for her and Arthan to be apart too; it gave him the space he needed to think. It was likely that she would come back to him at some point.

"How are things here?"

Arthan rested his cigar and leant back, the leather creaking beneath him. "We're managing. Gordon is still missing, apparently vanished off the face of the earth, leaving the rest of us to pick up the pieces of his half-finished projects. After she returned from her fruitless search for the boy, Marrin decided to come and work for us, which meets part of the resourcing requirements. Of course, you left us as well." Arthan glanced up, realising he may be giving Elliot the impression he wanted him back. "Are you—"

"I'm not coming back," said Elliot.

"Good." Arthan puffed on his cigar. "You've got a lot to deal with. It's best that you concentrate on that."

Elliot's lips twitched a little at this, but he nodded. "I do have rather a lot of new memories to think through." He walked his fingers on the arm of the chair. "So nobody has seen Gordon?"

"No."

What was Elliot thinking about? Arthan watched him sitting there, tapping his fingers and gazing at the wall. The boy seemed to be a little absent, his thoughts occupied, although he had always been that way. "You had better tell me what happened on the day Viros attacked."

Elliot shrugged. "Not much to tell. We fought. Viros Faded."

"Was there not a Host?"

Elliot shook his head. "Not as such. The power went into a small creature inside my head, a spy. I'm keeping it under control. So there are two of us, but really it's just me."

"So there is only one Grey sorcerer again." Arthan turned this information over in his head. He wondered about the nature of this small creature that had absorbed the power. It must have some semblance of a human mind in order to contain the sorcery. "I suppose I should tell you that I spoke to Paros. I told him we know he is a fraud."

This caught Elliot's attention. "When?"

"I called him. He remains petrified even though I told him Viros is dead, and so he wouldn't tell me much, but he did say that he felt something happen the day Viros died. It appears that he was being kept alive all these years by Viros, and I expect when Viros died, the Control broke."

Elliot nodded. "So now he will age and die like all other humans."

"I suppose he will." Arthan chewed on his cigar. "You will have a problem with that spy," he told Elliot. "You cannot contain a sorcerer forever, no matter how small."

"I can." Elliot stretched back in his chair. "Don't worry. I have a plan for Holly's baby too. There won't be any Fadings."

"A plan?"

"Yes." Elliot nodded to himself. "It's no use making choices if you don't have a plan."

Arthan peered at him, put his cigar to his lips, then froze as something gleamed in Elliot's eyes. Had he imagined it? Just for a moment, a different presence had seemed to pass across that measured gaze. A coldness.

With a chill crawling over him, Arthan looked at the young man opposite. He appeared to be the same person he had always been. The same wavy black hair, the same long arms and the same broad shoulders. But a Grey sorcerer had complete control over his appearance. It didn't matter what he looked like – there was no way to tell who was behind the mask.

"Who are you?" Arthan blurted out.

Elliot shrugged. "Does it matter?" He grinned. "I'm different now."

A personal note

Thank you for reading this book. It has been a wonderful escape to have this story as a companion to visit, read, write, put down and pick up throughout many years. It is even more wonderful to hear from people who have read it.

I would be hugely grateful if you consider leaving a review. Every review is important to me and I am keen to read your feedback. For other potential readers, your review will be crucial to help them understand whether this book might be one they would enjoy.

Whether you choose to leave a review or not, please get in touch if you would like to share any thoughts or questions. You can sign up below for my mailing list to hear about future books and to contact me. I love to hear from readers and I respond to every email.

Will Rice

willriceauthor.com

About the Author

Will Rice is a lifelong fan of fantasy fiction. He is absorbed by stories that are driven by imagination, by the answers that arise to the question: what if...

The Sorcerer Within is the first idea in a continual and never-ending stream that Will has held onto for long enough to transform into a novel. He hopes to do the same with many more.

Will has a degree in Mathematics from Oxford University, is a qualified pensions actuary and a Partner at Barnett Waddingham. In his spare time when not reading or writing he enjoys playing modern board games. Will lives in Buckinghamshire, UK, with his wife Jacquelyn and two children Harry and Lucy.

Printed in Great Britain
by Amazon

72471005R00194